THE ELEVENTH BROTHER

THE ELEVENTH BROTHER

A Novel of Joseph in Egypt

RACHEL K. WILCOX

Salt Lake City, Utah

Visit us at DeseretBook.com

Library of Congress Cataloging-in-Publication Data

Wilcox, Rachel K., author.
Eleventh brother : a novel of Joseph in Egypt / Rachel K. Wilcox.
pages cm
A novel exploring the story of Joseph, the son of Israel, in Egypt.
Includes bibliographical references.
ISBN 978-1-60907-854-6 (paperbound)
1. Joseph (Son of Jacob)—Fiction. 2. Asenath (Biblical figure)—Fiction. 3. Jacob (Biblical patriarch)—Fiction. 4. Judah (Biblical figure)—Fiction. 5. Egypt—History—To 332 B.C.—Fiction. 6. Bible. Genesis—History of Biblical events—Fiction. I. Title.
PS3623.I5326E44 2015
813'.6—dc23 2014031014

Printed in Canada
Marquis Book Printing, Montreal, Canada

10 9 8 7 6 5 4 3 2 1

Beginning of the Book of Breathings, which Isis made for her brother Osiris, to make his soul live, to make his body live, to restore him anew; that he might join the horizon along with his father . . .

—*The Book of Breathings, line 1*

CONTENTS

ANCESTORS OF JOSEPH AND JUDAH

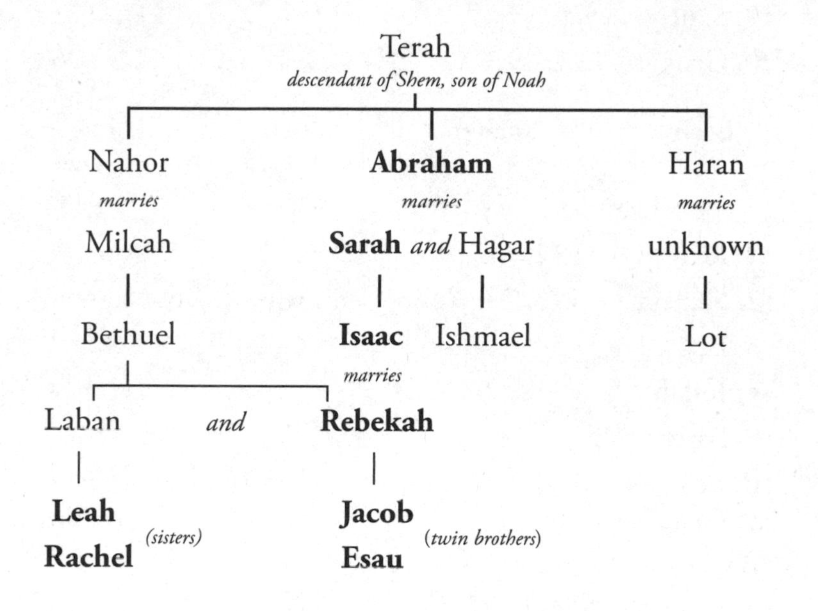

DESCENDANTS OF JACOB

Jacob

marries

Leah	**Rachel**	**Zilpah** *Leah's handmaid*	**Bilhah** *Rachel's handmaid*
1. Reuben	12. **Joseph**	7. Gad	5. Dan
2. Simeon	13. Benjamin	8. Asher	6. Naphtali
3. Levi			
4. **Judah**			
9. Issachar			
10. Zebulon			
11. Dinah			

PEOPLE OF EGYPT

Amon: A young aristocrat and assistant to Zaphenath-Paaneah

Amosis: Potiphar's first steward and overseer of the household slaves

Asar: An Egyptian prince

Asenath: Wife of Zaphenath-Paaneah and daughter of the high priest of the sun god Ra (called "On" in Genesis)

Djeseret: Wife of Potiphar

Ephraim: Younger son of Joseph and Asenath

Manasseh: Elder son of Joseph and Asenath

Potiphar: Captain of the royal guard

Sasobek: Name given to Joseph, son of Jacob, upon becoming a member of Potiphar's household

Senusret: King of Egypt, Son-of-Ra, God-on-Earth

Zaphenath-Paaneah: Name given to Joseph, son of Jacob, upon becoming the vizier, or *tjaty*, of the kingdom of Egypt

The descriptions, events, and concerns of the various characters, both Egyptian and Hebrew, arc meant to be appropriate for their time and place.

For further discussion of the characters and the historical setting in Egypt's Middle kingdom (such as why there are no "Egyptians" in the novel), please turn to "A Note to the Reader," on page 305.

PROLOGUE

Many years ago, in the desert wilderness beyond the borders of the Egyptian empire, a man named Abraham sought out the God of his fathers. And the God of his fathers spoke to Abraham and made a promise with him and with all his descendants after him.

Abraham's son Isaac had a son named Jacob. Jacob had twelve sons, and Jacob loved his eleventh son, Joseph, more than the others.

Joseph's brothers were jealous. They betrayed Joseph and sold him as a slave into Egypt. But Abraham's God remembered Joseph, as He remembered all of Jacob's family. And just as their separation had a beginning, the God of Abraham saw to it that it also had an end.

This is their story.

CHAPTER 1

Genesis 37:23–24

My son.

His father's face, warm and trusting.

I must ask something of you.

It was a simple task, only a day's journey, and his father smiled as he left.

His father, who trusted him and loved him, even if his brothers taunted him otherwise—his brothers, who were jealous, and anxious, and eager to inherit and be their own men.

You must understand, his father had said, *that there must always be one chosen for the birthright—one chosen for inheritance, for succession, for the covenant—*

One chosen for sacrifice.

The boy lay alone, broken open to the chill of the desert and the bleeding expanse of stars, enclosed on all sides by the earth that had received his body like a dead man's.

His memory scrabbled over the broken pieces: his robe,

stained with his mouth's blood, the cloth wailing, the knife driving in and out and the pieces of linen fluttering to the ground as he was dragged away, his arms bruised beneath their fingers.

He had struggled, thinking he could plead with them.

Then his body had collided with the wall of the well shaft, and he had fallen back, screaming.

A day, already, had passed. He knew that his brothers had stayed nearby at first because he'd heard them shuffling, murmuring in low snatches, but they had not answered his cries.

Now the desert was silent.

He lay staring up through the narrowed darkness. A trickle of water ran just beneath the surface of the dry well. He had worn the tips of his fingers raw from digging down toward it. Waves of nauseated hunger stirred him whenever he slipped, intermittently, into a place of no light.

His brothers had meant to kill him, but the knife intended for his throat had been turned instead on his robe, swift hands butchering the cloth as they would a sheep. He had simply been thrown away, the unusable, unclean remnants of the slaughter.

Reuben had begged the others not to hurt the boy, but he had been pushed aside, threatened with the same knife.

Don't kill him.

He heard Judah's voice in the tumult, felt his older brother seize him by the arm as he lay on the ground, his captors arguing like dogs over a carcass.

Don't kill him—Judah was breathless—*sell him.*

Mercy in the form of slavery. Atonement by pieces of silver.

Joseph had seen his brother's face in the moment before he was thrown away, and he saw Judah standing there, still, watching—

Just watching.

CHAPTER 2

Genesis 41:54

The rising of the new star came that year as it did every year. Shimmering in its ascent, *Sopdet*—star of Isis, harbinger of the land's renewed fertility and the beginning of the new year—glistened in the trailing stream of dying sunlight.

The man called *Tjaty*—the vizier, second-in-command to the king—watched the new star rise. He thought, as he often did, on the stillness of the night, the long sigh at day's end. Yet it was a mistake, he knew, to think the stars aloof or that the night had less to speak than the day. The day was for men to sweat beneath the heat, when the sun blocked the impulse to think beyond the immediacy of the hour. But the night, when the shadows grew long and the sun sank, was the time to gaze beyond the earth, to stare at all that was and wonder at the lives that might be lived beyond the veil of sun-bound days.

Closing his eyes, he remembered the words he had read that very morning as the sun rose on the first day of the new year.

Beginning of the Book of Breathings, which Isis made for

her brother Osiris. That was the way the text introduced itself, painted across the brittle, pounded papyrus:

Isis and Osiris, husband and wife, the woman who had called her husband back from the dead and restored the breath of life within his soul, and the man who had been killed by his brother for their father's throne and who then had passed below to gain power over death—to make his soul live, to make his body live, to make all his members anew—

He had been taught that the mere recitation of such sacred texts released a power within the written word, splitting open the marrow of whatever life was nestled deep within the characters. The vizier smiled slightly. If only it could be done, he thought, by speaking.

Or at least speaking it with his mouth alone in simple recitation, rather than reciting with his body, his breath, disciplining his every thought and action into the proper paradigms, speaking out the rituals with his very life before the gods would hear.

But then, he thought, at least they hear.

And then he heard footsteps scuffling across the open ground. Opening his eyes, he turned away from the night and toward the smiling woman who approached him with two little boys, one a little more grown than the other. Her hair was pulled back in preparation for sleep, her cheeks flushed in the warm air and her body shrouded in a light linen sheath. She held the boys' hands with the same calm comfort as the sky held the stars.

"They wanted to see the new star," she said.

Her husband smiled. The two boys scampered on ahead of their mother, thin, dark braids hanging from the side of their heads brushing against their bare shoulders. The taller of the two leaned on tip-toe against the low wall, gazing out across the garden at the outstretched fronds of palm trees and a cluster of blue lotus blossoms floating in the reflection pool. His younger brother struggled beside him, eager to see beyond the estate to the slow-drifting, wide-banked River.

For two years now, the River—*Iteru*—had failed to overflow its banks. And without the flooding, the River could not spread the rich, fertile black mud that allowed crops to flourish in the desert. The land that Iteru nourished took its name from the River, called after the dark mud that marked the boundaries of *Kemet,* the Black Land, the floodplain. All that lay beyond the reach of the River was *Deshret,* the Red Land, the barren place, the west desert where the People buried their dead.

"Do you see the River?" their mother asked, coming to stand behind her sons and tugging on the braid that hung over the younger boy's left ear.

The child giggled, squinting up at the sky. "Where's the star?"

"Do you know what it's called?" his father asked.

His older son nodded. "It's the star of Isis," he reported, leaning closer to his younger brother.

"Sopdet." His father smiled. "Her rising means that the River should be ready to flood."

The older of the two boys solemnly surveyed the

horizon where the River ambled across the plain. "But it's not flooding."

The vizier felt a tug on his hand and looked down at his younger son.

"Who's Isis?"

"Who's Isis?" The vizier bent down, hoisting the little boy into his arms. "There's a very old story about her. She was the daughter of Ra, and she saved her husband's life."

The little boy nodded, and his father looked past his son to his wife, Asenath, daughter of the high priest of the sun god Ra. "Her husband," he said, "was named Osiris. And Osiris had a brother named Seth, who was very jealous of him." He shifted his gaze, looking straight at the little boy, widening his eyes for dramatic impact. "And one day Seth *killed* him."

The child's eyes widened too.

"But," his father added reassuringly, "luckily for Osiris, Isis was very clever. And she found a way to save him. And that's why that star"—he looked up, and the child in his arms looked up too—"is named after her. She brings things back to life. And when the floods come, the River brings life back to the entire land. You see?"

The child nodded. His father smiled and kissed him on top of his shaven head.

"So where's Osiris now?" This time the elder boy was looking up in perplexity.

"Ah." The man smiled. "He's up there too." He gestured with his head toward the stars. "Don't you see him?"

"Right there." His mother bent down beside her son, pointing up and slowly tracing an outline in the sky, just below where the star of Isis hovered. "Look closely. That's his head, there, and then his body, with his arms stretched out to either side."

Both boys gazed up, the younger one's mouth hanging open.

"And there"—she looped her finger underneath the figure in a crescent arc—"is his boat."

The older boy looked at his father. "The gods have boats too?"

"Of course." The man met his wife's eyes, and they both smiled. "It's how they ride across the sky, like you ride along the River. You can always find Osiris with Isis. See how she watches over him?" The boys both nodded. "And you see how Osiris is made up of lots of little stars, all arranged together?" The man looked up again. "That's like you and your mother and me—all arranged together, to make up our family."

The younger child rested his head against his father's shoulder, yawning.

"How do you know that?" asked the older son, crossing his arms.

"How do I know what?"

"About the stars."

The man smiled. "I used to watch the stars at night with my father."

The older boy nodded, then, hearing the call of a night-bird, moved toward the sound.

Asenath looked at her husband. "I don't often hear you talk about your father."

"He was the one who told me to look at the way the stars hold together," he said quietly, looking down at his sleepy son. "How they bring peace and order into the sky. He told me that my brothers and I were like the stars."

Asenath looked at her husband, the moonlight glinting silver in his hair, seeing the creases around his eyes and the years etching slowly into his skin. "Have you been thinking about them again?"

He shrugged, putting a protective hand on his son's back.

"Zaphenath."

He glanced at her.

"The goodness you have done in your own life will be returned to you." She laid her hand over his. "That is *ma'at.*"

"And *ma'at,*" Zaphenath said, "is always represented as a woman, isn't it?" He leaned closer, kissing her lightly on the cheek. But she saw his eyes as he pulled away, and she looked at his face—a face with a dark, proportioned, almost ethereal beauty—and wished she could somehow capture what it was he saw, so that she could see it with him.

But the moment passed, and he simply looked away, back up at the stars.

CHAPTER 3

Genesis 41:39–45, 56–57; 42:1–14

On the morning after the rising of Sopdet, the first signs of Ra began to glow red beneath the horizon. The People called this first part of the new year the time of Floods. The earth itself would celebrate by pouring its bounty over the banks of the River, leaving the grateful inhabitants to slosh around outside their homes by boat until the waters receded in a wash of fertile richness.

But for the second year, the earth had ignored the rising of Sopdet, and for the second year, the time of Floods was occurring without any helpful rise in the River at all.

Zaphenath awoke first. He rose from his bed and moved alone through the house as was his custom—he preferred his solitude in this earliest hour. The family's private washroom was empty, and he lowered himself into the undisturbed water of the bathing pool. With a reflexive wince at the chill and a quick intake of breath, he closed his eyes and plunged his head back, submerging himself completely, suspended between earth and sky, before surfacing again, like Ra from the watery womb of the stars.

He pulled himself out of the pool with a series of tiny splashes and then quickly dried himself in the early morning light. Crossing the room, he opened a small wooden chest set against the wall and took out a sharp bronze blade with a wooden handle. He skimmed the blade along the length of his body, from his legs up to his bare chest; he took a little extra time around his jaw after the blade nicked the skin. Once shaved, he wrapped a fine-spun, pleated linen kilt around his waist. Then he lifted an expensive wig of straight, thick, shoulder-length black hair and fitted it over his head.

Shaven and properly wigged, he took up a small brush made of a single river reed and sprinkled a pinch of dark powder from a jar into a carved circular indention on a wooden palette. Mixing in a few drops of water, he dipped the reed and pulled the corner of one eye out toward his ear. Carefully balancing the brush, he swooped the dark liner down the inner length of his eyelid. He repeated the procedure with the other eye and quickly lined the outer part of his eyelids in the dark kohl mixture.

No one who had been in the country more than a few days would go without the dark liner after realizing the relief that the eye-paint brought from the glare of the white-hot sun off the sand. But the thought did flicker through his mind, and not for the first time, of what a roughened man his age who had lived his life out in the Deshret would think to see such attention given to one's appearance.

Zaphenath slipped his arms through the sleeves of a light linen tunic, spun so fine as to be nearly transparent against his skin. The material was creased with slim, soft folds and fell to his knees, extending no further than the kilt worn beneath. He cinched the tunic around his waist with an extra strip of fine linen and tied it to one side.

He reached for his amulet: a small golden disk dangling from a delicate golden chain, pounded thin like a burst of sun, with a single blue stone of lapis lazuli set in the midst of the burning orb. It had been a gift from Asenath when Zaphenath had been admitted to her father's powerful priesthood. Though Zaphenath was not a man to wear amulets and did not keep any small god-statues inside his house, he kept this one emblem of the Light-of-All-the-World, given to him by the woman whose very presence was light and life. He wore it around his neck, close to his heart, beneath the elegant and more elaborate golden chain presented to him by the king when he had become tjaty over all the land of Kemet.

Last of all, he slipped on the signet ring the king had presented to him as a symbol of his new identity. Also made of gold, the ring bore an inscription of the name he had received upon becoming vizier: *I am the king, and without thee shall no man lift up his hand or foot in all the land of Kemet, and thou shalt be called Zaphenath-Paaneah.*

Clothed in the authority of the state and its priesthood, his place clearly designated within a country highly conscious of its hierarchies, Zaphenath walked down the corridor that led from the private rooms of his villa and out into the central courtyard. Open to the sky, the courtyard marked the boundary between the public and private areas of the grand house. A handful of servants were already bustling through, carrying laundry or arranging flowers. Zaphenath nodded to those he passed as he headed toward a small room where he stored his scrolls and conducted his business when away from the king's court.

"Well," Zaphenath said, walking into the scroll room, "good morning."

A much younger man, also clothed in a linen kilt, was already in the room, bent over a low table with an unrolled length of papyrus. He was gesturing to one portion of the open scroll and talking to a man nearer Zaphenath's age, who kept his bald head uncovered and had a well-fed belly that protruded over the edge of his kilt.

The younger man inclined his head. "Tjaty."

The older man looked annoyed. "This young one thinks there's a problem with my record keeping."

Zaphenath stepped next to the table and looked down at the scroll. "You think there's a problem with the record keeping?" he asked, smiling slightly.

The younger man looked serious. "Tjaty, I'm trying to get all the necessary information assembled before we have to make a presentation"—here he shot a look at the servant, as if the man had perhaps failed to grasp the gravity of the situation—"to the king."

Zaphenath glanced down at the scroll. "Second month of Shemu."

The older servant shrugged. "I do the best I can, you know."

"You do very well." Zaphenath looked at his young assistant. "What scroll do you need, Amon?"

Amon looked at the older servant again. "The *fourth* month of Shemu."

Zaphenath bent down beside a wooden box set on the floor near the table. Nimbly untying the leather straps, he lifted the lid and pulled out another scroll, unrolling the papyrus far enough to verify the dates. "Here," he said, rerolling the scroll and handing it to his servant. "Try this one."

Amon held out his hand, and the older servant handed over the incorrect scroll.

Zaphenath took the scroll from Amon. "Someone must have put it back in the wrong order." He set the scroll back into the box and stood, glancing at Amon. "Not everyone has the headache of learning how to read."

The old servant grunted. "Do you need anything else?"

"Just those, I presume," Zaphenath said, gesturing toward a handful of other scrolls already set out on the table.

"Tjaty," Amon said, "we're going to be late."

"Well," Zaphenath said, "come on, then," and he turned and walked out of the scroll room.

Amon scooped up the other papyrus records and moved briskly after his master.

Zaphenath's older servant bent and carefully tied the leather straps, securing the box of scrolls once more.

Hot, sandy wind gusted around Zaphenath's bare legs as he moved along. He waved away a pestering fly that kept darting at his face.

"I'm sure the king will be eager to hear your report about the viability of the additional acreage," Amon said. He was doing his best to keep up while balancing the scrolls in his arms. Two guards walked behind them, with two more in front. "I've finished the comparisons you requested, and I think the plots that we've examined have high potential for future growth. The more marshland we can turn toward viable agriculture, the better for the recovery from the famine."

"So you think I should include the other sectors in my report?" Zaphenath asked.

"Oh," Amon nodded, "absolutely."

Zaphenath blinked in the glare of the morning sun, the dark kohl lining around his eyes deflecting only so much light off the sand. A trickle of sweat escaped from beneath his wig. "How is your father?" he asked, taking another swat at the diving fly.

The young man gave a serious-faced nod. "Well enough. He retains his strength."

"I'm glad." Zaphenath smiled. "I know he's proud of you."

They were beyond the riverfront area where the grand villas lay alongside the River. The crowds of travelers had begun to grow thicker; bodies pushed and jostled, and the mingled melodies of foreign languages rose from within the tumult. The loose linen garments, smoothly scraped skin, and made-up faces of the People were a sharp contrast to the scruffier merchants and sojourners who had come from the surrounding deserts and whose clothing and bodies bore the wear of several weeks of travel.

Zaphenath saw Amon wrinkle his nose slightly as they passed two ruffle-haired, bearded men wearing coarse woolen garments and arguing with each other in some incomprehensible language.

"You've never traveled beyond the borders of Kemet, have you?" Zaphenath said, watching his young assistant.

Amon shook his head. He glanced back at the bearded men. "There's no reason to go out into the Deshret."

Zaphenath glanced back as well. "The famine doesn't know that."

They pushed on, the guards prodding the crowd apart. A four-sided mud-brick structure, whitewashed and guarded, rose up against the horizon. The building was one of several granaries dotting the landscape, sheltering the grain gathered over the past several years against the foretold famine that had since swept across the land.

A line of people, their bodies glistening in the heat, empty baskets in hand, snaked up toward where the grain was measured and distributed. Grumbling workers lazily waved the waiting people through the line. Each transaction was carefully recorded by a squinting, sweating scribe sitting on a low wooden bench next to the doorway.

When the guards at the front of the line caught sight of the approaching visitors, they barked out an order that even the foreigners could understand. People quickly moved aside and created a path for Zaphenath.

The first granary guard they passed quickly lowered his head. "Tjaty."

Zaphenath thanked the man and glanced over his shoulder at the massed hopefuls, waiting with their empty baskets. Most were native workers arriving for their pay in grain. Some, however, stood with produce to trade or carried small ducks and geese, or even, if quite a lot of grain was desired, pigs or goats. A few of the hopefuls, especially the foreigners, had brought jewelry or precious metals to exchange.

The vizier moved toward the soldiers stationed beside the granary entrance, where workers within were hauling grain up from storage silos beneath the ground. Much of the kingdom's wealth lay in these structures, spread throughout the land and administered carefully by watchful overseers. The overseers, in turn, were carefully administered by Zaphenath, whose authority extended over nearly all of the resources of the land of Kemet and her powerful king.

The two officials greeted Zaphenath in the usual deferential manner.

"We need the report of your grain levels," Amon announced on behalf of his master, "for official business."

The sweating scribe had already risen to his feet, wiping his forehead. He held a wilted sheet of pounded papyrus, partially rolled, on which he had been recording the transactions.

"Levels are lower, Excellency," the official admitted. "The famine seems to be striking the foreign peoples much harder. They were unprepared."

Zaphenath nodded, eyes darting over the numbers. "As we anticipated, then," he murmured.

Amon held out his hand, and the scribe blew a dry breath over the freshest characters before handing over the record. Amon took the papyrus and unrolled the scroll several inches further, then nodded as well.

"Thank you," Zaphenath said. The scribe bowed. "And for your good service, all of you."

The two officials inclined their heads in acceptance of their superior's praise. Straightening, the senior of the two barked out, "All hail Zaphenath-Paaneah, vizier of the land of Kemet and the People!"

The native People bowed at the pronouncement of Zaphenath's identity. But a handful of coarsely appareled, heavily bearded men hesitated, observing the others before likewise kneeling. Their confused delay caught Zaphenath's eye. Usually merchants traveled alone, or perhaps in pairs, but these men did not appear to be merchants.

After a moment, Amon and the two officials followed the vizier's gaze.

Without turning, Zaphenath asked quietly, "Who are those men?"

The officials glanced at one another. "We'll find out,"

one promised. He gestured to the scribe standing beside them. "He can talk to them."

The scribe was clothed in a thin linen kilt, and his head was cleanly shaved. But Zaphenath looked at the bone structure of his face, the coloration of darkened skin that came from long exposure to the sun rather than by birth, and the shading on his cheek that indicated where a bold beard would have grown.

"Translate," the official ordered.

The scribe bowed and looked toward the kneeling foreigners in their shaggy clothes. Then he walked down the line toward the men, as ordered. Amon began to follow, but Zaphenath waved him back and followed instead, the familiar footfalls of two of his guards trailing behind him. By this time, several of the People waiting for grain had begun to raise their eyes, also watching.

"Are you one of the 'Aamu?" Zaphenath asked the scribe, falling into step beside the man. The 'Aamu, nomadic desert tribes who lived to the north and east of Kemet, usually stayed in the country only as other men's slaves.

The man looked at Zaphenath, then inclined his head, averting his eyes. "Yes, Tjaty."

The assembled grain buyers watched warily as the vizier approached. The fame of his predictions about the famine and the story of his elevation by the king had spread throughout the kingdom; it was whispered he was a man endowed with almost mythical powers of magic. When he slowed before the foreign tribesmen, the men hesitantly half-raised their faces. The whole bundle of visitors—how many of them were there?—had full beards, some thicker than others, and all peppered with gray and silver streaks, as if the withering desert sun had burned out all the color.

"Ask them who they are," Zaphenath ordered.

The scribe quickly addressed the men in a foreign tongue more often heard in the slave markets. The travelers glanced at one another and began murmuring back and forth. Then one whose beard was thicker and grayer than the others spoke in reply.

"We are men of Canaan," he said, keeping his eyes downcast respectfully.

The scribe turned to Zaphenath, but the vizier was already staring fixedly at the man's worn face with its broad cheekbones and heavy brows.

"They are Canaanites," the scribe reported.

"Ask them their business," Zaphenath said, his throat suddenly dry.

"We have come to buy grain," the Canaanite replied, his voice low, addressing the translating scribe.

Zaphenath's gaze moved over the faces of the other men, counting, feeling the pounding tighten within his chest. Eight, nine, ten . . .

Ten.

He scanned their faces again, blood thudding in his ears. Only ten.

"They are here to buy supplies," the scribe confirmed.

Zaphenath closed his eyes, seeing suddenly, in a bright

flash, a stalk of corn stretched out on the ground, prostrate beneath the onslaught of the famine *my sheaf arose, and yours stood round about* and the stars swirling in the expanse *eleven stars, and the sun, and the moon* and he tried to take a breath *you all bowed before me—*

"They wish to buy grain," the translator reported.

"They lie," Zaphenath said softly.

The translator leaned closer. "They—?"

Zaphenath turned his face toward the man who knelt at his feet. "You are spies from the 'Aamu," he said, "come to see the weakness of the People in this time of famine."

Eyes wide, the scribe stumblingly repeated the message to the immediate outrage of the Canaanites. Babbling their protests, the men's words tumbled over each other, and the one who had been speaking for them all vigorously shook his head.

"We are brothers," he insisted. "We are simply brothers—"

The people who had been fortunate enough to gather for grain before the excitement began were all watching now, although those closest seemed to be making a subtle effort to move away from the accused men.

"Ten brothers from Canaan?" Zaphenath dismissed the claim with a wave of his hand.

"More yet, my lord," the man insisted, nearly speaking over the translator in his haste. "We were twelve, but the youngest is not with us—"

"Another brother?" Zaphenath looked at him. "You have another brother?"

The man shrank back, not understanding the official's words but clearly unsettled by the tone of his voice. The scribe spoke to him to clarify the meaning. The man murmured an explanation.

"The youngest," came the translated reply, "is not with us. And the other . . . is not."

A breeze rose up, stirring the hems of the heavy desert robes, rustling across the sand in the quiet that followed.

Zaphenath turned and raised a hand. The Canaanite tribesmen cried out in protest, struggling in confusion against the approach of the guards until one brother, who until then had been silent, began to speak, raising and lowering his flattened palms, as if ordering the others to soothe themselves, to lie flat, to be still.

"Do not fight," he hissed. "This is a mistake. Do not fight them . . ."

The guards hustled the protesting men to their feet. Zaphenath saw the confusion in their stumbling movements.

"Tell them," Zaphenath said, voice low, "that one of them will bring this youngest brother back, if he exists. If he does not, then that one can tell of how the People deal with spies."

As they were led away, only one—the one who had spoken in an effort to calm the others—turned back.

But Zaphenath turned away from the man's gaze. He walked back toward where Amon and the officials were waiting for him and apologized for disrupting their work. The officials quickly shrugged, eager to express their lack of displeasure toward this man whose extraordinary command had just been exercised in their presence—the man whose influence was supreme over every law court in the country.

"Excellency." Amon inclined his head. "The king will be waiting for us."

And so the vizier went on his way, separated from all present by the almost tangible veil of power, while the officials gestured for the next citizens to move forward. Keep coming. Don't hold up the line.

But the scribe stood apart, watching the vizier and wondering why the man had used a translator when he so clearly understood everything that had been said.

CHAPTER 4

Genesis 42:17

Huddled in the darkness, the men from Canaan crowded into their own corner of the prison—the royal prison, though they were unaware of the distinction. They were separated from their freedom by a mud-brick wall, unbroken except for a single small window, cut out and barred with stiff wooden poles so that the guards could peer inside.

A handful of other prisoners, awaiting their own fates, shared the tight space, murmuring at the crowding arrival of this new band of men.

Judah found himself locking eyes, unintentionally, with a grizzled, thin-faced prisoner sitting in another corner and staring at the foreigners with dark, unblinking eyes.

"There was no reason to accuse us," his oldest brother, Reuben, muttered, speaking in low tones to the brothers who sat around him with their knees pulled up to make room for the others.

"Everyone knows these people look down on—what do they call us?—desert dwellers." The voice belonged to the second brother, Simeon, a tall, thin man with a slight beard, whose face favored their mother's more than his broad-shouldered elder brother's did.

"But we weren't doing anything," insisted Levi. "There was no reason—"

"How long will they hold us here?" asked Asher, who had been shivering despite the heat of the day. "Surely they won't just keep us—"

"They'll keep us," said Judah. He had sought to calm his brothers when the guards came for them outside the granary, and now he sat slightly off to the side. "Until one of us brings Benjamin back."

Reuben and Simeon looked toward him. Reuben shook his head. "Father won't allow it."

"What if they mean to trap us here?" Asher asked. "Even if someone brings Benjamin?"

"Benjamin won't leave," Reuben insisted.

"Then we all stay," said Judah.

Some of the other brothers were beginning to mutter, watching the exchange. Simeon turned away and spoke in a low voice to Levi and Reuben. Judah was only half-listening, feeling only too keenly the growing protest in his aging body, left here to sit on the unyielding ground in a foreign land, impossibly far from help or home. He closed his eyes.

What are you no no stop you can't no you can't no—

That had been a summer day too, without hint of shade or hope of relief, only the open hole in the ground.

My brothers my brothers please my brothers—

We have no right, Judah thought, to think we deserve mercy.

"Brother," he heard, and someone touched his arm. He turned toward the voice. Issachar, one of the youngest among them, though no longer young, was watching Judah in the dim light. "Are you all right?"

Judah nodded.

Issachar glanced toward Reuben, Simeon, and Levi, who sat together as if in council. They had been the first to be born into the family, and all had been born to Judah's own mother, Leah, first wife of his father, Jacob, and mother of seven of Jacob's children. Judah was the fourth of those children and Issachar the fifth, though four other sons separated them, sons born to serving women who had given birth to children on behalf of their mistresses.

It was somehow fitting, Judah thought, that of all the brothers held together in this prison, only the two sons of his father's second wife—Rachel, his mother's younger sister, the woman whom his father had loved above all others—were not among them.

Judah thought of those two half-brothers, boys who had been both favored and motherless most of their lives. Benjamin, the youngest of all the family, had never known his mother, and Rachel's other son . . . Well, as Reuben had told the official, her other son was not.

Judah closed his eyes, hearing the voice again.

My brothers . . .

And he thought, We are no brothers.

"Judah." He glanced toward Simeon, who was speaking to him. "Who do you think we should send back?"

Judah looked at Simeon, whose eyes stared through the darkness with their familiar sense of challenge.

"Whoever can be trusted," Judah said at last, pausing just long enough to let the first half of the statement linger, "to convince Father."

Simeon's eyes narrowed slightly. "And who would that be?"

"Someone who would not betray his family."

In the quiet, Judah could hear the scuffling of other prisoners, the low conversations in unknown tongues, and the hacking cough of a man who lay on the floor with his back to them.

Finally Reuben said softly, "That is old blood, brother."

"Reuben could go," suggested Gad, who until then had sat silently beside his only full brother, Asher, both sons of Leah's serving woman, Zilpah, and inheritors of Zilpah's waving hair and dimpled chin. "As the eldest."

Reuben flicked a loose pebble away, watching it bounce across the dirt. "Father's trust in me," he said, "may not be sufficient."

Judah looked away into the darkness.

At last Zebulon, Leah's youngest son, raised his eyes. "There is no heir," he said quietly, "so there is no clear choice about who should go, is there?"

There was no response to that, Judah thought in the quiet that followed, because there was nothing left to be said.

CHAPTER 5

Senusret

Khakhaperre—the man whose new name, upon ascending to the throne of Kemet, boldly proclaimed that the Soul of Ra had appeared—had been born as Senusret. He was named for a grandfather of several generations back, who, amidst a time of civil unrest and splintering governments, had risen to found the illustrious dynasty that had since ruled the land of Kemet. It was he who had restored order and unity to the People after the dark time of dissension and chaos. And it was as Senusret that Khakhaperre, fourth king of the dynasty and second to bear the name, preferred to be known.

When his tjaty entered the elegantly appointed receiving hall and bowed in formal greeting, the aging king simply waved his hand and beckoned his loyal counselor, trailed by his flush-faced young assistant, to approach.

"Zaphenath," the king said, smiling, "what reports do you have for me today?"

Senusret's great receiving hall, with its lofty pillars and brightly decorated walls, seemed quiet that morning. The usual court advisors were absorbed in their own conversations, and the artfully painted figures and characters adorning the interior felt subdued without the bustle and murmur of more crowded days. Senusret himself wore only an elegant wig and simple linen robes, forgoing the more elaborate pieces of costume that announced his position on earth as a Son of Ra and future god. His mortal face was not so deeply lined as the faces of men his age who had toiled in the fields, and the lines around his mouth and eyes maintained a certain gentleness in his expression.

Rising from where he sat, Senusret greeted his vizier, while Amon lowered his entire body, as best he could, in reverential respect.

"Good to see you again, Amon," Senusret said, gesturing for him to rise. "Let's see what news you have."

As Amon regained his footing, Zaphenath plucked one of the scrolls from the bundle the young man held. "The storage levels of the granaries are falling," Zaphenath told the king, unrolling the first scroll.

Senusret glanced at him, noting the almost abrupt tone in his voice and the unusual soberness of his expression. Zaphenath remained impassive, so Senusret accepted the offered scroll and studied the figures, frowning.

"The trend is similar throughout the region." Zaphenath pointed at the columns of numbers collected from granaries around the state. The king nodded, raising his eyes again. Zaphenath plucked another scroll, handing the first back to Amon. "However, we've established higher levels of supplies further inland, where fewer foreigners are coming to trade. We can easily transfer the surplus grain while maintaining a steady balance to feed our own people."

Senusret nodded, looking down at the second scroll. "How long will the transfer take?"

"It's already underway, Majesty." Zaphenath inclined his head. "We acted in anticipation of the decline. We should be able to begin redistributing and recalculating wages within the month. Kemet has the supplies to support her People and her neighbors, as long as we are mindful of our constraints."

Senusret smiled at Amon. "Your father could not have had a finer successor," he said, and Amon quickly lowered his head at the compliment. "Now tell me," the king said, looking back at his vizier, "what progress has been made on our irrigation systems in the Oasis?"

Zaphenath heard the sound of sauntering footsteps and a voice call out, "Tjaty."

Zaphenath turned and made his customary half-bow. "Prince."

Senusret's oldest son, named for his father, was away from the palace on a diplomatic errand, seeking to maintain the rather profitable trade relations the elder Senusret had established with some of their northern neighbors. This arrangement left the king's second son, Asar, with the run of the palace and, Zaphenath thought darkly, free to torment his father's senior official.

"My father thinks I ought to become involved in helping to oversee these land development projects in the Oasis," Asar said, waving his hand vaguely.

Glancing at Senusret, who merely smiled his assent, Zaphenath managed a weak smile himself. "It would be my honor." He reached for a new scroll, handing the other back to Amon, while Asar stepped closer and looked over Zaphenath's shoulder.

On the scroll was a diagram of a large plot of land. What Asar had been calling the Oasis was really a region of marshlands near the capital city, most frequently used for aristocrats' hunting and fishing trips. "The additional acreage you've identified, Majesty," Zaphenath said, after glancing over his shoulder at Asar, "can almost certainly become prime arable land with the proper drainage and development. Its central location will be particularly valuable for the resulting ease of distribution."

"Have you been to the area yourself?" Asar asked.

Again, Zaphenath glanced over his shoulder. "I have been out for several inspections," he said, "and my assistant recently returned from meeting with officials on my behalf." He glanced at Amon, who nodded. Zaphenath continued, indicating an inscription on the papyrus, "As it turns out, the lowered water levels right now are allowing us to develop a particularly good estimate regarding the viability of the marshlands."

"Perhaps," Asar said, pressing a hand to his chest and looking toward his father, "for the sake of accuracy, it would do to return to the place oneself before presenting a report to His Majesty."

Zaphenath raised his eyes from the scroll. "I assure you, Prince, the calculations are accurate and in accord with the most recent visits. Observe." Pointing to the characters written around the diagram, he began to explain the finer details of the drainage and development plan, including the mathematic calculations undertaken to produce a workable model of water flow and progressive estimates of additional crop yield, all while speaking at a steadily more rapid pace. Soon Asar's eyes began to wander.

"All right," the prince muttered, waving his hand again. Zaphenath inclined his head and turned back to Senusret, continuing his explanations.

Less than a minute later, Asar interjected, "Forgive me, Father, I have other business this morning." With a regal sniff, he took his leave.

Senusret watched his son go. "Asar is not so well versed in the matter yet," he said after a moment. "Perhaps a . . . less-detailed explanation, next time."

Zaphenath inclined his head. "My apologies."

Senusret smiled slightly. "You seem agitated, Zaphenath."

Keeping his eyes on the scroll in his hands, Zaphenath quickly rolled the papyrus closed, tapping the fringed end against his palm. "Not at all, Majesty."

Senusret looked at him, then, as if acknowledging that there was perhaps no more information to be had, simply shrugged. "Well, your calculations are excellent, if a little difficult for the average man to keep up with." He paused. "People tend to respond better to being led, not overpowered." He smiled again. "Gently, Zaphenath. Gently."

CHAPTER 6

Asenath

Asenath, daughter of the high priest of Ra and wife of Zaphenath-Paaneah, vizier of all the land of Kemet and special counselor to the king, looked up, listening, as the footsteps (which could only belong to her husband—none of the servants ever moved that fast) came striding down the family's private corridor. She sat on the floor of a comfortably appointed room with their two sons, the younger of whom was pushing a small, carved wooden horse in a circle, while the elder sat cross-legged, dutifully practicing simple characters with his ink brush on a broken shard of pottery. Then she watched as a figure brushed past the curtain, drawn to keep out the flies, and heard the footsteps diminish on down the corridor.

The children looked at their mother, and she glanced at them. It was a rare day, and never a good sign, for their father to fail to greet them all immediately upon his return to the house.

Asenath rose to her feet. "Watch your brother, please," she said, addressing her elder son, and the boy nodded dutifully. Moving from the room, she pushed through the thin curtain and walked quietly down the mud-brick corridor that stayed so pleasantly cool despite the heat of the day. Pausing outside the arched entryway into the room she shared with the man who had become the vizier and the king's most trusted advisor at the same time he became her husband, she took a deep breath and drew the curtain aside.

Zaphenath sat on their bed of cream-colored linens with his back to her.

"My love," she said, letting the curtain rustle closed behind. He didn't move. "Zaphenath."

He glanced back at his name, though the glance barely cleared his shoulder. His fine wig lay beside him on the bed, exposing his own dark, curling hair, which appeared thoroughly ruffled.

"Are you all right?" Asenath's voice was gentle in the quiet of the afternoon. "Did you present your plan to the king?"

"To the king," Zaphenath said, turning back away from her, "and his son."

"Asar?" she asked. "He was there?"

"The king," Zaphenath said, "has decided that the prince should be involved in the development project."

Asenath walked closer. "I know he can be difficult, but you've said yourself he's not a bad man."

"He's a jealous man." Zaphenath shook his head. "And has a particularly sore spot for his father's vizier. The king has to know that."

"Well," Asenath sat down beside him, "maybe that's part of why he wants you to work together." Zaphenath glanced at her. "The king is very tender toward him," she smiled, "and you know he lives under the shadow of his older brother." She gave her husband a little nudge. "You've certainly dealt with people who are more difficult than Asar, my love."

"I don't need trouble on this project."

"He'll be eager to please you if he feels he can." Asenath put a hand on his arm. "Think of the king's prisoners. No one else has been able to work with them as you have. Asar can be difficult, but he's hardly a criminal."

Zaphenath's glance implied that he was by no means sure such a development was out of the question.

Asenath smiled again. "At the very least, there's no need to provoke him, my love."

He gave her an irritated look. "I don't provoke him."

"You don't?" She leaned in, giving her husband a quick kiss on the cheek. "Then let it go."

Indignant, Zaphenath opened his mouth but could not seem to summon an adequate response. He looked away for a moment, then back at her. "You," he said, "have been mercifully spared much interaction with a certain side of human nature." He turned away. "The man you grew up with is very different from the one I have to deal with. And I've already been lectured once today by the king about being gentle and generous with his undeserving son."

Asenath frowned. After a moment, she leaned in toward him. He turned his face away from her and sat forward, hands clasped together, elbows resting on his knees. She pulled back and stared at him, a little perplexed and not a little hurt, but he did not look at her.

"What did the king say to you?" she asked at last. He didn't respond. "Zaphenath," she said, "this isn't like you." He sighed, lowering his head. "The prince is harmless," she said softly. "Really, my love, what is it?" But still he did not look at her. At last, she said, "All right," and stood up from the bed. "I'll let you be." She began walking back toward the curtained entryway.

"Asenath," he said, and she stopped and turned back around. He was sitting very still, his hair unkempt and his eyes a little wild. "I saw my brothers."

She felt a sudden change sweep through the room, and a strange, heavy silence in its wake.

"What do you mean?" she asked, as if he could mean anything other than what he had said.

Zaphenath swallowed, looking away. "They came for food."

She took a step closer, holding out one hand in an unasked question. "But . . . where are they? Did you speak to them?" He nodded. She took another step. "What did you say?"

"They're being held," he said, looking back toward the wall, "on my orders. Until I decide."

She stared at him, or at least at the back of his head, and asked finally, "Did all this with Asar happen after—?"

"Yes," he said shortly. Then he looked back down at his

hands, and she could see, for the first time, that his fingers were trembling. "Once someone has done to you what has been done to me," he said, and his voice was quiet, "then you can lecture me on why I shouldn't worry about the prince."

Slowly now Asenath moved closer, and slowly she sat back down on the bed. When she reached out, almost hesitant, to rest a comforting hand on his shoulder, he did not move either to acknowledge her touch or to reject it.

"They looked like savages," he said. "That's what Amon thought. All beards and wool." He looked over at her. "They didn't recognize me."

"How could they?" Asenath ran her fingers up through his curls. "You look like one of the People. You are one of the People."

"I'm not." He looked down. "I'm a Canaanite."

"You are Zaphenath-Paaneah," she said. "You are tjaty of all Kemet—"

"I was a slave."

She took his face in her hands, turning his gaze back toward her own. "The man who was a slave," she said firmly, "is the same man who is the king's most trusted advisor. The same man."

"I'm not the same man," he said, and his voice sounded hoarse. "I'm not the same man at all." He blinked, turning away and putting his hands up to either side of his head as if to ward off a headache threatening above his ears. "Your people are all about being firm in proper punishment," he said, quietly, "exercising anger when anger is justified, maintaining order in the world by maintaining order between people." He shook his head. "And nobody knows who I am. I hardly know who I am."

Asenath looked at him, at the way his fingers clenched at his hair and his eyes stared off and away, and she reached out, resting her hand on his back. He bowed his head and covered his face with his hands.

CHAPTER 7

Genesis 34; 35:16–19, 22

The desolate majesty of the horizon stretched out across the plain, sprawling in a dusty, undulating sea and thoroughly encompassing the little gathering of tents propped together in the temporary solitude of safety. A tall man with thick, curling white hair stood alone in the midst of this camp of desert wanderers, facing two of his sons—dark-haired young men with glowering dark eyes, arms crossed defiantly against his anger.

A woman with a young face stooped down beside a younger, solemn-eyed boy who stood watching. "Joseph," she whispered, a loose, dark curl falling across her cheek, "come away from here."

"The men of Shechem promised peace." Jacob, he of the white hair, gestured accusingly at the sons standing before him. "You have made us a family of murderers—"

"Our sister was betrayed," Simeon snarled. "It was for her honor—"

"She would have been protected," Jacob snapped back. "What life have you given her?"

"Take him away from here," murmured Reuben—that was the oldest brother's name—and the young woman, she of the dark curl, glanced at Reuben, who stood behind her, feeling the lightness of his touch on her back.

"I want to see Dinah," Joseph said, looking up at her. "She's all alone."

"She's all right, Joseph," the woman said quietly. "The other women have to help your mother—"

"Bilhah." The woman turned, looking toward where another, older woman had appeared, beckoning sternly from around the corner of a nearby tent. When the second woman saw Reuben, her eyes narrowed, and Reuben looked down, eyes suddenly fixed on the top of his younger brother's head. "Bilhah," the woman repeated, hissing so her low voice would carry the distance, "we need your help—"

Bilhah also looked down at the boy—the beloved and only son of her mistress, Rachel—but Joseph was looking past her, toward this other woman, his mother's sister, who was older and taller and had borne seven children. He took a step toward her, but she gave a firm shake of her head, gesturing to Bilhah, who caught his arm.

"Not yet, Joseph," Bilhah whispered. "The baby's not here yet. I'll go see your mother"—she tried to smile—"and you go see your sister."

She left him, not looking at Reuben as she brushed past. Joseph stood watching as the two women disappeared around the corner of the tent. Then he looked up at his older brother, and Reuben smiled and crouched down, putting an arm around the boy.

"Your mother will be fine," he whispered. "Go and see Dinah."

"Your sister's marriage"—Joseph suddenly heard his father's voice again, breaking like waves against the outer edges of the camp—"would have made peace with a people who would have protected this family."

"Queen to a man who violated her," Simeon shot back, and Joseph felt Reuben tense beside him. "Marrying her does not atone for what was done. Nothing can forgive—"

"You dare to speak of forgiveness?" Jacob advanced closer, broad and strong in his aging years. Simeon gazed back at his father for only a single furious moment before lowering his eyes. Jacob had moved close enough to strike his son or to himself be struck. But neither of them moved. "You are a child," Jacob said, his voice low, "who understands nothing."

"Come away from here," Reuben murmured, rising and steering Joseph away by the shoulder. "You should be with Dinah."

Joseph crept softly into his sister's tent in case she was sleeping, but she was not sleeping. She lay on her back with mute, open eyes, barely shifting her attention as her little brother came creeping in.

"Dinah," he said, as he moved closer to where she lay, stepping across the sheepskin carpets lining the ground and kneeling beside her. She looked toward him. Her eyes were pale and shadowed.

Joseph brushed a loose strand of hair off her forehead, the way he had seen his mother do.

"How is she?" Dinah asked, her voice quiet.

Joseph shrugged. "I don't know."

Dinah's hands rested on top of her stomach, her body loosely robed. Joseph rose to a seated position and rested his own hands together in his lap. They sat together without speaking.

"Did . . . the prince hurt you," Joseph asked at last, "again?"

Dinah's face was fair and still half-childish, with long, inky-dark hair and a delicacy that resembled her little half-brother more than the other boys. "No," she said.

"Simeon . . . wanted to protect you," Joseph said, and she glanced back at him.

"I saw him die." Her eyes were glazed. "I saw what Simeon did."

Joseph reached out, touching her arm as if to pull her back from that strange and silent place that had swallowed her whole.

The covering of the entrance to the tent was drawn back again, and Joseph looked over his shoulder as another brother ducked in. With bristly dark hair and a round teenaged face just losing its boyishness, he had his father's broad expression and his mother's brisk movements. He tip-toed lithely over the sheepskins, settling down next to Joseph.

"I was wondering where you went," he said, ruffling his little brother's hair. "Reuben said you came to keep Dinah company." He looked at his sister and smiled at her. "Are you hungry?" She shook her head. "We can bring you something."

"What's happening outside?" she asked, voice still quiet.

"Father's with Simeon and Levi," Judah said, keeping his voice light. "The other women are with Rachel."

Dinah looked at him. "It's been a day already."

Judah shrugged and looked down at Joseph. He put his arm around the boy who so resembled Rachel—his father's beloved second wife, who had been in labor with her second child since the previous morning—with the same dark eyes and beautiful, curling hair. "Don't worry," Judah said, "your mother will be fine. Sometimes it takes a long time for a baby to come. She's just worn out, because . . . we had to move quickly."

Dinah pushed herself off her sleeping mat and sat up, taking a slow breath. "Because of me."

Judah reached out, taking Dinah by the arm, as if to steady her. "Not because of you."

She looked at him. "She's done so much, taking care of me . . . and . . . we had to leave . . ."

"Stop," Judah said, shaking his head once.

"I can help take care of you," Joseph said, quietly. Judah and Dinah looked at him, and Dinah tried to smile.

"Thank you, sweet boy," she said softly.

Judah smiled too. "Your mother will need you to help take care of your new brother."

"Is it a brother?" Joseph asked.

Judah grinned. "Probably."

"Will he look like me?"

"Oh," Judah said, "most certainly. He'll be very handsome."

Joseph looked at Dinah. "Or if it's a girl," he said, "she'll look like you." Dinah smiled too, but her smile was sadder. Then Joseph looked back up at Judah. "But," he said, "I bet he'll be a brother."

And Judah smiled.

Sleeping, lying on his back in the darkness with the camp quiet all around, Joseph opened his eyes.

And as he did, he found himself staring, rising, up into the stars, watching the brilliant patches of light swirl and spin, and he was stunned, breathless, and his body rushed higher into the sky—tumbling, free and safe and whole, and the stars encircled him as he hung suspended in the sky, enclosing his entire being in a pulsing, trembling globe—and up above, beyond the burning, he saw the great dancing disk of the sun embrace the silvery, shadowed moon, the one passing over the other and subsuming both into a glorious, shimmering flame—and he closed his eyes and the stars themselves began to speak, calling him by name—

Joseph—

Joseph—

"Joseph . . ."

His eyelids fluttered. His little body lay curled on a sheepskin where he had fallen asleep in his sister's tent. Dinah was rubbing his back.

"Joseph," she said again, and he raised his head, blinking the darkness from his eyes. Dinah looked as if she were about to speak, and Joseph blinked again, looking up at her. There was something strange about her face and the stillness of her body.

"Are you all right?" he asked.

She was not all right, because she had come to tell him that the world was not all right.

She had come to tell him that he had a brother, a big, healthy baby boy born in the wilderness of their afflictions, a child their father had named *Ben-jamin,* Son-of-My-Right-Hand, and that the baby was sleeping in Bilhah's arms. But Bilhah herself was weeping, and Leah sat beside her in the stillness of the shadows with Zilpah at her feet, and Jacob walked alone in the desert, and the moonlight ran freely down his face.

Dinah had come to tell Joseph that his mother—his beautiful, brave, beloved mother, Jacob's most cherished wife, his "Little Ewe"—had given Jacob his twelfth son in a wash of blood that could not be stopped.

And Joseph—who had listened while Bilhah explained to him that it was love that brought children into the world and that the love of his parents had brought him and now this new little one into life—could not understand why love should demand such a hideous sacrifice.

CHAPTER 8

Dreams

Darkness—darkness and dryness encased by loose, pebbly sand, and his fingers raw from clawing at the earth that gave way in a hissing stream—the white sky high above beating down the day's heat and gazing unblinking into the empty well shaft dug deep into the earth where no life breathed—the walls of the pit collapsing into greater darkness, with other groans, other bodies—he could hear voices—and the darkness came as searing as the harsh white desert sun, and he cried out—and nobody answered, and nobody came—

Stirring, Asenath opened her eyes and saw her husband silhouetted in the dim light, trying to catch his breath from some dream that had startled him awake.

"Are you all right?" she murmured.

"It's nothing," he whispered, "go back to sleep." He slid his legs over the side of the bed and moved to his feet, tying his linen kilt around his body as he walked from the room. He moved alone down the corridor and out onto the private porch that overlooked the gardens. He closed his eyes, trying to slow his breath.

From behind, he heard the sound of soft, approaching footsteps, and Asenath came and stood beside him.

"What is it?" she asked.

He rubbed his hands over his face as if the night air were some sort of reviving water bath he might splash across his skin. "Dreams," he said. "Nothing."

"More dreams?" She was watching him as he stared out toward the great, dark, lapping River. "About your brothers?" When he didn't reply, she looked out toward the River as well, where a gradual lightening was beginning to seep across the sky. The low croaking of night noises carried in from the garden. "There are not many moments," she murmured, "when a man gets to glimpse the sun's sacred progress so closely." She glanced at her husband. "This is the most sacred time at the temples, when Ra returns to the world. When a soul goes to meet him, the soul begins there"—she pointed toward the horizon—"where the heavens and the earth meet. Where Osiris rises from the underworld. The in-between moments"—she looked at him—"are when all things are closest together. The in-between places are the passageways."

Zaphenath watched the line of the horizon growing slowly brighter, Ra shining his brilliance back into the world, summoning up souls to ascend with him on into the heavens.

"Out in the desert," he said quietly, "you're always moving toward a horizon that can't be reached."

Asenath smiled. "In the desert," she said, "every horizon

blends into another, and there is neither beginning nor end. The horizon is both time and eternity." She placed the palm of her hand against her husband's chest. "Take a deep breath, my love." He looked down at her, and she looked up at him; then he closed his eyes, and his chest rose and fell slowly beneath her touch, and she felt the pounding of his heart beginning to slow. "To breathe," she said, her voice gentle in the early quiet of the morning, "is to embrace the gods and be embraced in return. The most sacred rituals center on restoring breath." Her words were joined in a delicate duet by the croaking of river frogs over the wall. "Restoring the living with the dead."

The Book of Breathings, which Isis made for her brother Osiris . . .

He opened his eyes and looked at her, his wife, daughter of the high priest of Ra. "Isis causes the soul and body of Osiris to breathe," he said, reciting the words and smiling, "*to make his soul appear in glory in heaven in the disk of the moon, and his body to shine in the womb of the stars.*"

Asenath smiled too. "The stars are always the first place of rebirth."

"Your brother gave me that text," he said. "Maybe you know the mystery of why Isis brings Osiris back to life."

Her eyes found his. "So that all things can be joined anew." She reached out again, resting her hand over his heart. "My love," she said quietly, "what are you going to do?"

Zaphenath didn't answer her. But he looked up and beyond, toward where the rising sun and fading moon and the stars all hovered together for a single, unbroken moment in the horizon.

CHAPTER 9

Genesis 42:17–24

Judah could not tell whether he had actually slept during any of the time he had spent curled on the hard dirt floor of the prison. The drifting, muted conversation of the guards lulled him in and out of a dim, in-between sleeplessness, and his neck twinged with a warning ache as he began to move. It was now the second morning since he and his brothers had been left, without further explanation, in this place. Two strangers had been taken out the first night and had not returned; where they had been taken was not something Judah cared to know.

He did wonder, however, just what the penalty was for spying in this mighty kingdom, beholden to none but itself. Why did no one come to speak to them, or explain what they might expect, or offer so much as a single chance to explain themselves? And another thought danced at the periphery of his mind, circling back and back again and looming ever larger with each return—how long could their families survive? How long before their wives and daughters and sons began to starve? How long until their aged father ceased to wake?

Rolling over, wincing, Judah looked up at the fissures in the mud bricks blocking the sky. His brothers had all remained close together, some sprawled sleeping, others speaking in low voices; it was still unclear who would be given the chance at freedom coupled with the onerous task of begging their father for Benjamin. Judah had finally removed himself from the discussion, feeling disinclined to bicker with Simeon or Reuben or any of the others, and instead tried to sleep, or at least lie with his eyes closed and try to dream. But in the darkness, no dreams came.

Snatches of thought came, though, with pricklings of memory, and he could not remember when he had last seen so many flitting visions of another brother's face in all the years since the boy had been lost. He said nothing as others spoke hopefully of misunderstandings, of mercy. They did not deserve to hope for mercy.

A rising tide of voices, rippling into the otherwise undisturbed murmurs of low conversation, nudged him from his thoughts. He looked toward the growing sound. The other prisoners began looking over too, while the brothers seemed to draw closer together, protectively, against whatever uncertainty might be rallying against them now.

Steadying himself to his feet, Judah winced over to the solitary small opening in the wall, squinting to peer out. He saw a man clothed in fine-spun linens and an elegant wig standing in the central room outside their holding cell, surrounded by more guards, speaking to a prison official. He was accompanied by a bare-headed fellow in much simpler, unadorned dress. The wigged man kept looking over toward where the brothers were being kept. Judah glanced at his brother Zebulon, who had risen to stand next to him in an effort to see what was happening.

"Do you recognize him?" Judah asked. "I can't see his face."

"It's the man who accused us," Zebulon said softly.

One of the guards turned and approached the cell. Judah and Zebulon backed away, stepping into the shadows. Judah could hear the men outside speaking rapidly to each other, and then their accuser's face, with his dark-lined eyes, appeared in the opening. His elegant gold chain, bespeaking his wealth and authority, was dim around his neck in the poor light. He stared in at them and then he turned, speaking in a low voice. The bare-headed man stepped closer.

"The vizier of all Kemet returns to speak with you," the man announced.

The vizier—could they possibly have had the misfortune to offend the greatest official in the country? Judah wondered in blistering disbelief—spoke again to the translator, who nodded. "You are still suspects," they were told, and Judah felt a deep breathlessness, "and proof of your identity will be required. However," the translator paused, and the vizier spoke again, the foreign interchange nearly inaudible within the cell, "because the vizier is a merciful man, he will allow you to return to your families with your grain."

A murmuring wave swept through the brethren. Judah saw Simeon, one of the chief proponents of the imminent mercy that would surely be shown to them, look around, smiling to himself as the other brothers looked toward him. After all, it was he, aside from Reuben, who was the most senior among them—the one, it was quietly said, who felt he should have received the birthright after his older brother's disgrace with one of his father's wives.

"However," the translator continued, and the brothers waited, "one of you will remain behind."

The murmuring swelled again as the vizier pointed, saying something first to the translator and then turning to the guards, gesturing with his head in the direction of his outstretched hand.

"This man," the translator said, "will remain."

Simeon cried out in alarmed astonishment.

Reuben put a hand on his arm. "Brother—"

Simeon jerked his arm away.

"You will begin your journey today," the translator announced, even as one of the guards unbarred the small door that led out of the cell, "and return with this youngest brother you claim. It is not the vizier's wish that you or your family should starve."

Outside the cell, Amon, who had been sent out of the room on an errand before the conversation with the foreign prisoners began, returned, approaching his master.

"I have given the orders to have their grain sacks filled, Excellency," he said, "and their animals will be brought and prepared for the voyage back to the Deshret." He paused. "Tjaty?"

His master nodded abruptly and cleared his throat. "Thank you."

Two of the guards were moving in among the prisoners, shouldering their way past the bearded men who stood around the prisoner singled out for ransom.

Then Amon heard something that he did not quite understand and glanced back toward his master.

Zaphenath had turned his face away. "Tell them they are free to go," he repeated.

Amon gave the order for the translation.

As Judah moved out of the cell, he looked toward the vizier. At the same moment, the vizier turned and met Judah's gaze with rich, dark, haunted eyes—such eyes, Judah thought, as he had not seen since—

But then one of the guards held up an arm, and the great man moved past without another word, leaving the prison and the men from Canaan behind.

CHAPTER 10

Abraham 3:3, 11–12, 15
Genesis 37:9–11

And I saw the stars, that they were very great, and that one of them was nearest to the throne of God; and there were many great ones which were near to it; and the Lord said to me: These are the governing ones . . .

Joseph, son of Jacob, sat on the floor of his father's tent. His young head, covered in abundant dark curls, bowed over the scroll held open on his lap, with the bobbling, dripping illumination scattering the space with shadows and making it difficult to read the foreign characters in the dim light.

And he said to me: My son, my son, I will show you all these. And he put his hand on my eyes, and I saw those things which his hands had made, and they multiplied before my eyes, and I could not see the end . . .

Joseph's own dark gaze darted over the strange and wonderful words, inked carefully onto the pounded papyrus scroll by his great-grandfather's own hand. His lips moved quietly over the foreign sounds.

And the Lord said to me: Abraham, I show you these things before you go into Kemet, that you may declare these words . . .

The writings had been passed first to Abraham's second son, Isaac, and Isaac had passed them to his second son, Jacob, and now Jacob had begun to teach his own son—the eleventh of his body but second in line for the birthright, even as Jacob and Isaac had been before him—what these writings contained. When Joseph asked his father who among his brothers had seen the scrolls, Jacob acknowledged that Reuben had seen them, "but," he added darkly, "he failed entirely to understand them." Besides Reuben, only Joseph had been allowed to read the most sacred writings for himself. Although Jacob instructed all of his sons in the strict way of the covenant inherited from his grandfather Abraham and all the boys could read the basic words of the writings, the actual handling of the scrolls, the learning and study by heart until the words were so deeply ingrained as to be beyond the power of any earthly being to remove, was a task for a birthright son. These words were his inheritance.

"What do you understand from this?" Jacob asked, sitting beside Joseph, waiting until his son had finished reading the passage.

Joseph thought for a moment, and Jacob could not but see, as he so often saw, how closely the boy resembled his beautiful mother: her dark curls, her large, inquiring eyes, the gentle symmetry of her face. But the resemblance was greater than the boy's appearance—he tended, at times, toward Rachel's slight, almost shy, aloofness with his brothers, even as Rachel had seemed forever reluctant to challenge her older sister's jealously guarded eminence as Jacob's first wife and mother of so many of his children. Instead, Rachel had quietly raised Joseph while his brothers fought and wrestled together under the desert sun, and Joseph was drawn to her company over any other, knowing, with his mother, that he was the oldest and only and most beloved and that they were more a part of one another than any other two people in the camp.

Joseph also had his mother's quiet powers of keen and compassionate observation, and—this was what stabbed at Jacob the most—he saw in Joseph's interactions with his brothers the same sense of exclusion he had watched Leah exert against her sister, an isolation decreed in revenge for not being the favorite. Yet Leah and Rachel had been sisters, and their sense of blood devotion had managed to transcend the rivalry that they had inherited with their marriage to the same man. Rachel almost always remained gentle with Leah, somehow able to feel Leah's sadness rather than her anger, and Leah, in spite of her jealousy, could be extraordinarily protective of her acutely sensitive younger sister. Theirs was a relationship into which Jacob had never been fully admitted, and it seemed to him that was as it should have been.

But Joseph, who had been born to Rachel after Leah had already given Jacob seven children, was not a full brother to any other child in the camp save little Benjamin, the last of Jacob's children. And Benjamin, who looked much more like Jacob than he did his mother or his older brother, was really Leah's child—Leah, who had lost a baby of her own so shortly before Benjamin's birth and had wept at the thought of her sister bearing a healthy child in her place; Leah, who had nursed and nourished and doted on Benjamin, her love for him the penance she sought for such selfish thoughts before her sister's death. Aside from his sister Dinah, who pitied him, Joseph had never found another friend so loyal as his mother.

Jacob, too, had never found any friend greater than his beloved Rachel.

And so, while Joseph sought out his brother's friendship whenever it was dangled, tantalizingly, before him, in a very true sense he was an only son, a lone child in the midst of a family, even as Jacob's own father, Isaac, had been.

Just what, Jacob sometimes wondered, has this boy inherited from us?

"It appears," Joseph said at last, his voice still oddly unfamiliar after having so recently shifted into the depth of a young man, "that the Lord governs all things, though sometimes"—he glanced at his father—"he uses representatives to govern."

"He governs," Jacob agreed, "yes. He creates governance and order for all things but never compels his creations." Joseph nodded. "And as he chooses governors among the stars"—Jacob put a hand on Joseph's shoulder—"so too does he choose governors among men. This is why there is so much for you to learn, before you become a governor within our family. It is a heavy inheritance. But," he smiled, "one for which you will be eminently capable."

Joseph bowed his head, accepting the compliment, and smiled as he glanced back up. "When it says, 'that you may declare all these words,'" he asked, "does it mean that Abraham was meant to tell these things to the people in the Divided Land?" The Divided Land was the name among the desert people for the country of Abraham's foreign sojourn—a northern and southern kingdom united tentatively under a single powerful ruler, prone to dissolution and revolution and ever seeking to tame the wildness of the elements and the darkness within men.

"The Lord often means for us to teach what he has taught us." Jacob smiled. "This scroll comes from the record Abraham made while he was there."

Joseph looked at his father. "But why did he go to the Divided Land when this was his promised land?"

"A terrible famine," Jacob said gravely. "He could not have survived here." He paused, then said, "The Lord's promises do not always come in our time."

Joseph looked back down at the manuscript, but he did not continue reading. After a moment, Jacob asked, "Do you have another question?"

Joseph pointed at a particular passage. "*The Lord said to me,*" he read, "*this is the sun. And he said to me, this is the moon. And he said to me, these are the stars, or all the great lights.*" Then, raising his eyes, he said, "It's like my dream."

In the flickering shadow light, Jacob's face looked deeply lined. "Which you had the sense to tell your brothers about."

Joseph looked back at the text. "But it was just like this." He swept his hand over the words. "And I've seen it more than once—the stars, all around me, and the sun, and the moon, passing over each other—"

"And bowing to you," Jacob said. Joseph's cheeks flushed, and he looked down. "Your brothers are the stars, and your mother and I the sun and the moon?"

"No. I . . . I don't know." Joseph glanced at his father. "It's just . . . always been the same, even after she . . ."

Then he grew quiet.

Jacob reached out, pressing his hand to his son's arm. "Come with me," he said and rose to his feet. Joseph, nearly as tall but not nearly so broad, stood up after him, and Jacob held out his hand for the scroll, which Joseph carefully rolled up and handed to him. Jacob moved toward the entrance of his tent, scroll in hand, and pushed the outer flap aside, stepping out into the desert night. Stepping out after him, Joseph raised his eyes, staring up at the great wash of stars. At first, he could hear the laughter coming from the other tents and the intertwined voices of light-hearted conversation. But as he stared up, all else in the world began to fall away, and he simply stood, gazing and open to the night sky.

"The heavens," he heard his father say, "possess different degrees of light—the sun brighter than the moon, the moon brighter than the stars." Jacob turned to his son. "My father told me he believed that men also express different degrees of light, whether it be in understanding, or compassion, or intelligence, or faith." He looked back up. "But see how they are all arranged together, each giving light in its own way, each respecting the course of the other because each is bound to the others—traveling and returning together, in and out of the seasons." He looked back at Joseph. "I like to think that you and your brothers are like these stars, formed and bound together on your course."

Joseph stood with his head tilted back, following his father's gaze up into the sky.

"As we come to understand our place in the world," Jacob murmured, "we also find our place in the worlds to come." He swept his hand across the horizon in a broad gesture. "As we ascend through the understanding of the stars, the moon, even the sun—as we acquire that same level of light and all that it entails—we return ever closer back to God." He nodded and then said quietly, "We pass through burnings as great as we can stand." He put a hand on Joseph's shoulder. "You will have to teach and guide your brothers, Joseph, when I am gone—you will be the head of our family." Joseph looked up at his father. "But you must do it carefully." Jacob looked down at his son. "The strength of the sun obliterates the light of the stars, doesn't it?" Joseph lowered his eyes toward his sandaled feet, feeling his father's hand tighten in an affectionate squeeze on his shoulder. "You have many gifts, Joseph, and great capability.

But whatever dreams come to you in the night, I trust you understand why it is not . . . helpful is one word . . . to tell your brothers."

Joseph sighed. "Yes." He shook his head. "But I think—they think I'm your heir because you favor me."

"On the contrary," Jacob said. "They fear their own light is not as bright as yours." His face seemed suddenly sad. "And there are those who think that diminishing another will make them brighter." He was quiet before adding, "It was what my brother thought of me. And my father's brother thought of him."

Joseph looked up. "You had to leave your brother to save your life."

Jacob looked back at his son, and his face was serious. "And then we were reconciled," he said. "You are always a part of your brothers, and they are part of you, even if it takes all of you many years to see it." He looked up once more. "Knowing that the stars are all bound together is more important than their precise arrangement. And until you understand that"—he glanced once more at his son—"you cannot think to go beyond them."

Joseph nodded, and stood still, and looked up at the sky.

A moment passed, and Jacob touched Joseph's shoulder. Joseph glanced toward his father. "Come," Jacob said, holding out his arm, and Joseph turned, walking beside him. "I have something to show you."

Joseph ducked back inside his father's tent and waited,

watching, as his father crossed to the far side of the flickering interior. Jacob bent down, kneeling beside a wooden box that Joseph had seen before and that he assumed, like any other wooden box, carried inconsequential clothing or supplies. So he watched closely as his father pushed back the lid and carefully, almost reverently, lifted out an airy, cream-colored bundle. Jacob placed Abraham's scroll inside the same box; then he rose, turning.

"Joseph," Jacob said, moving back toward his son, "this robe"—he held out the almost transparent cream-colored cloth—"was given to me by my father, who received it from his father." He began to unfold the delicately spun garment, and Joseph watched as Jacob revealed an open, flowing robe with long sleeves, the kind to be worn over a man's tunic. The robe was embroidered with delicate, linear patterns running the full length of the material, and as Joseph looked closer, he saw what appeared to be a series of two interlocking squares forming an eight-pointed, star-like design, with a circle enclosed within the interlocked space. "Now," Jacob said, "I believe you are ready to receive it." He held up the robe as Joseph slipped his arms into the waiting sleeves. "It is a symbol of your birthright," Jacob continued, speaking quietly, "and of the authority possessed by the birthright son by virtue of the knowledge and wisdom he inherits."

Joseph reached down, pressing the material between his fingers—as fine a consistency of cloth as he had ever imagined, light and almost papery, different from the woolen robes he and his family wore, different from any material he had ever known—and he turned, watching the robe ripple with his movements.

"It is linen," Jacob said. "From the Divided Land."

"And this?" Joseph asked, pointing to the interlocking square design.

"Ah," Jacob said. "That is the symbol of Melchizedek."

The boy's eyebrows raised. "The king?"

"The king," Jacob smiled, "and the priest."

CHAPTER 11

Senet

Ushering the tjaty into the royal palace complex, part living quarters for the royal family and part administrative offices of the state, the guards bowed and allowed the vizier to hurry down the elegant corridor that led toward the private rooms of the king. He moved alone, unaccompanied by either young Amon or the usual armful of scrolls, and was followed only by the echo of his own solitary footsteps. Another pair of guards stood outside the entrance to the king's rooms, and Zaphenath waited while one of the men entered to confirm that the Son-of-Ra, God on Earth, wished to hold this particular audience. Once approval was received, the guards pulled back the imposing wooden doors, painted in bright red to repel the advances of any untoward demons, and allowed the vizier to pass through.

"Ah," he heard, "Zaphenath," and he inclined his head respectfully. The king was wearing a fine-spun linen robe, his eyes lined and his bald head uncovered. He was sitting on a long, low wooden couch, comfortably cushioned and held off the ground by four delicately carved, lion-like feet, facing another reclining couch of similar workmanship. Set on a low table between the two couches was a long, rectangular box covered in gold and inlaid with three rows of gleaming squares. Small ivory playing pieces were positioned variously across the board. Senusret gestured to the reclining couch opposite his own. "Sit."

Zaphenath sat. "It appears that you have a Senet game in progress," he said, looking down at the table.

Senusret waved a hand. "My son felt disinclined to finish his turn."

"Ah." Zaphenath studied the placement of the pieces. "I recall that Senet has never been much to his liking."

"Mm." Senusret murmured his agreement. "He seems to have trouble striking the delicate balance between skill and chance that the game requires. Well." The king's hands were clasped lightly together, his lips pursed as he studied the board. "He will learn."

Zaphenath leaned down and picked up one of the slim sticks lying beside the Senet board, one of a handful tossed upon the table to determine the moves of a player's turn.

"This is partly why I would like Asar to become involved in our project," the king said. Zaphenath raised his eyes, placing the stick back on the table. "He desires very much to be a good servant of the kingdom." Senusret shrugged. "His skills are not as strong as his older brother's. And so he pretends not to care and covers himself with bluster." He picked up one of the ivory pieces, tapping it thoughtfully against the board. "I am hopeful that he may be able to learn from you."

Zaphenath pressed his fingertips together, looking down at his hands. "You know," he said at last, "my only desire is to serve you and your kingdom."

"There is no one of greater ability in all my kingdom," Senusret told him, "than yourself."

"Your words are very generous, Majesty." Zaphenath paused. "Nevertheless, I am not sure that I—that is, there are others who—"

"Zaphenath," Senusret said, a little shortly, setting the Senet piece back down, "I haven't placed you in your position simply because I think you are competent, or clever, or honest." He looked up, pressing one hand against his chest. "You have a connection to all that is most important. And you let that connection guide you. That," Senusret raised a finger, "is why I have made you my most trusted official. And that is what my son needs most to learn."

Zaphenath kept his eyes focused on the Senet board. The game was modeled, it was said, after the reversals and glories and spins of fate that might govern a man's life, with different squares offering various rewards or requisitions to the player who obtained them. One square alone glowed with the stately *ankh* figure—a single vertical line with a horizontal platform and looping circle on top—symbol of life in this world and the next. At last, Zaphenath said, "I will strive to be worthy of your trust."

"You always are." Senusret gathered up the throwing-sticks, tapping the wooden ends against the tabletop to even them out, and extended them toward his vizier. "Throw, if you wish."

Zaphenath watched the king for a moment, as if trying to ascertain whether the offer was serious; then, taking the sticks, he rubbed them briskly between his palms and dropped them onto the table. Senusret smiled as his vizier moved the nearest ivory piece onto a safely neutral square.

"Very good." The king held out his hand, and Zaphenath gathered up the sticks and handed them back. "I am hopeful that this is something else my son can learn from you. To listen." Now Senusret rubbed the sticks between his hands and let them fall. "Ah," he said, "excellent, an extra turn," and moved his piece. He glanced at his vizier, then spoke as he gathered up the throwing-sticks. "Something has been bothering you, Zaphenath."

Zaphenath was watching the board. "There are many responsibilities, Majesty."

"I have seen when responsibility weighs upon you." Senusret raised his eyes. "Or are you telling an old man that his discernment is beginning to fail him?"

Zaphenath smiled slightly. "I would not dare."

The king dropped the sticks and moved another piece. "So." He looked up again. "What is it?"

Zaphenath gathered up the sticks but then merely sat, holding them in one clenched hand. Senusret remained as he was, leaning forward, waiting. At last, Zaphenath looked up. "I have never sought to deceive you," he said, "about my life." Senusret waited. "Where I was born." Zaphenath glanced back at the board. "Or how I came here."

"Zaphenath," Senusret said, waving a hand as if to clear the air of smoke, "I know how you came here." Zaphenath nodded, looking down, one hand still clasped around the throwing-sticks. "Has something been said to you?"

Zaphenath shook his head.

Senusret kept his focus on the vizier's face. "Then it seems an odd time for a bout of self-reflection."

Closing his eyes, Zaphenath said, "Some men from Canaan came to buy grain. I accused them of being spies."

Now Senusret raised both of his eyebrows. "Spies? From Canaan?" He chuckled. "Are the desert tribes planning an invasion?"

"Of course not." Zaphenath sighed. "The men were—are—my brothers."

Senusret sat back from the table, and Zaphenath looked down at the Senet board in the silence that followed.

"How long has it been?" the king asked at last.

"Twenty years." Zaphenath set the sticks down on the table.

Senusret was quiet for a moment, then, looking at his vizier, asked, "Twenty years? And you couldn't come up with anything better than spying? High treason, at least?" Zaphenath looked up at that, and Senusret smiled. "You will force me to lecture you on the abuses of power, Tjaty."

"I didn't know what to do," Zaphenath admitted.

The king waved a hand. "You are a more merciful man

than I might have been. I suppose they know who you are now?"

But Zaphenath shook his head. "I let them go." The king looked at him. Zaphenath didn't raise his eyes. "All but one."

Senusret's eyebrow inched up. "What do you intend to do with the one you kept?"

"I'll use him to make the others bring my younger brother back." Zaphenath paused. "Our father is still alive. Once he dies . . . my brother will be unprotected."

Senusret was quiet. "You believe they would harm him?"

"I know the danger of trusting," Zaphenath said, "where trust is not merited."

Senusret looked at him. Then, reaching out, he placed the tip of his finger on top of one of the Senet pieces, tilting it. "Where is your captive now?"

"In the prison." Zaphenath paused. "I won't keep him there long. Just . . . long enough."

Senusret looked at his vizier. "Long enough for what?"

"He will not be a burden on the state, Majesty."

"It is not the state," Senusret said quietly, "that I fear may be damaged by the burden."

Zaphenath did not reply.

After a long pause, the king rose to his feet, and Zaphenath, glancing up, rose as well. "You seem very weary," Senusret said. He reached out, putting a hand on his vizier's shoulder, and waited until Zaphenath met his eyes. "Your grandfather understood a great deal about the unity underlying all things." He looked at his vizier. "And he knew the value of kindness where no kindness is deserved."

Zaphenath looked at him and then bowed. "Good night, Majesty." And he took his leave.

CHAPTER 12

Genesis 37:8

Closing his eyes, Zaphenath drew a great gulping breath and plunged beneath the water, his wake rippling out in wobbling arcs. He surfaced again with a splash, whipping his head back and scattering droplets like stars across the sloshing murmurs of the pool. Running his fingers through his hair, tiny streams trickling down his skin, he sank into the water again up to his neck. The private outdoor pool was guarded within the garden of his walled estate, situated near the gray-barked fig trees, with their great outstretched branches quivering in the slight evening breeze.

Dipping his head back into the water, Zaphenath closed his eyes. The deadening weight lapped into his ears, magnifying the world beneath the ripples. In his mind, he could hear the king's voice, as if in echo.

You seem agitated, Zaphenath.

He let his body sink beneath the surface.

"You take it too personally," Judah said.

His younger brother Joseph walked beside him, arms crossed in brooding contemplation. "Shouldn't I?"

"Simeon is jealous." Judah shrugged. "That's just his way."

The brothers were strolling back toward the edge of their father's camp, the open plains glowing gently in the fading light. The other brothers had returned to the camp earlier, but Joseph stayed behind to help Judah round up a pair of lambs that had wandered away from the flock and were bleating piteously when the brothers finally came upon them. Now the lambs scampered out ahead, kicking up tiny clouds of spreading dust with each hoof strike against the dry earth, eager to be reunited with their mothers.

"We'll have to move the flocks before long," Judah mused when Joseph didn't respond.

Joseph glanced over. "Father won't want me to go."

Judah shook his head. "It's not that. He needs one of us to stay here."

"But if I never go," Joseph said, "I don't see how anyone will ever—"

"They'll respect you when they have to," Judah said. "They'll have no choice."

Joseph looked down, smoothing the front of the robe their father had given him, Jacob's decision of who would be his heir made visible to all. "They think Father means to make me something I wouldn't be without this."

Judah glanced at his brother. "The rivalry is older than

you are." He looked back toward the setting sun. "It's a lot of years to undo."

Joseph watched the two scraggly lambs, trotting now, slowing as one swished his tail. "Do you think it would be this way if my mother were still alive?"

Judah shrugged. "Reuben and Simeon and some of the others may go their own way eventually."

"You think they'd leave us?"

"The way Father's brother, Esau, did." Judah shrugged again. "Why not?"

Joseph shook his head. "Reuben was the birthright son before I was."

Judah smiled tightly. "Father doesn't trust him." He kicked at the dirt, scattering a loose cluster of pebbles. "However much Father loves any one of us"—he watched the breath of dust rise up from the ground—"he loves this family most of all. He wants to protect his people." He glanced back at Joseph. "You were raised apart from us in so many ways—I can see why Father would choose you. You're—different from the rest of us. It's better."

Joseph was quiet for a long moment. "Did Simeon expect the birthright? Is that why he hates me?"

"He doesn't hate you." Judah seemed to hesitate. "I don't know what he expected. He told Reuben that Bilhah would be Reuben's wife one day anyway and that he deserved her. Even if Father was still alive."

Joseph looked at him. "I didn't know that."

"You were younger." Judah crossed his arms. "You wouldn't have known."

"Did he mean for Reuben to be disinherited?"

Judah shrugged. "If Father had married Rachel first, like he meant to, you would have been his heir to begin with. The birthright was never meant to belong to Simeon." He shook his head. "You shouldn't be blamed."

"But my mother was blamed," Joseph said. "Leah was angry with her. Jealous. I do think some of the brothers see that, in me." He shook his head too. "It was their father who arranged it. It wasn't my mother's fault."

"And it wasn't my mother's fault, either," Judah said. "But they made a life for themselves in spite of it, didn't they? They stayed together. They cared for each other. Even at the end . . . my mother was the one with Rachel."

Joseph nodded, looking down, then turned his face back up toward where the cooking fires glowed, beckoning them onward. Judah smiled a little weakly. "We're all still brothers," he said. The chattering voices of the camp were starting to drift out across the open ground. "The blood bond is not a light thing. Simeon will respect that."

They passed back into the camp, with the bleating of the sheep ringing around the periphery. As they walked, passing the tents, Joseph suddenly heard a scampering of little feet. He turned and smiled at the curly-haired boy running toward him. Though he was only five, it was already evident that Benjamin looked less like their mother than Joseph did and had more of his father's broad cheekbones and shoulders. The child had a certain distinctive gentleness around his eyes, though, and the same rich, curly hair.

"I've been helping Dinah," Benjamin reported with breathless self-satisfaction.

Joseph chuckled, bending down to speak with his brother at eye level. "I'm sure you were a good help."

Still smiling, Benjamin looked up at Judah. "Why are you both late?"

"We had to find some lambs," Judah told him, ruffling Benjamin's hair.

"And you brought them back?"

"Of course," Judah assured him. "In our camp," he winked at the little boy, "we watch out for each other." He glanced at Joseph, and Joseph smiled. "That's what makes us family."

CHAPTER 13

Genesis 42:35

The sun was sinking slowly below the horizon, setting the sky ablaze, as the caravan returned. First the excited voices of little children heralded the approach of the familiar line of lumbering camels led by their weary masters; then the women began ducking from the tents, some pulled along by tiny impatient feet, others talking and walking together, wrapping their woolen shawls more heavily around their shoulders to protect against the coming chill of desert night. One of the women, with silver streaks spreading through her once-dark hair, moved more slowly now, as if physically burdened by being the only woman in the camp whose memory stretched back to the days when there had been twelve brothers.

She heard the approaching footsteps and turned, smiling, as a curly-haired man took her tenderly by the arm. His beard was still dark and full, not yet brushed with the silver that had crept upon his brothers.

"How is Father?" Dinah asked.

"Resting," Benjamin told her. "I'll tell him they've returned when he awakens."

In the dying light, the travelers were mere shadows against the darkening sky, with those who approached listing away into shadows themselves. Dinah squinted as she and Benjamin drew closer, hearing the chatter of the women and children (some of whom were young men and women now themselves), eager to see their returning husbands and fathers. Benjamin scooped up one of his sons and kept moving toward his brothers, but Dinah slowed and stood, watching the families embracing. As she stood, she saw her brother Judah, standing alone, unharnessing the provisions from his camel's back as the animal stood, chewing lazily, with a thin wisp of spittle dangling from its mouth.

Dinah moved toward him.

"You're back at last," she said.

Judah turned.

And she stopped, staring at him in the darkness—seeing, suddenly, a flash of a much younger Judah's face, the raw horror in his eyes and the hoarse confession in his voice—

"What is it?" she asked.

Judah reached out, taking his sister's hand. "Simeon was kept behind," he said, voice low, "but he's alive. He's alive."

Dinah stared at him.

"We were accused of being spies." Judah closed his eyes, putting his free hand up to his head. "I don't know why. Simeon has to stay until we return." He couldn't look at her. "With Benjamin. We have to take Benjamin."

Dinah stood, eyes fixed on her older brother's worn,

weary face, and the voices around her suddenly seemed to be swirling, stumbling—

Benjamin, who had glanced back, set down his son and moved through the gathering crowd. Judah glanced over his shoulder as Benjamin approached.

"Are you all right?" Benjamin asked, touching Dinah on the shoulder.

Dinah looked at him. "Simeon was kept behind."

"We were accused of being spies," Judah said, already weary of telling the story. "We'll go back for him. It's a misunderstanding."

"A misunderstanding?" Now Benjamin was staring at him. "Where is he?"

"He'll be fine." Judah turned to his camel, hoping his own uncertainty had not bled into his voice. "Help me unload some of this." Benjamin reached up to help Judah balance the heavy sack of grain.

"The officials"—Judah's voice was dark on the word—"want some sort of proof that we are brothers, not spies. Our numbers made them suspicious." He swung the sack heavily to the ground with a muffled thud, and though it took him a moment even to realize that he had heard the faint jangling sound, he stopped and peered down at the sack.

"They want you to go back," Dinah said.

"Me?" Benjamin sounded incredulous. "Why?"

Judah was untying the heavy rope sealing the top of the grain sack. "Someone told them about you," he said. "They seem to think that you'll prove whether we're actually a family, not whatever they think we are." The rope flopped onto the ground, and Judah ruffled the sack open. And stared.

A smaller bag was nestled comfortably within the mouth of the sack, poking up from where it had worked its way into the grains over the jostlings of the journey. Benjamin and Dinah looked down as well, then glanced at each other. Slowly stooping, Judah clenched his fist around the mouth of the smaller bag and pulled it out, sending trickling streams of grain down the tiny creases in the material. He looked back in the direction of his other brothers, but they were all speaking to each other and their families and eagerly unloading their own sacks, entirely unaware of the strange new devilry at work.

"So," Judah murmured, gazing at the offending bag clutched in his hand, "he plans to torment us still."

"If you think I had a better choice," Joseph said, arms crossed, facing his brother, "tell me what it was." He was older, taller than he had been when he and Judah had chased lambs together, when Judah had assured him that in time things would get better.

Judah said quietly, "You'll make enemies, if they think you'll always run to Father—"

"They're Father's flocks," Joseph snapped, "and if his own sons are stealing from him—"

"You know," Judah said, stepping closer, "they don't trust you. You have to understand how they see it, not just"—he altered his voice—"the higher moral principle involved." He stuck a finger against Joseph's chest, where the folds of Joseph's robe did not cover the tunic beneath. "You have to think about the whole family. If we come apart—"

"Unity at any cost," Joseph said, "will destroy us, too." He glared at Judah. "What would you have done, if Father had sent you and you saw that they were trading the sheep for themselves?" His voice was gaining a harder edge. "Ask them to stop?"

"As the birthright son," Judah said, "you should consider your position once Father is gone."

They faced each other over the barren ground.

"It would be easier," Joseph said at last, "if you helped me to stand up to them." He waited, but Judah said nothing. "Our brothers respect you," Joseph said, his voice quieter. "They look up to you."

"I don't want to be involved."

"We're all involved." Joseph narrowed his eyes. "You just don't want to help."

"Joseph," Judah said and then took a slow breath before speaking. "You need to be careful." He grew quiet. "They weren't doing what they did because they thought it was right." He paused. "You have to try to understand them, even if you don't like them."

"It's not disliking them," Joseph said. "It's distrusting them."

"Especially if you distrust them," Judah said, "you have to try to understand what they want. You can't just"—he waved a hand—"condemn them, accuse them. You can't overpower them just by arguing, even if Father supports you."

"So what would you do?" Joseph crossed his arms. "Negotiate a share of the profits?"

"No," Judah said, sounding impatient. "Watch them. Figure out what they want. Everybody wants something." He held out an open palm. "Everyone has a price."

Joseph looked at him.

Judah, waiting in the quiet, looked back.

Joseph turned and walked away.

CHAPTER 14

Genesis 42:36

Judah ducked out of the evening light and into his father's darkened tent, blinking in the sudden dimness. He heard the rustle of fabric behind him as Benjamin, who had held the tent flap open, stepped in behind him. Judah waited while his brother moved past across the soft flooring of carpets and sheepskin. Their father, Jacob, was resting on a low couch, his white beard as brilliant as ever.

Benjamin knelt beside Jacob, putting a hand on the aged man's shoulder. "Father," he said, "they've returned with food."

Judah saw the old man's eyes open; he saw his father's eyes focus keenly on his face. "Judah." Jacob smiled, rising to sit. "How was your journey?" His voice carried easily through the tent. Judah moved closer.

"Safe," he reported. "And the People were generous with us."

Jacob nodded. "Good," he said, stretching. "Good. We could not have gone on much longer without you."

Judah nodded, taking a slow, deep breath. "Well," he said at last, "God has always watched over our family."

Jacob raised an eyebrow, eyeing his son in the dim light. "What has moved you to speak of God?"

Benjamin looked away at his father's emphasis on *you,* but Judah simply raised the small bag that he had found nestled in the grain, holding it out so his father could see. "This pouch was hidden in my sack," he said. "It's the silver we used to buy the grain."

Jacob stared at the strange apparition. Then he held out his own hand, flicking his fingers in a beckoning gesture. Judah handed him the pouch of silver. Jacob weighed the roughly made material in his palm before loosening the neck of the little bag and peering inside.

"There is some strangeness at work here." Judah paused. "We were also accused of being spies."

"Spies?" Jacob looked up. "Why would anyone think you are spies?"

"I don't know." Judah swallowed. "But Simeon was kept behind."

A sudden, strangled hush fell through the tent. Benjamin reached out to put a hand on his father's shoulder, but Jacob pushed his youngest son's hand away, rising from his couch, his thick woolen garments doing little to cloak the lingering broad strength of his chest. He took a long step toward Judah.

"You have come," he said, gesturing with the jangling

silver sack, "to tell me that another of my sons is taken from me? That is what you have come to say?"

"Father—" Benjamin began, but Judah, glancing at his brother, raised a hand for quiet and looked at his father, who, even in his fiery white-haired age, stood still taller than his fourth son.

"It's a misunderstanding," Judah said, facing Jacob. "They asked that we bring Benjamin as proof that we are a family. Then Simeon will be freed."

He saw his father's lip twitch before he spoke. "Benjamin?" Jacob turned around, looking back at the young man who stood, hesitant, behind them. He wheeled back on Judah. "You dare to come here and tell me you have left Simeon and intend to take Benjamin for bargaining?" He shook his fist, jingling the bag. "With your silver in the sacks? They will accuse you of being thieves, not spies!"

"Benjamin," Judah said, trying to keep his voice calm, "is the proof they demand."

Jacob turned his back with a growl, retreating toward his couch.

"Father"—Judah stepped after him—"I know what it is to lose a son."

Jacob stopped, then slowly turned. His dark eyes fixed on Judah's face.

"On my life," Judah said, "no harm will come to him."

The wrinkles around Jacob's eyes deepened as his gaze narrowed. "That promise," his voice low and even, "is a promise you cannot make." He turned, and his gaze flicked over his shoulder. "We are finished speaking."

Benjamin, Jacob's youngest son at only seven years old, looked up, startled, sitting with an open scroll across his knees. Jacob too paused in the middle of the passage he was reading aloud as the covering over the entrance to his tent flapped back and Benjamin's older brother came striding in.

"They're saying you don't trust me to go with them."

Joseph's shoulders had filled out since Jacob had given him the linen coat of the birthright, and he looked, from what his seven-year-old brother could tell, like a fully grown and very handsome man with his newly grown beard.

With a sigh, Jacob sat up straighter. "I've already said—"

"Is it true?"

"That I don't trust you?" Jacob asked, holding the gaze of his seventeen-year-old son—the son he had trained and taught and reared by his side, the son over whom he had taken such careful watch after his mother's death, the son he had named as his heir—and Jacob wondered why this son should take such a sudden interest in aligning himself with his brothers instead. "You stay with me," Jacob said, "because you have a different work than they do. Who has been saying that I don't trust you?"

Joseph crossed his arms. "It's just . . . what they say."

"Who?"

Hearing the tone, Benjamin quickly lowered his eyes, pretending to be studying the scroll. Joseph lowered his eyes as well.

"Whoever it is," Jacob said, "I'm sure they have their reasons to say what they do. Joseph"—he waited until his son raised his eyes—"if I did not trust you, why would I make you the heir of this family and the covenant we carry?"

Joseph looked at his father. "Because of my mother?"

Jacob's face hardened. "My love for your mother," he said, and Benjamin, caught awkwardly between them, stared even more intently at the scroll, "would not cloud my judgment as to who should lead this family. Nor is it her fault that only she has given me capable sons. I will not hear her name abused in this camp."

"No one was—" Joseph began, but Jacob held up a hand.

"No more," he said. "And if you want to be respected, then you must tell your brothers so yourself."

Flustered, glaring, Joseph turned and left without reply.

In the sudden quiet, the kind that fell over the desert after a great thunder stroke, Benjamin looked up at his father. Jacob's eyes were closed, and for a rare moment he seemed to sink into the appearance of an old man, a stooped and wizened carrier of many burdens.

But when Jacob opened his eyes and looked back at Benjamin—who had his same dark eyes, with his father's face and his mother's gentle, observant nature—Jacob smiled, tiredly.

"It will work itself out," he said.

Benjamin, still a little wide-eyed, nodded.

It was Dinah who saw Joseph striding away from Jacob's tent. Glancing at Bilhah and Zilpah, who sat beside her grinding grain, she gave a quick excuse and got to her feet, moving after her younger brother—younger half-brother, as the others would point out.

"Joseph," she said. He turned, looking a little annoyed at being delayed in whatever hot-headed trajectory he was on.

"Maybe you want me to grind corn with the women?" he asked.

"You wouldn't know how." Dinah smiled. "Where are you going?"

Joseph crossed his arms. "Everyone's making fun of me because I'm not going to take the flocks. They said Father doesn't trust me with any real work."

Now Dinah crossed her arms as well. "And you believe them?" She shook her head, reaching out a hand. "They're just jealous—"

Joseph stepped back, turning and moving his shoulder just out of her range of touch.

"People pity me," he said, "or they hate me. No one respects me."

"Joseph," Dinah said, "you know Father respects you more than anyone—"

But Joseph just waved a hand and walked on.

Dinah stood, watching his retreating back and the swishing of the elegant robe that set him so apart.

"Dinah?" Judah was walking toward her, carrying a small lamb that was agitatedly flicking its ear at a fly. "What's wrong with Joseph?"

"The same thing," she murmured, still looking after him. "Only now he says that everyone either hates him or pities him." She glanced at Judah. "Can't you get them to back off a bit?"

"Is this about not going to take the flocks?" The lamb gave a little bleat and began struggling. Judah held the animal tightly to his chest, trying to soothe the tiny creature. As the lamb calmed, he looked back at Dinah. "It shouldn't matter."

"Well, clearly it does." She glanced at him. "He's already alone in so many ways. He doesn't need trouble from the rest of you."

Judah looked after Joseph's retreating back. "He can be . . . a little intense, you know." He shrugged, readjusting his grip on the lamb. "Maybe it's hard for you to understand. He is . . . part of it."

"Well," Dinah turned to her brother, "maybe if you all stopped ganging up on him and making him feel he isn't one of you, he might not be so intense." The lamb gazed up expectantly, swishing its tail and giving another bleat. Dinah reached out, tickling her fingers across the wooly little head. "It may be the way of the desert that the strongest always prevails"—the lamb gave another flick of its ear—"but in the covenant, God prevails on behalf of all."

Then she turned, walking back toward the other women.

"Father."

Judah bent down beside Jacob, crouched within the milling herd of sheep as his father inspected the hoof of a limping ewe. A vibrating din of animal noise filled the air, mingling with the shouts passed between the brothers as they prepared to travel with the flock and the first of the new lambs toward fresher grazing grounds.

Jacob didn't look over. "Yes?"

Judah looked down at his hands, scratched and covered with dirt from the day's work. "If you have reservations," he said, "about sending Joseph with us, I would look out for him."

Now Jacob did look over, letting the ewe put her weight tentatively back on the wounded foot. "You think I don't trust him?" His emphasis lingered just slightly on the last word.

"I'm sure your trust is always well placed," Judah said, pretending to look at the ewe's hoof. "But if I can be of help, I would be." He looked up, meeting his father's eyes. "That's all."

Jacob looked back at his son, surrounded by the woolly moving bodies, then rose to his feet. Judah rose with him.

"Well," Jacob said, putting his hand on Judah's shoulder. "I'll remember that."

Judah nodded.

Jacob turned and made his way on through the flock.

Justified! Thou art pure, thy heart is pure, cleansed is thy front with washing, thy back with cleansing water . . . justified, in these standing waters . . .

Thou enterest . . . by the great purification, with which the Two Ma'ats have washed thee . . .

—*The Book of Breathings, lines 9–13, 18*

CHAPTER 15

Genesis 37:23–24

My son.

His father's face, warm and trusting.

I must ask something of you.

It was a simple task, only a day's journey, and his father smiled as he left.

His father, who trusted him and loved him, even if his brothers taunted him otherwise—his brothers, who were jealous, and anxious, and eager to inherit and be their own men.

You must understand, his father had said, *that there must always be one chosen for the birthright—one chosen for inheritance, for succession, for the covenant—*

One chosen for sacrifice.

The boy lay alone, broken open to the harsh chill of the desert and the bleeding expanse of stars, enclosed on all sides by the earth that had received his body like a dead man's.

His memory scrabbled over the broken pieces, stumbling, like a wounded thing—his robe, stained with his mouth's blood, the cloth wailing, the knife driving in and out and the pieces of linen fluttering to the ground as he was dragged away, his arms bruised beneath their fingers.

He had struggled, thinking he could plead with them.

Then his body had collided with the wall of the well shaft, and he fell back, screaming.

A day, already, had passed. He knew that his brothers had stayed nearby at first because he'd heard them shuffling, murmuring in low snatches, but they had not answered his cries.

Now the desert was silent.

He lay staring up through the narrowed darkness. A trickle of water ran just beneath the surface of the dry well. He had worn the tips of his fingers raw from digging down toward it. Waves of nauseated hunger stirred him whenever he slipped, intermittently, into a place of no light.

His brothers had meant to kill him, but the knife intended for his throat had been turned instead to his robe, swift hands butchering the cloth as they would a sheep. He had simply been thrown away, the unusable, unclean remnants of the slaughter.

Reuben had begged the others not to hurt the boy, but he had been pushed aside, threatened with the same knife.

Don't kill him.

He heard Judah's voice in the tumult, felt his older brother seize him by the arm as he lay on the ground, his captors arguing like dogs over a carcass.

Don't kill him—Judah was breathless—*sell him.*

Mercy in the form of slavery. Atonement by pieces of silver.

Joseph had seen his brother's face in the moment before he was thrown away, and he saw Judah standing there, still, watching—

Just watching.

When the rope was lowered down to where he lay, Joseph stared at the dangling strands, uncomprehending, before he reached out, pawing at the rough, fraying ends. A voice shouted down, telling him to bind his wrists together. Fumbling with clumsy, swollen fingers, eventually he managed to obey.

With a jerk, his body was lifted off the ground, and he was hauled up out of the darkness, spitting as his face collided with the gravelly sides of the pit, wincing at the rope chafing against his wrists. Another pair of hands reached down and grabbed him under his arms and hauled him up over the edge, flooding his eyes with light and lowering his stinging body gently back to the earth. He tasted the rich trickle of fresh blood.

A man bent down, shielding his face from the flickering light. The boy heard voices speaking in a quick, chattering tongue. His eyes fluttered, and he saw the man, a stranger, who had hauled him up and was sitting crouched beside him, slowly winding a rope back into a coil. Had he expected his brothers? His eyes rolled back, and he could not speak. He lost all sense, and the world was darkness.

When he awakened again, he was lying on his side and no longer felt the scorch of the sun. He could still hear strange, muted voices talking to one another, as if coming from somewhere far away. As he tried to open his eyes, drawing more fully to the surface of consciousness, the voices became louder. He blinked, wincing, and felt a presence draw closer and crouch beside him. He felt a hand on his arm.

"Boy." Blinking, forcing his eyes back open, Joseph looked up into a calm, weathered face. "Can you drink?" Joseph nodded, and the man turned, gesturing urgently. Someone handed over a water pouch, and the man offered it to Joseph's lips, holding the slick opening against the boy's mouth.

"How long were you down there?"

Swallowing, Joseph moved his mouth away from the water. "Two days," he croaked.

The man gave a low whistle. "In this heat?" He was helping Joseph sit up. "You must have a lucky star." Joseph, eyes still raw, squinted. He had been lying in the shadow of an accommodating camel, and the beast remained kneeling beside him, chewing thoughtfully. Looking around, still blinking, he saw half a dozen other loitering camels and half a dozen other men tending to their animals or speaking quietly to one another.

Then Joseph noticed another small group sitting by themselves.

He looked back at the man who had bent down beside him. "Did you find me?"

The man shook his head, waving a hand. "Some tribesmen found you."

Joseph felt the dirt around his eyes as he squinted. "Who are you?"

The man smiled and gestured toward the horizon. "We are traveling to Kemet." He paused, trying to ascertain whether Joseph had understood. "The Divided Land."

Joseph felt his eyes turn again toward the small band seated together on the ground. One of the men was staring at him, while the others sat with their backs turned.

Sell him. Don't kill him. Sell him.

Joseph heard the words echoing around his head like a cry in an empty cave.

"I thank you," he swallowed again, tasting another sip of blood from his dried lips, "for saving me. My father will repay you. His camp is close," he turned, pointing, "to the east . . ."

"We have come from the east." The trader shook his head. "There are no camps."

Joseph looked at him. "That's impossible."

"You're disoriented." The trader reached out, pressed a

hand to Joseph's forehead. "You've had a fever. There's no one coming for you, boy. It's just the desert."

"Let me go," Joseph snarled, moving from the man's touch.

But the trader merely put a quieting hand on Joseph's shoulder. "If I let you go," he said, "you will die."

"No," Joseph shook his head, voice breaking, "it's a mistake—my brothers . . ."

And then his eyes caught sight of his wrists, bloodied from the rope, and he looked down at his stomach, thin and caved, and how he was naked except for a small cloth wrapped around his hips. His brothers had left him nothing—no clothing, no family, no identity.

The trader looked at him—sadly, it seemed. "If your people come for you," he said, "they may have you. But I cannot leave you here."

He rose and snapped his fingers. One of the other men approached.

"Give the boy something to wear," the trader said, "and some food."

His fellow traveler nodded, moving away. After a moment, the man reached back down, holding out a hand. Joseph looked up at him; then, hesitantly, he allowed the trader to help him gently to his feet. "If my brothers did to me," the man murmured, keeping one hand on Joseph's arm to steady him, "what they have done to you, I might take my chances in Kemet."

Joseph turned, looking back in the direction where his father's camp should have been, but all he saw was the desert heat bending the trembling waves of light above the sand, hovering in the emptiness of the horizon.

CHAPTER 16

Judah

Judah, son of Jacob, stood at the edge of his father's camp. He watched the sun disappear over the horizon, and the sky sink through bruised shades of deepening violet into a night the color of dried blood. He had endured the weeping, the cursing, the torn clothes and the dust and his father's raging—he had endured it silently, refusing the companionship of his brothers, afraid to speak to Dinah, unable to bear the sight of Benjamin.

Please, Reuben had said, *don't hurt the boy. He is our brother. He is our father's son—*

Simeon had not listened—none of them listened—and Judah had stood there, frozen, watching as the brothers gathered around, not knowing what to do, knowing suddenly and horribly what was about to happen and yet he did nothing, nothing, until someone knocked Joseph over and the others set on him and stripped him and struck him and he cried out, and they were beating him, shaming him, tearing his coat to pieces, tearing him to pieces, and it happened so quickly, and they were hurting him, they were hurting him—

Sell him.

It would buy time. Simple mercy had no sway, neither he nor Reuben nor anyone else was strong enough to control the mob, and so—

Sell him.

Joseph had heard him say it, he knew, because Joseph had looked up and stared at him, as if confused—not understanding, Judah knew, feeling the tightness in his throat, that he was trying to save his brother's life.

Sell him.

When Reuben had made his way back alone to the pit with the rope that would draw his brother back to safety, he had fallen to his knees, gazing down over the side, calling out and looking around, wild-eyed, crying the boy's name over and over again—

But there was no answer.

The pit was empty.

Joseph was gone.

We killed him, Judah thought. We took his coat. We tore him to pieces.

The brothers were supposed to go to Shechem—the place that had witnessed another slaughter, another violation of one of Jacob's children—but they had moved the flocks on toward Dothan, and still somehow Joseph had found them, still somehow he had come, as if the desert meant for them to find each other in the scorched and windswept emptiness.

Judah had promised his father that he would protect Joseph. He had given Joseph the assurance of his friendship.

Then he had watched while Simeon beat him.

It didn't matter that he had not known what to do. He had witnessed it. He was guilty. They were all guilty.

A flash, and he saw Joseph's face again—his wide, red eyes, his skin purpled and broken, not at all the way a sacrificial lamb ought to be treated. He saw Joseph staring up at him, wondering why Judah, Judah, of all of them, stood there and did nothing, only said—

Sell him.

Now it was done. The sacrifice was over. There was no ram in the thicket, and no angel. Joseph's brothers simply returned from the desert, bound together by his blood.

Two of the brothers had slaughtered a goat with the same knife that had been used against Joseph and his beloved robe. They dipped the fragments of the garment into the sticky, slippery gore. All of them stood together to present the robe to their father, leaving him to draw his own conclusions. Not one of them said another word about it. Not one of them knew what to say.

Standing beneath the dark night sky, Judah still did not know what to say.

Crossing his arms tightly, protectively, he raised his face toward the emerging stars. The horizon stretching beyond the camp was full of ghosts—whispers, shadows slipping in and out of the heat and the chill, lost travelers, and eternal sojourners—but as long as they were not his brother's ghost, he could face them. He could face anything now.

Anything, except what he would see if he turned back to the camp.

Anything, except what they had done.

He might have asked for forgiveness, but he knew there could be none. The birthright was destroyed, the covenant shattered, and the brothers themselves had done it. He had done it. There was no God of his fathers who would embrace them now in mercy. They were exiles, wanderers, cast out into the briars and thorns, doomed to wander the world as shadows.

Judah lowered his head and took a slow, deep breath of soft desert night.

If he was doomed to wander, then he would go to seek that horizon, the ever stretching-out boundary of the known world, and he would go beyond it to what was unknown and had no recollection of what had been done in the wilderness at Dothan. He would become a severed orphan like his betrayed brother, make no claim on his father or fathers or their all-seeing God. It was not penance, but freedom did not have to be complete to allow its seeker to at least dip his hands, splash his face, let the trickles run over his skin for momentary relief.

There were places where the power of what had been did not extend. He would seek them out and blend away.

He would escape beyond the edge of memory.

CHAPTER 17

Asar

"Tjaty."

Zaphenath turned, standing alone in the passageway leading from the king's chambers, holding in his hand a papyrus document related to their most recent meeting. He had stayed long after the other officials, verifying the last details of a legal case in the process of being settled, and now he was finally setting off to return home after an unusually tiring day. Now, seeing the man approaching, he felt wearier still. He lowered his head in required respect.

Asar was striding steadily closer, a light smile on his face.

"I suppose you were meeting with my father," Asar said, pausing a few paces away and placing his fist on his hip, shifting his weight to one leg.

"We've had a difficult case," Zaphenath told him. "With luck, it will be finished soon."

"Mm," Asar said, "no doubt you are a great help to him."

Zaphenath inclined his head. "I hope to be."

Asar waved a hand. "And I'm sure my father hopes I will be able to learn from you."

Zaphenath watched him. After a moment, he said, "It is my honor to have your opinions on our project, Prince."

Asar raised a slight eyebrow. "Oh," he said, still smiling, "well, thank you. Tell me, how is Asenath?"

"She is well." Zaphenath shifted his fingers around the scroll in his hand.

"Please," Asar said, "do send her my regards. The court has lost a little of its sparkle since you took her away from us."

Zaphenath inclined his head. "I'll tell her."

Asar was watching him too. "Good."

"Well," Zaphenath said at last, "good night." He walked past Asar, on down the corridor.

"Actually," he heard and turned back around, "I meant to ask you"—Asar took a casual step closer—"you reminded me, when you mentioned that court case. I heard some talk about some sort of disturbance at one of the granaries."

Zaphenath looked at him. "A disturbance," he repeated.

"Yes," Asar murmured, "a disturbance involving some Canaanites." He waited. "Have you heard anything about it?"

Zaphenath shifted the scroll in his hand again. "Nothing worth speaking of."

"Oh," Asar shrugged. "Well, never mind, then." He waved his hand again. "I suppose it must not have been much of a threat to the kingdom after all."

"I'm not sure I would classify any disturbance at a

granary as a threat to the kingdom." Zaphenath took a slow breath. "What part of this disturbance is of interest to you?"

"It's not much of an interest to me," Asar said, "but I thought it might be of interest to you."

Zaphenath tilted his head back slightly. "To me."

"Because it involved Canaanites," Asar told him, "accused, I think, of being spies." He clasped his hands innocently behind his back. "Do you think there is a threat of Canaanite spies?"

"No," Zaphenath said shortly. "I do not. The matter was a misunderstanding and has been resolved."

"It's amazing," Asar mused, "isn't it, how much distrust still exists towards the Canaanites, in spite of my father's work."

Now Zaphenath looked straight at the prince. Asar returned his gaze evenly.

"As I said," Zaphenath said after a moment, "the situation was resolved."

"The People are still nervous," Asar said quietly, "that our country could dissolve back into disorder and disunity. Take away their prosperity, and you uncover all their fear."

"Prince," Zaphenath said, "please, be plain with me."

Asar took a step closer. "I hear that there are some—not me, of course"—he smiled—"who wonder whether our country is vulnerable, let us say, to foreign influences in our weakened state."

"The famine has stricken everyone," Zaphenath told

him, "and this country remains the strongest of any of her neighbors. There is no danger."

"But I rather fear that the People may not believe you." That smile. "Perhaps"—he crossed his arms—"that is part of why my father thinks I should be involved. To give the People a symbol." He looked at the vizier. "To feel assured about who is in control."

They stood, facing each other.

"As I have said before," Zaphenath said at last, his voice soft, "it will be my honor to receive your opinions, Prince."

With a bow, he turned and walked on.

"I'll take the scroll straight back," Asenath promised, smiling, standing in the entryway of the villa. "Thank you for bringing it."

Amon, who had dropped off an additional papyrus document that Zaphenath had rather uncharacteristically forgotten to pick up after his meeting with the king, smiled too. "Thank you, my lady." He raised the hand not encumbered with the records he was taking back to the official state offices. "Good night to you."

"Good night," Asenath said, nodding, "and thank you for your help to him." Amon smiled again and started across the garden, trotting on toward the gates of the estate, his body silhouetted in the fading light.

Asenath turned with the scroll in hand and moved

back into the house, pulling the heavy wooden door closed. Servants had already lit the candles lining the walls of the open inner courtyard in preparation for the coming darkness, and Asenath passed through their flickering shadows as she moved toward her husband's private study, secluded from the public area of the house. She found him but not as she had expected, pacing around, or reading with his eyes darting impatiently over the words, or sketching out plans for some new project.

He had removed his wig and was standing with a small, polished bronze mirror.

"Zaphenath," she said, and he looked quickly over. His eyes were lined in the custom of her countrymen, and the removal of his wig revealed the beautiful hair of the desert tribe he had been born to.

She smiled. "What are you doing?"

He pulled at a loose curl of hair. "I'm thinking of shaving my head."

"Why?" She moved closer toward him. "Is your hair bothering you?"

"I wear the wig every day anyway." Zaphenath looked back into the mirror, focusing on his distorted reflection. "It's just added heat."

"But your hair is so lovely," Asenath said. "No one has hair like yours."

"Exactly." He set the mirror down on a low wooden table. "Is that for me?" She handed him the scroll, and he unrolled it, glancing quickly over the characters. "Ah," he murmured.

"I'll get started on this." But she stood there, watching him, as he shuffled the scroll closed. Then she crossed her arms. He looked up. "What?"

She made a face. "What?"

"I have a lot to get done—"

"Really?" she said. "Like shaving your head? Zaphenath." She shook her head. "You're not yourself."

"I'm tired." He leaned down, placing a quick kiss on the top of her head, and brushed past, scroll in hand. Just as he reached out to pull back the curtain hanging over the entryway to the room, she said, "Zaphenath—"

He glanced over his shoulder.

She swallowed. "Come with me to the prison."

"The prison?" Zaphenath tried to laugh. "What have you done?"

She shook her head. "I want to see your brother."

He stared at her, and it seemed for a moment as though he might say something. Then shaking his head, he said, "No."

"No?" He ducked out of the room in a rustle of curtain, but she followed after him. "Why not?"

He waved the scroll, not looking back. "I'm not discussing it."

"I'm not one of your courtiers," Asenath said, catching the curtain and ducking through after him into the corridor. "You can't just 'not discuss it' with me." The candlelight reflected off his back as he moved along ahead of her. "You can't pretend he doesn't exist—"

"Who's pretending that my brother doesn't exist?" Zaphenath wheeled around. "I can assure you," he said, pointing the scroll at her and then sweeping it in a gesturing arc along his linen clothing, "I am acutely aware that my brother exists."

"I want to see him."

"There's nothing to see."

"Please," she said, but he turned from her.

"My love," he said without looking back as he kept walking, "I have a lot of work to do."

She, following him, slowed, then stopped, and watched him walk across the open courtyard of the house toward his public meeting rooms. She watched as he brushed aside the curtain to his scroll room and disappeared from her sight.

And then she followed him.

CHAPTER 18

Genesis 43:1–14

Jacob's wooden staff crunched into the dirt, a steady, percussive rhythm underscoring the bleating and hoofsteps of the sheep as he walked alongside his grazing flocks. The sun seemed to catch in the fiery brilliance of his hair, and his gray-bearded son Judah thought, not for the first time, how truly little of his father had been leached out by the passing of years in the desert. Even now, Jacob's voice did not falter, and his hands did not tremble. Occasionally he would rest through the heat of the afternoon or ask Benjamin to read a passage to him when the light was dim and his eyes were weary, but he still walked calmly among his flocks and stood as the unchallenged center of his family.

Today, Judah walked alongside him, quiet, not wishing to disturb, letting his father walk as he pleased, his staff striking the earth and his feet still finding their steady step.

"Your flocks have grown," Judah observed, "even with the famine."

"A blessing," Jacob murmured.

"There are so many to feed now." Judah glanced over,

but Jacob merely struck his staff down once more. "And two new babies in your camp."

Jacob nodded. "The Lord has prospered us."

"With so much prosperity," Judah glanced at his father again, "it will be difficult to keep everyone fed for much longer."

Jacob prodded at a sheep blocking his path, and the animal trotted back into the herd. "There's only one place with food."

Judah watched their shadows slip out ahead, splayed across the ground, while Jacob tapped his staff, prodding another bleating sheep out of the path.

"Father," Judah asked, "what do you want us to do?"

Jacob slowed, and then stopped, resting his hands on the top of his staff. He looked out over his milling flock. Judah stood quietly beside him. It was only now, as Jacob's body had begun to stoop, that Judah could nearly speak to his father face to face. It was Reuben who had always looked the most like their father—the same strength, the same physical presence.

But Reuben was not here.

"We have no choice," Judah said softly. Jacob looked over, his fierce white eyebrows directed toward his son. "There is no more food." Judah shook his head. "We have to go back." Jacob sighed, turning his gaze out toward the desert. "I promise you," Judah said quietly, "Benjamin will be safe."

Jacob grunted again. "Safe." He glanced at Judah.

"Reuben promised me the life of both of his sons in return for Benjamin's safety." He shook his head. "One life does not restore another."

"Benjamin," Judah said, "will redeem Simeon."

"You had to tell him there was another son." Jacob looked over at Judah. "Why?"

"He asked us." Judah looked at his father. "He asked whether we had another brother." Jacob frowned, looking away again. "If we don't bring Benjamin, all of our people are lost. Send him with me." Judah's voice was quiet and firm. "Let me be his surety." He reached out, setting a hand on his father's arm. "You can require him from me."

Jacob turned his eyes toward his fourth son. After a moment he spoke. "You will take twice the money," he said, "that you gave before, and we will send gifts to this man who has kept your brother a prisoner." He nodded to himself. "As we sent to my brother, Esau, when we made peace with each other."

Judah too nodded in quick agreement. "We'll give the best of what we have. I know they value turquoise from the desert mines, and silver—"

"And then," Jacob said, "God willing, he will have mercy upon you." He raised his eyes. "And upon me."

Zaphenath raised his eyes from the scroll spread open on his lap. "Yes?"

Walking otherwise uninvited into her husband's scroll room, Asenath gathered up her linen skirt in one hand and sank down onto the floor next to him.

"My love," he turned his attention back to the scroll, "I'm truly busy."

She looked down at the writing as well but did not move. "How are things going with Asar?" she asked at last.

Zaphenath unrolled the scroll further, frowning. "Just today, he was so good as to speak to me about the matter of popular prejudice regarding those of Asiatic origin."

"Probably because I married such a handsome one."

"You certainly married an older one."

She sat there quietly before she said, "I want to see your brother." He didn't respond. "You haven't seen your family for twenty years—"

"My brother," Zaphenath said, eyes flicking over the characters as he read, "is the reason I haven't seen my family for twenty years."

"Mama!"

Asenath and Zaphenath both looked quickly over to the entryway, where a small, quivering Ephraim stood with his little body partly hidden in the curtains, clutching a trembling fist to his mouth. Asenath was quick to her feet and across the room.

"What's wrong, little one?" she asked, bending down and putting her arms around the boy. "Bad dreams?"

Ephraim nodded with a shuddering intake of breath,

and Asenath scooped him up as he let out a little wail. Zaphenath set the scroll aside and got to his feet.

"It's all right," Asenath said, looking over Ephraim's little shaved head, but Zaphenath reached out, taking the child from his mother and holding his son gently in his arms. Ephraim curled up against him.

"It's all right," Zaphenath murmured. Asenath rubbed the little boy's back as Zaphenath held him. Slowly, their son's breathing began to gentle, and Ephraim's eyes closed. He rested his head against his father's shoulder.

"He's a vivid little dreamer." Asenath glanced at Zaphenath. "I suppose he gets that from you."

Zaphenath's dark eyes met hers, and he looked down at his sleeping son, cradled in his arms. "Benjamin was hardly older than our boys," he said, softly, "the last time I saw him."

"Maybe he has sons of his own." Asenath smiled. "Imagine how big your family has become."

"My family," Zaphenath said, "is right here."

Asenath looked back down at her sleeping son. "But you have a brother."

Zaphenath shook his head. "Benjamin would barely remember me."

"You have a brother here."

He shook his head. "In twenty years," he said, his voice quiet and hard, "not one of them ever came to find me." He would not meet her eyes. "I have no other brothers."

"Zaphenath." She laid her hand on his arm. "I want you to find peace."

"And you think," Zaphenath said evenly, "that going back into a prison is going to do that?"

Ephraim stirred, mumbling something before growing still again.

"I'll go put him back down," Asenath whispered.

Zaphenath shook his head. "Let me take him."

He brushed through the curtain leading out of the room, and Asenath stepped out after him, watching as her husband walked down the shadowed corridor with their son resting quietly in his arms. And she stood there, waiting, in the candlelit darkness, until her husband returned, slowly drawing closer until, close enough, he looked at her, and she looked at him.

"You are everything I have," he whispered.

She leaned in against him, feeling how tightly he held onto her. Closing her eyes, she whispered, "I love you too."

CHAPTER 19

Simeon

"Tjaty." The surprised guard of the royal prison stepped aside with a bow.

The vizier held up a hand in thanks to the guard on the night watch, and the woman with the vizier—surely it couldn't be his wife, but who else would he bring here?—smiled, her face partially hidden by the shadows. Leaving their own contingent of guards outside, the vizier led the way into the small inner room that was the holding cell for royal prisoners, lit only by the faint flicker of torches.

"Over here," he said and moved closer, peering in through the small opening in the cell's wall. Two men lay stretched out on the ground within, while a third sat leaning against the opposite wall, head lolling. Then he turned back and pointed to one of the men lying curled on his side.

Asenath stepped closer and leaned up on her toes, gazing in at the foreign man's bearded face, his peppery hair streaked with age, his skin lined with years of travel beneath the sun, and his tall, lean body folded in protectively as he slept. His woolen garments were dusty with the dirt of the cell, and he slept with his head propped against the crook of his elbow.

Turning back, Asenath looked over her shoulder at her husband. He had already moved away. His hands were clasped lightly behind his back, his bearing every whit that of a dignitary.

She thought, You've slept here too.

She turned once more toward the desert man who lay in the dirt, curled into the dreams that hopefully gave him some escape from the grim and strange life that had overtaken him. Then she glanced over her shoulder again.

"He's an old man," she said, speaking almost too quietly to be heard. "Is he being taken care of?"

"Of course." Zaphenath glanced back at the guards. "All the prisoners here are treated well."

She looked back at the sleeping man. "He doesn't look anything like you."

"Did you expect him to?"

She touched her fingers against one of the rough wooden poles driven through the tiny opening, guarding the men within. "Tell me his name again."

"Simeon."

"Simeon," she repeated, moving her mouth over the foreign sounds. "Why him?"

"My own reasons." She heard her husband take a slow breath. "Have you seen enough?"

But she was still gazing in at Simeon.

And then Simeon, who until then had lain unmoving,

began to stir, stretching out one arm and rolling over onto his back. Asenath stood absolutely still, watching as Simeon lifted a hand to his face and rubbed his eyes before rolling back onto his side, fluttering his eyes open, yawning.

He blinked, squinting in the dim light.

He saw her.

She knew it from the way he stared, suddenly perplexed, as if trying to understand what it was he saw standing there, watching him in the darkness.

Zaphenath, hearing the rustle from within the cell, moved closer and took his wife's arm.

She glanced back as he touched her, just as the prisoner raised his head. And for a single, suspended moment, she stood between them like a balance—her husband's hand on her arm, and his brother's fixed gaze extending out from within the cell—and the two men looked past her from opposite sides of the bars, one in regal dress, the other filthy and exhausted, and they saw each other.

Zaphenath stared at his prisoner, seeing the hesitation and the way he held himself back from the full embrace of the flickering torchlight. This man, whom he had seen only in the shadows, had a stranger's face, with a faded beard and dirty foreign clothes, and the years in the desert had drained away so much of what should have been familiar—and yet, couched in the worn lines and the fleeting expression, the wry, flickering eyes and the darting gaze, were vestiges of the brother he had known.

Did I expect the desert to make them immortal?

In his mind, they had never aged—they were still the strong, hot-headed bullies who had beaten him, not old and frightened men. Time had been cleft out there in the desert, seizing them all in a frozen and unchanging spasm, for time and all eternity, after the Joseph who had gone to seek his brothers had been murdered and torn apart like the betrayed Osiris. And he had somehow believed that his brothers, his family, and all the world that was had also died in that moment, trapped forever in the unforgiving embrace of broken time, left behind in the desert never to grow old, never to return home, to remain forever in that single moment from which there was neither redemption nor release. The violence of that day should have sealed them all with the desert's unchanging, unblinking memory of who they had been when the universe was violated and tilted, spinning wildly and irrevocably away from the known world, and neither mercy nor time could undo what had been done.

But time had undone it.

Zaphenath saw it, in the face of this stranger who had been his brother, now a man who had lived a whole life of which Zaphenath knew nothing. Simeon—the young fury, captured forever in Zaphenath's mind in that moment of terrible rage—had no relation to the dirty prisoner who cowered before him. Yet this prisoner, who now also could not comprehend what was happening to him, was Simeon—and in that moment it was as if the universe tilted again, and the rift that separated who he was from who he had been came rushing back together, and here they were, staring at each other, reunited on the other side of time.

Zaphenath could have spoken to him. No one in that small room besides the prisoner who lay on the ground would have understood the words. In all of Kemet, there was no other being who carried the memory of who Zaphenath had been in that other life in the time before time split, no one who could speak to that other part of him, no one who could cross over and bring that severed half back to life by acknowledging that it had once existed.

But he did not speak.

Asenath felt his touch fall away from her arm.

And then she heard him speaking softly to one of the guards.

" . . . released tomorrow morning," he was saying, "and have him brought to my house. We will hold him there until further notice."

The guard acknowledged the command.

CHAPTER 20

Genesis 43:15; 39:1

A young boy went scampering toward the edge of the camp, hurrying toward the stomping congregation of camels and followed in close pursuit by his younger brother.

"Papa!" the child called out. "Papa!"

Facing toward the rough tents that stood encamped together like an island of refugees, Benjamin smiled, bending down to catch his sons in their tumbling embrace.

"I'll be back as soon as I can," he promised, hugging them, "and we'll bring plenty of food for you. Now," he reached out, putting one hand on each of their shoulders, "you'll watch over your grandfather for me." They nodded solemnly.

Jacob was standing beside Benjamin, and the aged patriarch's robes billowed out around his body, carried on a dancing spiral breeze that rose out of the desert. He looked out over his sons, all men now with sons of their own. They were all his hope of the future, all that remained of the women he had loved, all the fulfillment of the ever-elusive promise of his birthright. Now they would go down together, disappearing over the horizon into an unknown and hostile land, carrying Benjamin to barter for their survival.

And Jacob could not but think of his own grandfather Abraham, who also had been asked to put his son on the altar of promised future prosperity, who had been asked if he were willing to lose him forever for the sake of the covenant.

Rising back to his full stature, Jacob's youngest son, the child he had named in his greatest hour of sorrow, turned to him. "You can rely on your grandsons while we're gone."

Jacob smiled. "Do I have need yet that they should watch over me?"

Benjamin smiled too, shaking his head. "You watch over all of us, Father."

Jacob took Benjamin by the arm and looked intently into his face, seeing, as he always did, the shadows of Benjamin's mother and brother in the way his son smiled. "The Lord watch over you," he told him.

Benjamin nodded, clasping his father's arm in return.

How many years, Jacob thought, how many years since I stood here with your brother?

They embraced.

Do not forget yourselves, Jacob had told his sons. *Kemet is a powerful place. Be safe. Be wise. Do not forget whose sons you are.*

Still holding his last child to him, Jacob closed his eyes.

"I'll come back," Benjamin murmured. "I promise."

Jacob nodded and released him. "Yes," he said, "God willing." He felt a hand on his shoulder.

"Father." Judah glanced past Jacob toward Benjamin. "The provisions are prepared." He paused, then looking at Jacob, he added, "We're ready to leave."

Jacob nodded. Benjamin tried to smile, then turned and moved toward where his camel and its burdens waited, his young sons trailing after him. Judah stood beside Jacob as Jacob watched him go.

"On my life," Judah said quietly, "I'll bring him back to you."

Jacob turned and looked at Judah—at this son who, alone amongst all his sons, had offered to protect Benjamin with his own life, bartering himself for the survival of their family and their father—and Jacob reached out, resting a hand on Judah's arm.

"If I be bereaved of my children," Jacob said, "I am bereaved."

Judah met his father's deep, rich eyes with his own eyes, the same eyes.

"I cannot go with you to save our family," Jacob said. "You will go in my place."

Judah nodded. "We will return as soon as we can."

"Judah." His father's eyes were focused intently upon him. "You will go in my place." Judah looked at his father, and Jacob held his son's gaze. "God watch over you."

Judah put his hand over Jacob's. "For your sake, Father," he said quietly, "I believe He will."

The man named Given-of-Ra—so named by his father, who also carried the name he had bestowed on his eldest son—sat cross-legged in his private chamber with his head bowed over an open scroll.

I answered, Here am I.

And he said, Behold it is I, be not afraid, for I am before the world was, a strong God who exists before the worlds, and a mighty God who has created the light of the world.

Bring me a pure sacrifice. And in this offering I will show you the Aeons, and reveal to you that which is secret; and you shall see great things you have never before beheld; for you have loved to seek me, and I have called you my friend.

The man traced his finger along the characters, so carefully copied down from the original text kept by the priests at the place called Iunu, the great Temple of Ra, the holy site commemorating the first moment of creation—where heaven and earth and gods and men could be joined in symbol as they hoped to be joined, someday, in eternal realities.

His own copy of this text was a rarity, presented to him as a gift when he too was admitted into the secrets of the priests. It was a strange document, written by a desert sojourner who, he'd been told, was no mere symbol or child's story concocted to ease the transmission of some abstract or difficult teaching. On the contrary, he had it on authority from his own father that the man had actually existed, had actually seen things and spoken in his own flesh to the priests, and they had written those things down and kept them and studied them, until the time when the text had been given into his care to be studied and searched and pondered over.

His eyes turned back to one passage in particular that he could not get out of his mind any more than he could understand its significance:

Bring me a pure sacrifice. And in this offering I will show you the Aeons . . .

What secret was hidden here, couched in such a straightforward command? What sacrifice had this man offered that had so unlocked the heavens as to show him great things never before beheld—to reveal the sweeping secrets of creation? What was this strange offering that the gods so desired that they would barter the revelation of their handiwork with a mortal man?

And what mortal was capable of offering such a gift, such a sacrifice?

His own name, Given-of-Ra, was evidence that gifts, including a man's very life, proceeded from the divine to men. His two younger brothers and younger sister had also received such names from their father—the second son being designated Son-of-Ra, and the third proclaimed Born-of-Thoth, the god who communicated the intelligence of Ra and represented the heart of all things. His mother had wanted to call his dark-eyed little sister Beautiful One, for she had been beautiful even as a baby, but his father desired more than beauty for his child, and she became Daughter-of-Neth, named for the goddess of creation and the mother of Ra himself.

The lives of all of them were gifts, and all of their identities spoke of his parents' conviction of the divine moving among men. But how might men move among the gods?

Given-of-Ra, his father's eldest son, had read over this particular scroll many times since his father had presented it to him, but he was yet to discover any further hint to what this sacrifice might be or what ceremony was required in its offering. He was acquainted, of course, with the rites performed by the sun-priests to appease and entreat the powers of Ra in the god's eternal sustaining course. But he knew of no ceremony that might open the very secrets of how the sun was set in motion or the purpose of its particular orbit, or how to so justify a man as not only to be brought into the presence of the divine but to share in the governing secrets of the worlds.

The possibility that a man might hope for an eventual joining with Ra, passing through the horizon to the place of judgment and on into the eternal realms, had long been captured and recorded in the sacred writings of the priests. But this particular writing seemed to speak of something deeper, something further, to hint that at least one man had traveled beyond the horizon in his lifetime and had propitiated the gods sufficiently to allow him not merely to serve and worship but to be admitted into actual fellowship.

Could such a thing be possible, he wondered, not just once? Might it be sought again by another? Was it simply an isolated occasion of vision, or had this man left more than simply a record of what had been—left, perhaps, a pattern to be followed, with secrets to be discovered in emulation?

His father had never told him what the document really was, whether a record or a pattern, a personal history or a ritual text, and his time with his father had been brief after receiving it. But the questions taunted him, teased at him, as if they wanted him to follow, to seek them out, as if they meant to haunt him until he did.

"Potiphar."

He raised his eyes, looking toward the curtained entryway that led out of the small private study where he liked to sit in contemplation amidst his collection of scrolls. The dark-eyed young woman who had spoken his name was smiling at him, leaning in from the outer corridor, her body partly sheathed in the beaded strands of curtain that covered the open entryway. Her large black eyes were elegantly lined with kohl, and her dark hair fell past the slim straps looped over her shoulders, holding up a thin linen dress. A bright blue stone set in a circle of pounded gold hung around her neck on a golden chain, a gift from her husband to remind her of the overarching power of Ra that watched over their priestly family.

"Your steward is back," she told him.

"Ah." Potiphar carefully rolled up the mysterious text and rose to his feet. Setting the papyrus back in the open box where he kept the sacred scrolls, he stretched his arms and smiled, moving toward the young woman. She smiled back at him as he slid an arm around her waist and leaned down, giving her a quick kiss. She wore her long black hair naturally that afternoon, separated into several braids and uncovered by any of her wigs, and her sparkling eyes stood out from her smooth, sun-brushed skin. Her face was not quite so remarkable as to stand out from the other well-mannered and well-dressed women born into the world of the king's court, but she seemed to have a natural affinity for attraction—an easy, knowing coyness, a charming, friendly banter—and he had been one of many men who noticed her.

Who still, he thought to himself with a slight smile, noticed her.

For his wife's part, the decision to marry one of the king's most esteemed young courtiers was not a difficult one. That the man was handsome and young, still in the prime of his strength and an important member of the king's inner circle through his current position as captain of the king's royal bodyguard—well, there was a great deal to be admired and coveted by the other women, and when he had pursued her particularly, it had been to her great pleasure.

But the pomp and celebration of their marriage had soon grown quiet, and the activities of the court and her childhood friends had been replaced by the stillness of her new home and the passing of days. A year had gone by, and another, and yet one more, and still the placid sophistication of the home remained unruffled by tiny squeals or uncertain footsteps. The two of them never spoke of it.

"Come along with me, if you want," Potiphar said, taking her arm.

She smiled.

Brushing through the curtained entryway, they moved arm-in-arm, walking down the corridor away from the private rooms of the house and out into the open central courtyard. A servant opened the heavy wooden front door, bowing, and they stepped out into the bright sunshine of early summer, with Potiphar's young wife putting up a hand to shield her eyes. Potiphar's steward, the man who managed his estate and household staff, stood waiting for his master with four other men, their chests bare, heads uncovered, standing with downcast eyes as Potiphar approached.

"Amosis." Potiphar smiled, patting his wife's hand as she slipped her arm away.

His steward bowed. "I have found three more men to tend to your fields, Potiphar."

Potiphar glanced from Amosis to the men who stood beside him. "These three?" he asked, gesturing to the bareheaded man who stood directly next to his steward and the two who followed him. The men stood slightly shorter than their new master (though taller than his broad, stout steward), with well-defined arms and weathered skin that spoke of previous exposure to the life of a field-worker.

Amosis nodded. "They said they'll be willing to work hard for a good master."

But Potiphar was looking toward the fourth man, standing at the end of the line, his head bowed and his hands clasped behind his back. This one's arms were not nearly so broad as the other men's, and his skin looked burned beneath the dirt and dust of the road. His head was covered with dark, loose curls—the sort of hair, Potiphar thought with a smile, that his wife might envy—and the young man's jaw was shaded with an unkempt dark beard.

Potiphar nodded toward the man. "Who's this one?"

Amosis looked down the line. "One of the 'Aamu. An Asiatic brought in on a recent caravan."

"Can he understand anything?"

"A little."

The slave raised his eyes, and Potiphar saw that he had a young man's face, unlined, with a certain disarming delicacy.

"Can you understand me?" Potiphar asked, speaking slowly.

The slave hesitated, then nodded.

Potiphar looked back at Amosis. "What were you told about him?"

"Seems he was picked up by an Ishmaelite caravan," Amosis said with a shrug. "Quiet. No trouble. Said he was found in the desert."

"Found," Potiphar repeated, glancing back at the bearded slave, who was watching the exchange as though trying to follow what was being said.

Amosis lowered his voice slightly. "Those tribes sell each other to slave traders from what I hear. That's how the trade is."

Potiphar was quiet a moment. "How much was he?" Amosis told him. Potiphar looked a little surprised. "Who sold him to you?" Amosis gave the name, and Potiphar looked back at the ruffle-haired young man. "You see how valuable Asiatic slaves have become in Kemet?"

The young man's expression did not change.

"I don't think he can understand you," Potiphar's wife murmured, standing behind her husband.

Potiphar paused a moment, then speaking slowly, asked, "What is your name?" The slave looked at him. "Your name," Potiphar repeated.

The young man glanced at Amosis, then back at Potiphar, then said quietly, "Joseph."

Potiphar nodded. He looked back at the native field slaves. "I'll look forward to good work from you," he said. "You belong to the house of Potiphar now, and we watch over our own." Amosis grunted, nodding in affirmation. "Well." Potiphar glanced back at the foreign one and found the young man still watching him with those intense dark eyes. He nodded slightly. "Take them out for a wash," he told Amosis. Then he turned back toward his wife, offering her his arm.

"Come on, then," Amosis said, gesturing away toward another part of the estate. The native slaves moved with him, understanding the order, but the desert boy paused. Amosis turned back around, gesturing with his hand. "Come on," he said, and the boy, after another hesitation, moved after his fellows. His eyes gazed across the estate—open pools of water surrounded by palm trees, tumbling patches of brightly fragrant flowers, fig trees lining the property within the walls.

"Your master is an important man," Amosis was saying, "captain of the king's bodyguard, head of all the soldiers and the prisons and one of the king's most important counselors. People say he may even be vizier one day."

The field-workers nodded appreciatively, but the Asiatic slave was still looking around the garden. The boy's back was straight and his head as yet unbowed. He was a strange one, really, pretty almost like a woman, and projecting an uncanny sense of comprehension, even though he seemed to understand only a little of what was said to him. He had been that way in the slave market, too, watching, waiting, returning the gazes of the men who came to haggle over him.

"Joseph." Amosis repeated the name as Potiphar had, stumbling slightly over the sounds and gesturing to the boy with one hand as the slave looked over at him. "This way."

Joseph followed, walking with the other slaves out of Potiphar's elegant garden and passing through the gates of the estate, crossing out onto the dusty road. They moved in a line, walking away from the villa and on down toward the lapping, murmuring River that flowed lollingly past, stretching far across to the opposite bank. The water was flanked on both sides by abundant greenery—thin grasses bending in the breeze, tall reed stalks jutting up out of the shallows, and some wondrous, delicate flower, unfolding in white and blue blossoms and perched on a spreading green pad resting gently on the undulating current.

Wading carefully through the plant life, still clothed only in a loincloth, Joseph stepped into the chill of the water, at such contrast with the beating heat of the day. Steeling himself, he bent down and began to wash the water up over his dusty, dirty skin. The rivulets began trickling away the heat and humiliation, with the physical layer of memory sloshing away into the river as he washed, and splashed, and scrubbed. Wading out a little further, he bent his knees and sank down into the River, dipping his head back and immersing his entire body.

When he emerged with the others, fresh and dripping, Amosis led them back across the road and through the gates of Potiphar's estate. This time, the little procession moved away from the villa and went further on into the private garden. They followed a walkway lined with palm trees, their wet feet slapping the dirt and leaving a speckling of water in their wake as they headed toward a small mud-brick building at the edge of the walled estate. Pausing, Amosis said something to the other three men, pointing across the garden to another mud-brick building of identical composition, and the three walked obediently in the direction of his outstretched hand. Then Amosis turned back to Joseph.

"Come," he said, gesturing. Joseph followed him, and Amosis pulled back a woven mat hanging over the entry space of the closer mud-brick building. The straight-walled room was mostly bare with a single fire pit situated toward the far side of the room. A series of tightly woven mats were unrolled and lined up on the floor. One end of each mat touched the wall, with coarse linens and wooden boxes marking the head of the sleeping spaces.

"House slaves sleep here," Amosis told him, following Joseph inside, and Joseph looked back at the steward. "House slaves," Amosis repeated, pushing back the entryway's woven covering again and pointing in the direction of their master's home. "You," he pointed at Joseph, "work at the house." He pointed through the open entryway across the estate. "The house." Joseph looked over his shoulder, toward the villa, then back at Amosis, and nodded.

"Now," Amosis let the covering fall and pointed to the sleeping mat nearest the curtained entryway, barren of either wooden box or linens, "you sleep here." He turned and moved toward a large wooden crate, stored apart from the sleeping spaces. He bent down, lifted the lid off, and pulled up another bundle of folded sleeping linens. He turned, holding the linens out, and Joseph stepped closer, taking the bundle in his arms. Amosis pointed, and Joseph set the linens on the mat that was evidently his new sleeping place.

"Good." Amosis lifted another object out of the box and rose to his feet. "Kneel down," he said, pointing to Joseph and bending his knees. Joseph, looking as though he were guessing at what Amosis wanted, balanced his body carefully down onto his knees. Amosis stepped closer, and Joseph saw that the object in the steward's hand was a blade—a shimmering, polished bronze blade—and his eyes fixed on the sleek, sharp edge. Amosis glanced down at the blade as well and then looked back at Joseph.

"Like this," he said, and raised the blade to his own head, pretending to run the edge over his naked scalp. Joseph kept staring at him. Amosis sighed, stepping closer, and placed a steadying hand on Joseph's head. He could feel the boy's blood pulsing quickly under the skin. Joseph closed his eyes, and Amosis drew the blade carefully along the top of his scalp—once, twice, and the dark curls began tumbling loose, flopping onto the cold dirt floor.

When the boy's head was completely bare, Amosis stepped back. Joseph glanced up, then lifted his hand and touched his fingers to the freshly exposed skin. Amosis was already turning to the boy's face, and Joseph closed his eyes as his young beard was sheared, falling among the curls on the floor. Satisfied with his work, Amosis stepped back again and this time held out the blade to the boy. Joseph took the blade uncertainly, watching as Amosis gestured to his own bare chest before pointing at Joseph's unshaven skin.

"Every slave must be clean," Amosis told him. "You wash every day, and shave."

When Joseph handed the razor back, Amosis gave an approving nod. The dirty desert creature had been quite transformed with the help of a bath and a blade. He looked almost civilized enough to enter the house.

"Your new name," Amosis told him, speaking slowly in hopes the boy would understand, "is Sasobek." He put a hand on his chest. "Amosis. I am Amosis. You"—and he put a hand on the young slave's shoulder—"are Sasobek. Son-of-Sobek. You know Sobek?" Amosis slapped his hands together, like a snapping mouth. "Crocodile god. Sasobek."

He paused, watching the boy's lips silently form the name. "Sasobek," Amosis repeated.

"Sasobek," the boy said.

Amosis nodded. "Now you are one of the people of Kemet." He put his hand back on the boy's shoulder. "Kemet. You are Sasobek, of Kemet. You understand?"

The boy averted his eyes. After a moment, he nodded.

"Good." Amosis stepped back, gesturing with his hand. "Come."

Rising uncertainly to his feet, brushing a strand of fallen hair from where it clung to his shoulder, the boy whose name was now Sasobek stood and followed Amosis back into the sun.

CHAPTER 21

Sasobek

Lying in the damp heat of the night, the new slave Sasobek lay curled on his side, his closed eyes flitting back and forth, his head cradled protectively in the crook of his elbow.

He dreamed that he was standing in the desert, naked except for a linen kilt around his hips, yet he did not feel the sun's heat, did not even feel the sting of the sand against his bare feet. He turned and looked around but saw nothing except desert stretching out and out, as far as the horizon in every direction. Looking up at the harsh, white-blue glare of the sky, he held up his hand to shield his eyes with shadow, and still there was nothing, nothing but fierce, open air, as inhospitable as the desert below.

But then he heard a sharp, crackling rise of voices and turned back and saw, where before he had seen nothing, a shielded outcropping of rock, a natural shelter in the midst of the desert. He moved closer to it, still holding his hand to shield his face and squinting through the trembling waves of heat. The voices grew louder as he drew closer. He touched the rock that should have been too hot to grasp but was not, and he pulled himself up so he could glimpse whoever had gathered to take refuge.

"Joseph!"

His brothers Levi and Asher looked up, waving, from where they were sitting in a circle with other desert shepherds. Joseph slid down over the other side of the rock at their friendly beckoning, and Levi moved over, opening a place for Joseph in the circle. As he drew closer, Joseph felt suddenly self-conscious and bare, wearing only his loose linen kilt, but Levi just smiled, waving him closer. Joseph was trying to see the other faces in the group—bearded, smiling, looking like his brothers but not his brothers—as if he should know them, had known them, but knew them no longer.

Then his heart beat faster as he suddenly recognized his father—his beloved, trusted father—sitting there in the circle. The patriarch turned his great white head.

"Father." Joseph could barely get the words out. He tried to raise his voice, desperate for his father to hear him. "I've been trying to find you . . ."

But his father was talking and laughing with the others and turned away as if he had not seen him.

"Father," Joseph tried again. "It's me." He pressed a hand to his chest. "I've been waiting for you, but you haven't come . . ."

As if hearing something vague, like a buzzing fly, Jacob glanced toward his son, scrutinizing Joseph's lean, linen-clad appearance, and pointed to something lying in the midst of the circle. Joseph looked down.

A lamb lay stretched across the sand at his feet, the head thrown back and its wool partly shorn with blood staining its open belly.

"You are your mother's son," he heard his father say. His mother, Rachel, whose name meant *Little Ewe.*

Joseph stepped back, feeling a heavy, haunting warning.

"Your brothers are happy now," his father told him. "There is peace for our people . . ."

His father was holding a knife.

Joseph's feet stumbled in the sand, suddenly unable to find their proper grip, and he heard Levi calling out after him as he ran, tried to run, but his feet were sinking down, and down, and his hands collided with the ground in a spray of sand—

A hand on his shoulder, gentle, drawing him up—he turned and looked into the face of a woman standing there beside him, her hand steadying on his skin and her smile gentle. Somehow, he thought, he knew her—

He reached out, toward her face—

The vision faded as his eyes opened, and he surfaced once more into consciousness, reaching out in the soft darkness—

He gasped, and his body jerked back, away from the crouching desert scorpion and its quivering tail.

Choking, Joseph tried to swallow, but his mouth was ragged and dry. Evidently having concluded that this skinny, unrecognizable foreigner was no real threat after all, the scorpion lowered its tail and scuttled away.

Still trying to gather his breath in the heavy, unfamiliar night, Joseph raised his eyes toward the mud-brick ceiling closing off the stars.

He knew, at last, that his father was not going to come for him.

"My lady."

Djeseret, wife of Potiphar, turned from where she sat before her mirror, carefully relining her eyes with a brush dipped in thick black kohl. The golden disk surrounding the blue-stone amulet around her neck sparkled with her movement, and her eyes, framed by a thick, shoulder-length wig, settled on the short, well-rounded woman standing in the entryway to the room.

"Please, my lady," the serving woman was saying, "a breeze came up and scattered some of the master's scrolls. He left them out, and . . . I don't know where they should go. He'll be so angry . . ."

"Oh." Djeseret set the kohl brush down and rose from the small wooden stool, coiling her long, loose dark hair over one shoulder with her slim fingers. "I'll come help you."

"Thank you, my lady," the serving woman stammered. "Of course I don't know up from down with those things . . ."

Djeseret just smiled. Leading the way, she brushed back

through the curtained entrance to her room and moved down the open corridor toward her husband's private study. But as they reached the entryway, both women stopped. There, crouched on the floor, was the new foreign slave with one of the tumbled scrolls in his hands.

"You!" the serving woman snapped, and the slave looked up, startled. "Those are the master's. You can't just—"

But the mistress of the house glanced at her serving woman, held up a hand, and looked back at the young man. He had risen quickly to his feet, plucking up another fallen scroll as he rose.

"Where are the others, then?" the serving woman demanded, sweeping her hand across the room. "Been meddling in here, have you?" The new slave glanced at an open box on the floor, and the women could see a handful of other scrolls already neatly stacked within. The serving woman raised her hands in accusing frustration. "You can't just put them anywhere you please!"

"They go here," the young man said, his accent clinging determinedly to the words.

The serving woman set her hands on her hips. "And how do you know that?"

"Don't worry," Potiphar's wife cut in. "I can sort them out." She walked across the bare floor of the study toward the slave who stood holding two of the fallen scrolls. She held out her hands, trying to give him a reassuring smile, and he quickly handed her the scrolls. She took the first one and unrolled the papyrus, glancing over the inscriptions; then, glancing at him, she handed the first scroll back and unrolled the second. "These are sacred scrolls," she murmured and looked at the wooden container on the floor. The slave quickly bent and set the scroll back with its fellows, then lifted up the small scroll box and held it toward her. Her eyes flicked between the wooden box and the young man's expectant expression. She set the scroll she was holding back in the box and plucked out a third, unrolling it carefully.

"Should I fetch someone else?" The serving woman was standing in the entryway, quivering like a hound for the chase. "Amosis?"

"No," Djeseret said, speaking quietly, looking down at the unrolled scroll. She glanced over her shoulder. "It's fine. You can go."

A moment of quiet passed; then, shooting another look at the interfering foreign slave, the woman ducked away and disappeared in a ripple of curtain.

When the serving woman was gone, Djeseret raised her eyes to look properly at the young man who was standing there, still holding the box. Thin, worn looking, nervous, he could not be much older than she—he might even be younger—and he was infinitely further from home.

She spoke slowly, taking care to enunciate the words, pointing to the foreign servant and to the scroll in turn. "How did you know where to put the scrolls?"

He shrugged. "I read them."

She raised an eyebrow. "You read them?"

He pointed to the tiny ink strokes on the exposed

papyrus, still unrolled between her hands. "Here." He pointed to the word. "Sacred."

She pointed down at the characters written in careful columns across the scroll. "Can you read this?"

He looked down and was quiet for a long moment. Then, looking a bit sheepish, he glanced back up at her and nodded.

Keeping her finger pointed toward the characters and raising her voice slightly, as if increased volume would make the language easier to understand, she asked, "How can you read our language?"

He looked back down again, then said, "My father."

"Your father?" Now she looked thoroughly confused. "Is your father from Kemet?"

He shook his head. "No." She sensed that he was trying to summon the right words. "He had . . . scrolls." He pointed at the parchment. "And I read them."

She was watching him closely now. "Why did your father have scrolls?"

He was quiet again, and this time it seemed that he was struggling for words he had no real way of capturing, so she waved a hand. "It doesn't matter," she said and reached for the scroll box. Their fingers brushed as he handed her the box. "My name," she told him, "is Djeseret."

He inclined his head respectfully.

"Who are you?" she asked him.

He looked up and was silent, as if unsure how to answer. At last he said, "Sasobek."

Potiphar walked with slow-crunching footsteps toward his villa, carrying a small papyrus scroll in one hand and watching as the sun sank in brilliant splatterings of gold. His body was only somewhat less weary than his mind after what had become a tediously long day at the king's court. He'd had to deal with three different prisoners and reorganized the watch of the royal guards, and he felt a sense of relief at seeing the soft candlelight wafting out into the evening air, beckoning him toward a meal and the comfort of rest.

Greeted at the front door by a servant who stood aside for him to pass, Potiphar headed across the central courtyard of the house and down a flickering corridor. As he walked, he could hear voices and scuffles coming from other parts of the villa, carried through the mud walls, and his stomach grumbled. It was certainly past the time when he would have liked to eat his dinner.

Brushing through the curtains hanging over the entrance to his bedroom, Potiphar stretched and made his way toward his bed with its fine, carved wooden frame and soft linens. Tossing the scroll aside, he pulled off his wig and sat down, letting out a slow breath. He was just running a hand over his bare, shaven head when his wife appeared at the entrance to the room. Smiling, he rose to his feet to greet her as she moved toward him.

"You look tired," she said, giving him a kiss.

"A little," he admitted.

"Busy day?"

"Too busy." Potiphar shook his head. "And not over yet." He sighed. "Really, I don't have time to manage the affairs of this household and the affairs of state at the same time." He gestured back to the scroll, lying on the bed. "I still have to look over the agricultural plans tonight."

"Can't Amosis do it?"

Potiphar grunted. "Not unless he's suddenly been blessed with literacy."

Djeseret smiled. "Perhaps when you're vizier—"

"That," Potiphar said, "is an honor and an office to which I do not aspire. Dealing with prisoners is one thing. Taking on the law of the entire country is another."

"Everyone says there would be no finer man to do the job."

He shook his head, smiling, and then paused, seeing someone suddenly appear behind the curtains leading into the room. "Yes?" he called. The curtains parted, and one of his house servants—the Asiatic slave, the new one—looked in, hesitant. "No one sent for you," Potiphar told him, but Djeseret turned around.

"No," she said, "stay." She looked up at her husband. "I asked him to come." She held out a hand toward the slave. "It's all right," she said. "Come." The slave came closer, and Djeseret reached out, putting her hand on the boy's arm, as if seeking to steady him in Potiphar's presence. She looked back at her husband. "He can read."

Potiphar glanced from his slave to his wife. "Read?" He sounded incredulous. "What does he read?"

"Some of your scrolls were knocked out of place today," Djeseret said, "and he knew how to put them away—"

"Which scrolls?" Potiphar asked, voice sharpening.

"There was no damage," Djeseret assured him.

"Those are my private writings," Potiphar said and looked again at the slave.

"I understand," Joseph said, speaking at last in his accented speech. "I know them. They are sacred."

Now Potiphar stared at him with more perplexity than annoyance. "How would you know these writings?"

"My father," said Joseph.

Potiphar looked over at his wife. "What do you know about this?"

She shrugged. "He couldn't really explain more than that."

Potiphar looked at Joseph and then back toward Djeseret, who nodded encouragingly. Potiphar took a step closer to his new slave before stepping suddenly back and picking up the scroll he had left lying on the bed.

"All right," he said, holding out the scroll. "Read this."

Joseph took the scroll, and Potiphar crossed his arms, watching as Joseph unrolled the papyrus and looked down at the characters inscribed around what appeared to be a diagram of a field. Potiphar could see the slave's eyes moving and saw the young man frown slightly. Potiphar glanced at his wife, a little smugly, but Djeseret stood there calmly and waited.

Finally, Joseph raised his eyes. "A field plan," he said.

Potiphar blinked and glanced again at Djeseret, who smiled.

Joseph had already turned back to studying the scroll, his eyes darting over the characters. "To—create—more harvest." He raised his head. "For the year." Then, almost meekly, he offered the scroll back to his master.

Staring at Joseph, Potiphar took the scroll. "May I ask how a young Asiatic slave learned to read our language?"

Joseph glanced quickly at Djeseret.

"He seems to read more than he can speak," Djeseret told her husband and glanced at Joseph.

Potiphar considered this. Then he took a step closer, clasping his hands and holding the scroll behind his back. "Sasobek," he said, and the slave looked at him. Potiphar remembered those same observant eyes from the day Amosis had brought the foreign boy to the household, staring back from a face that had looked much more foreign then than it did now. Potiphar brought the scroll from behind his back. Joseph hesitated before reaching out and taking the offered document. "Do you know," Potiphar asked, "what a scribe is?"

Joseph blinked, then nodded.

"I will train you," Potiphar told him, "and you will take care of my records." He looked at him. "Is this pleasing to you?"

There was silence, and then, after another moment's hesitation, Joseph nodded again.

"Ah," Potiphar said, "you understand?"

Another nod.

"Well," Potiphar said, "good." He tapped the scroll with his finger. "Take this"—he pointed in the direction of his study—"and put it with the others. Yes?"

Joseph gave a slight bow and, carefully holding the scroll, turned and walked from the room, brushing through the curtain.

When he had gone, Potiphar looked at his wife. "I've never seen such a thing."

"Nor I," she said, and laughed, putting her arms around her husband's waist. "He's a little wonder, isn't he? Very solemn."

Potiphar just shook his head and leaned down to kiss his wife on the cheek.

Lying quietly that night, after checking his bed to make sure the lurking scorpion was nowhere to be seen, Joseph did not sleep. The other servants of the house lay around him in the darkness, breathing slowly, while he alone stared up into the quiet. He kept trying to focus his thoughts on the image of the field plan, trying to remember the descriptions and indications for planting recorded on the document and trying to understand why something about it seemed . . .

imbalanced. He had a sense, turning the diagram over in his mind, that there was something better, that it could be improved . . .

What could he do about it, though? It was his father—

Joseph stopped the thought, frowning. It was his father who had the gift of prosperity.

Well, that might be, but his father was not there.

Joseph had held out hope, at first, that his father would come, a hope that sustained him through those first stark, sunburnt days and comforted him in the mind-spinning fear that descended with the first nights. Surely and inevitably Jacob would learn the truth and come hurrying after the caravan. When the caravan arrived in Kemet, Joseph imagined that his father would appear in the marketplace with silver to trade for his beloved son—because his father would not just abandon him; his father would never let him go; his father would come and find him, and it would not be hard, for there was only one place the slaves were brought . . .

But neither his father nor his treacherous brothers had come.

Instead, they had allowed him to be sacrificed. He thought it bitterly as he came to understand it, as the days passed and his hope was worn away, eroded beneath the weight of his growing realization.

And to whom had he been sacrificed? What had been the purpose of the offering of his flesh and his life and his memory? Was it the God of his fathers who demanded such propitiation, who would forever bless his father's family with survival and promised increase now that he, the focus of all their contentions, had been removed?

Where had the God of his fathers been that day in the desert?

Abruptly, as he always did, Joseph turned from the welling darkness that threatened when he lingered too long over that question. His thoughts turned instead, and suddenly, to his sister, Dinah—Dinah, who had always been so kind to him, who had watched over him, who had taken such a special interest in him after his mother died.

And then he thought of his master's wife, Djeseret. She would be about Dinah's age. She had been kinder than he thought she would be.

He closed his eyes, and soon he slept.

Across the room, the scorpion still crouched, hidden, in the darkness.

CHAPTER 22

Countrymen

"Excellency."

Zaphenath turned from where he sat with a small group of officials in the midst of discussing the king's Oasis development project. Although the proposed site of the development was not far from the capital, based in the region where the king was already building his pyramid, some of the officials were still hesitant about the prospects of transforming the marshland into agricultural acreage. The guard made a slight bow. "You asked to be alerted when the Asiatics returned."

It took Zaphenath a moment to understand what the guard had said. When he did, a strange, almost light-headed rush washed through his body, and his hands felt suddenly cold.

"Have they been detained?" he asked.

"As you ordered, Excellency."

They came back, he thought. They came back for Simeon.

The guard bowed and left, and Zaphenath turned back to the other men, including the king and his son. Senusret raised his eyebrows, but Zaphenath avoided his eyes. Asar merely smiled.

"Let us continue," Zaphenath said, clearing his throat and returning the attention of those present to the diagram sketched onto the unrolled papyrus. "With the improvements we've discussed, these areas can easily be drained and cultivated, but we will have to install more sophisticated drainage trenches."

"What about the labor costs?" one official demanded. "We can conscript the workers, but there's still a cost."

Zaphenath shrugged. "If you want to invest in this land," he said, "the necessary labor costs will have to be undertaken too. Otherwise your crop will inevitably be threatened by high water levels and the investment is senseless. Moreover," he said, his voice a little testy, "the additional crop yields we would gain by converting a portion of the Oasis for agriculture would be far more beneficial to the country right now than the usual royal fishing trips."

The man who had asked the question turned to the fellow next to him and murmured something under his breath. Zaphenath ignored them.

"Please," Senusret said, redirecting the attention of the grumbling officials and glancing at Zaphenath. "Continue."

Asar was sitting back, arms crossed, watching the discussion with a slight smile on his face as Zaphenath continued speaking. And he remained quiet as the other officials asked questions. It was only when the other men were rising to leave, their business concluded for the time being, that he asked, "What was that about Asiatics?"

The question muted all other chatter. Zaphenath looked over at the prince, who sat waiting for a response.

"It's a state matter," Zaphenath said.

"Ah," said Asar, "well, then it's probably too complicated for me."

A few chuckles met the remark. "I'd be happy to discuss the matter with you privately," Zaphenath told him, "if that is what you'd like."

"Oh," Asar said, waving a hand and rising to his feet, "that's fine. I understand if you don't want me asking about it."

Some of the other men in the room began to look at one another.

"I mean," Asar was still smiling, "it's an unsavory business to have to meet personally with suspected spies. Though I understand, of course." He looked straight at Zaphenath. "I'm sure it's the simplest thing to do, seeing as they are your own countymen."

Zaphenath could feel the other officials in the room focusing on him, their gaze triggering a spreading flush up the back of his neck.

"I think," Senusret said, "our business is finished here." He gave a nod, and the other officials, taking their cue, began to shuffle out of the room, a few glancing over their shoulders as they left. Zaphenath bent down to roll up the diagram with the field plan he'd sketched out, but Senusret held up a hand. Reluctantly, Zaphenath straightened again. "You too, Asar," the king told his son. The prince crossed his arms, while Zaphenath bent back down and finished rolling up the papyrus, waiting for the room to empty of the others.

"Well," Senusret said at last, when the three of them were alone. "Asar, if you have a sincere question for my vizier about state matters, please ask him. Otherwise, I'm sure he has other business to attend to."

Holding the scroll in both hands, Zaphenath looked at Asar, who glanced back at him.

"Well," Asar said at last, "I haven't said anything about the spies." That slight smile again. "But since other people may talk, I just wondered what exactly your relationship is to these people."

"My responsibility," Zaphenath said, "is to oversee all legal proceedings and disputations. That is my relationship."

"Oh," Asar glanced away. "I didn't mean to offend you. I must not be the first person who has asked."

Zaphenath looked over at Senusret, who frowned. Then he looked back at Asar. "To be frank, Prince," he said slowly, "you are certainly the only person who has asked." He paused, and his voice was a little terse. "May I ask if I have caused you some sort of displeasure?"

Asar glanced at his father before looking back at Zaphenath. "It's just what you and I have spoken of before, Tjaty. The matter of appearances is important for the People. And these men are your countrymen."

"In that way, Prince," Zaphenath said, while Senusret looked from his son to his vizier, "I have no countrymen." He took a slow breath. "I would hope," he said coldly, "that my birthplace does not cause the prince to suspect my loyalty to the king or to my country. I am a man of Kemet." He bowed slightly in Senusret's direction. "If we are finished here, there is indeed other business that I need to attend to."

Senusret nodded. Zaphenath bowed again, turned, and took his leave. But within moments of passing the guards and crossing back out into the corridor, he heard footsteps—the dismissed prince, following behind him.

"Tjaty—"

Zaphenath turned.

"I did hear one thing," Asar said, voice lowered, "that I'm sure couldn't be true, but I meant to ask you. Privately."

Zaphenath watched the slight, almost imperceptible glimmer rise in the prince's eyes. "About that boy who works for you—Potiphar's son." Asar paused and looked at him. "He is Potiphar's son, isn't he?"

Zaphenath's whole body grew very still. For a long moment, he did not reply. At last he said quietly, "You may accuse me of being a spy, and you can say what you want to your father." His voice grew sharp. "But you will never—and I warn you, Prince—cause trouble for a man as good as Potiphar." He stepped closer and shook his head once. "You understand nothing."

And he walked on.

CHAPTER 23

Scribe

Hunched over the worn papyrus, the slave whose name had once been Joseph sat crossed-legged on the ground with a thin, reed-like writing utensil, a stylus, lying on the ground beside him. He closed his eyes, straightening up and squinting hard, as if the effort he exerted would somehow clear the jumble of characters crowded together on the battered scroll. It was one thing to know enough to recognize certain words within a known context, but to have to strip this complex language down to its most primal units and learn them one by one—each character representing a sound, or a combination of sounds, or sometimes an entire expression—there were just so *many* of them.

Yawning, he opened his eyes again and looked back down at the papyrus sheet with its intricate markings—names and ideas and abstract concepts all transmitted through these fragile sketches on a material of flattened river plants. For some time now he had been practicing reading those fragile sketches and writing them out himself on broken shards of pottery, sitting with other young scribes in training for hours a day in the nearby temple while the priests taught them the sacred art of the Word. Great creative potential was unleashed through the act of writing, they were told, as well as the act of reading and speaking aloud the words that were written, as if the breath of the scribe imbued the copied symbols and rituals with life, blending what was written and what was real, and releasing into being that which until then was represented only symbolically as text.

As the young trainees were executors of this sacred craft, exceptional behavior was expected of them. They would be important members of the community throughout their lives, yes, but most important, they were to stay solemnly aware of the sacredness of the powers with which they were now endowed as masters of the Word.

All of which was very grand, Joseph was sure, but during the nights when he sat alone in Potiphar's house, trying to fill up the gaps in his mastery of even the basic spoken language, he could often feel a low, pounding tension radiating behind his eyes, and he slept with the pain when he could read no longer.

He rubbed the back of his neck, straightening up again in a stretch, before focusing once more on the document in front of him. It was a story about a courtier who fled from Kemet at the death of the king only to find chaos and disorder beyond the country's borders, out in the regions where the Asiatic tribesmen dwelt in states of various incivility. He had just gotten to the part where the exiled courtier prayed to return to Kemet, in spite of the prosperity and riches he had acquired in his foreign sojourns, when he suddenly sensed someone watching him.

He raised his eyes and smiled.

Djeseret stood, leaning her shoulder against the brick arch lining the entryway into the room. "What do they have you reading now?" she asked.

"It's about Sinuhe," he told her. "This is how you say it? Sinuhe?"

"Ah," she said, "the Tale of Sinuhe," and moved across the floor in a rustle of thin linen. She was wearing one of her long, full wigs, and golden jewelry, inlaid with green stones, bound her upper arms and wrists. He smiled as she sat down beside him. "Where are you?"

Joseph looked down at the manuscript. "He wants to go home."

"Has he found success and riches yet?"

Joseph nodded. "But he still wants to go home."

"He does go home," she said, "eventually." Then she glanced at him. "Does it . . . make you think about—?"

"This is my home now." He didn't meet her eyes. "Potiphar is kind to me."

She smiled. "Potiphar thinks you're very smart. He was telling me that the way you reorganized the field-planting project has been a huge success. He said your suggestions were brilliant."

Joseph glanced at her. "I just saw it," he admitted. "In a dream."

She laughed. "Your dreams are much more useful than

mine. You must have a gift." The golden bracelets on her wrist jangled as she gestured. "Blessed by the gods. Maybe by Sobek himself, hm?" She nudged him. "Sa-Sobek, Son-of-Sobek."

"Ah," he said, "Sobek," and picked up his stylus. The wooden rectangular slab where the stylus rested when not in use had two small, circular indentions carved into the wood, one of which was filled with black ink and the other with red. Joseph dipped the stylus into the small pool of black ink and, in the upper corner of the much-copied record, set to work, his wrist flicking deftly around the design. With a grin, he pointed to the tiny crocodile now crouched along the uppermost border in the corner of the manuscript. "Sobek."

"Can you write your name?" she asked.

He nodded and drew what looked like the small figure of a goose in front of the crocodile. "Sa-Sobek," he said. "I think the crocodile will eat the goose."

Djeseret laughed again, and Joseph chuckled with her. "And you're using the sacred writing, too," she said, "not just the scribal script. Potiphar will be very impressed." She smiled. "Can you write my name?"

He thought for a moment, stylus poised. Then dipping it quickly back into the ink, he sketched out the characters, using the space underneath the crocodile and the goose: a serpent, followed by a knot, then an open mouth, and finished by a little mound that looked like a half-risen sun peeking over the horizon. "Djeseret," he pronounced.

"I like how you drew the serpent," she said, and he smiled. "And what about your real name?" He glanced at her. "Joseph?" She looked down at the papyrus. "How do you write it in your language?"

Next to the crocodile, and moving faster than with the foreign characters, Joseph drew the simple strokes quickly—a few dashes, a circle, a backward-facing hook.

"Joseph," he said.

She looked down at the foreign name. "Do you think much about your people?"

He shook his head.

She was quiet a moment. "Do you have brothers?" she asked. "Sisters?"

He glanced over, his head bare and his eyes lined. "One brother," he said. "One sister." He smiled a little. "She is kind, like you."

Djeseret smiled too. "A small family, then."

"My mother wanted many." He shrugged. "But . . ."

She nodded. "I understand." Her smile became a little sadder. "Me too." She held up her fingers with the number. "I am married four years but no children."

Joseph looked up toward the ceiling, thinking. "My mother—nine years."

"Nine years," she repeated. "Are you the oldest?"

Joseph's expression seemed to indicate that his thoughts were outpacing the language he had to express them. Finally, he just said, "Yes."

She was watching him. "I'm sure they miss you."

"My mother is dead." He swallowed. "She was very good. Very beautiful, in all ways." He pressed a hand over his chest. "She is still . . . close to me."

Djeseret lowered her eyes. "I'm sorry."

He gave another shrug. She looked back down at the papyrus, and it seemed that neither wanted to meet the other's eyes.

Finally, Djeseret said, "I felt very lonely when I first came to live here. I had to leave my family. Not like you did, but . . . I still missed them." He glanced at her, and she gave a weak smile. "It's hard to come to a new place. For a while you don't fit." She paused, trying to rethink her words. "You have no place."

He thought about that, then nodded.

"But you'll find a place." She tapped the papyrus. "Maybe you'll be like Sinuhe too and find lots of riches in your new country."

Joseph looked at her. "Sinuhe was free."

"Well," she said, "maybe someday your master will make you a free man. That can happen."

He raised his eyebrows. "Yes?"

"Of course." She smiled again. "Why do you think Sinuhe wanted to come home to Kemet? This is the most civilized place in the world."

Joseph set his stylus back down on its platform with the little ink pots. "So," he asked, "you have found your place?"

"I've tried to." She shrugged. "I guess . . . I don't always know what my place is." She rubbed one hand over her arm, jangling the golden bracelets around her wrist again. "Sometimes I think Potiphar is . . . disappointed, maybe, that he chose me for his wife."

"Oh, no," Joseph shook his head. "I'm sure he's very glad. And you are lucky." Djeseret wouldn't fully recognize the sudden conviction in his voice, couldn't know that he saw the shadows of his sister when he looked at her. "Potiphar is a good man."

She lowered her eyes. "Yes." She looked back, and Joseph, seeing the sudden sadness in her face, reached out instinctively, setting his hand on her arm, the way he so often had with Dinah. She blinked, and looked down, and then looked back up at him.

"I'll let you get back to work," she said, her smile wobbling. She pushed herself back to her feet, setting her jewelry tinkling softly with her movements. Joseph looked up as she stood and watched as she moved away. She didn't glance back at him as she brushed through the entryway and out of sight, and he was left sitting alone, holding the papyrus where their names were written—hers bridging the gap between his new name and his old one, binding the two halves back together.

CHAPTER 24

Genesis 43:18–23

Head lowered, Zaphenath moved down the road leading to the royal prison, walking quickly, when he caught sight of the serious-faced Amon hurrying up the road toward him.

"Tjaty," the young man panted, falling into step beside him, "I'm sorry I'm late."

Zaphenath glanced at him. "For what?"

Amon wrinkled his nose. "Weren't we supposed to meet to review the granary levels?"

Zaphenath thought for a moment, then rolled his eyes. "Of course," he muttered, "you're right. Forgive me." He beckoned for Amon to keep moving alongside him. "Talk to me while we walk. Something else has come up."

Amon began rattling through the numbers he could recall while Zaphenath listened. Then seemingly out of nowhere, he glanced over and said, "Amon?"

Cut off mid-sentence, Amon asked, "Yes?"

Zaphenath paused a moment. "I assume you know how I came to know your father."

Amon looked at him, and Zaphenath could see, as he so

often saw, a flash, a flicker, a haunting whisper of a face that had once been so very familiar. Then Amon nodded.

"Has anyone ever asked you about why you work with me?" Zaphenath asked. Amon glanced away and shook his head. Zaphenath saw the hesitation. "Amon." Amon looked uncomfortably back at him. "It's important that you tell me." Zaphenath kept his eyes focused firmly on the young man's face. "Do you understand what I'm asking?"

"Yes." Amon looked away. He was small and lithe, with the sort of elegant features that Zaphenath himself possessed, the inheritance of boys who closely resembled their mothers. "But I don't think I look anything like you."

Zaphenath blinked. "Is that a joke?"

Amon sighed. "It was supposed to be."

Zaphenath glanced toward the sky, so expansive and piercingly blue, and his hands shifted uneasily on the scroll clasped behind his back. Then he heard Amon say, "You don't need to worry, Tjaty. I know what happened." Zaphenath looked at him, and Amon smiled slightly. "My father told me." Then he held out a hand. "Do you want me to take the scroll?"

Zaphenath, watching him, handed over the papyrus.

"Are you going to the prison?" Amon asked. "I'll come with you."

Zaphenath was quiet for a moment before he said, "Then there's something else I must explain to you." He paused. "And, perhaps, ask of you."

Benjamin, son of Jacob, glanced up at the structure's mud-brick ceiling, as he had done every few minutes since he and his brothers had been escorted with minimal ceremony into what appeared to be the designated place for their reunion with the man who had imprisoned Simeon. Their camels, laden with gifts from their father and quite out of place amidst the small braying donkeys that the local people used to haul their burdens, had already been led away, albeit with the promise of eventual return. The brothers themselves had been escorted from the entrance of the city to the royal prison, whose interior was really quite comfortable and cool and where, this time, they were allowed to remain outside the holding cell.

Now they stood quietly together, waiting, under the wary eyes of the guards. Indeed, the last several miles of their journey into Kemet had been marked by the particular acknowledgment of the guards at each outpost along the highway leading in through the borders of the land. Someone had known they were coming, and someone had put out the word that they were to be watched for.

"Is that where you were held?" Benjamin asked, voice quiet, gesturing with his head toward the enclosed space at the other end of the room. Judah, who was standing beside his youngest brother, glanced over and nodded. Four men, Judah had confirmed for himself, were still imprisoned there. They gazed up at his foreign face with distrusting eyes when he peered in.

"Do they not like Canaanites?" Benjamin asked, his voice still soft.

"Not these," Judah murmured, glancing around at his brothers.

Benjamin nodded, looking up at the ceiling again, and swallowed. "So where's Simeon?"

"Not where we left him." Judah took another quick look toward the enclosure he had scrutinized so closely when he first entered the room—scanning the faces once, twice, and once more in disbelief—but his brother was nowhere to be seen, and Judah had no way to ask the guards what had happened to him. All he could do was wait, with his father's most beloved son standing wide-eyed beside him, and pray that he had not made the mistake of his life in bringing Benjamin back here.

He could hear footsteps approaching and turned toward the sound, feeling the energy among his brothers—tense, alert, and watchful—and a sudden shakiness in his hands, revved by the pounding of his heart.

The silhouette of a man appeared in the entryway of the prison. Judah squinted, trying to see against the glare of the sun. Then he watched as the figure stepped inside, moving with a certain deliberateness, pausing in the sudden cool. The guards inclined their heads respectfully, and Judah glanced at Benjamin, who stood, watching. The official (Judah assumed he was some sort of official) was clad in a crisp linen skirt, and his lined eyes stood out sharply against the framing that his wig afforded his curiously boyish face. Judah could not help but glance down, a little self-consciously, at his own coarse desert dress and at his hands, still covered with dust from the two-week journey.

The official, whose face was entirely unfamiliar, did not speak; instead, he stood, simply looking at the bearded brothers. After a moment, they began to lower their bodies and press their knees against the hard prison floor. Lowering himself along with the others, Benjamin raised his eyes, hoping to sneak another glance. Realizing that the man was staring straight at him, he quickly focused his gaze instead toward the ground.

Seemingly satisfied, the official turned to the guards, speaking quietly, and the guards nodded. Turning back to the family, the official walked closer, stepping slowly, keeping his eyes firmly on the faces of the assembled men. He stopped when only a few remaining paces separated them. One of the guards stepped up alongside him.

The man turned to the guard and spoke quietly. The guard nodded.

"You may rise," the guard said, his accented words indicating that some time had passed since his last use of their language. As the Canaanites shuffled their way back to their feet, the guard asked, "Where is your remaining brother?"

Judah moved forward, taking Benjamin by the arm and stepping out of the protective gathering.

"This is our brother," he said.

Reuben moved after them. “Please,” he said, and lowered himself once more to his knees. “I do not know what caused the mistake,” he spoke with averted eyes, “but when we returned from our last journey, we found the silver we had used to buy the grain mistakenly placed”—he was picking his words carefully—“within our sacks. We’ve brought back the correct amount and more, with gifts for the vizier.” He shook his head firmly. “We are not thieves.”

The official tilted his head slightly toward the guard as the man gave a hurried translation, looked at Reuben, and shook his head. “There was no record of any missing payment,” they were assured.

Judah dared to raise his eyes, watching.

“No,” Reuben insisted. “I am sure—”

The official waved a hand, speaking quickly, and the guard shook his head. “We keep very careful records. Everything was paid in full.”

For a moment, Judah stared in disbelief and then lowered his eyes again, lest he should appear disrespectful.

“Then let us give the money as a gift,” he heard Reuben say, “and we will present the vizier with other gifts as well.”

“The vizier thanks you for your gifts,” the official told them, “and you will be most welcome to present them, but first, you are to come with me.” He gestured for Reuben to rise from the ground as the guard translated. The official clapped his hands, and the guards in the room advanced. Instinctively, Judah put an arm in front of Benjamin, pushing him back into the throng of brothers, but the man called out another command, and the guards paused.

"You are to be escorted to a safer place," the guard assured them, turning to the brothers, the slightest of bemused smiles on his face.

The other guards stepped closer and, appearing somewhat less menacing, indicated that the brothers should follow. Judah watched the finely dressed official turn and walk from the room, becoming a darkened shadow as he marched back out into the sunlight. Looking uncertainly at the others, Judah followed, and his brothers moved along after him. The watchful, suspicious gaze of the remaining prisoners followed them to the last.

CHAPTER 25

Genesis 39:2–6
Abraham 1:1–2, 15; 3:11–12, 15

"We may have some company," Zaphenath announced, leaning into the sunlit room where his two sons played on the floor. Asenath, who sat beside the boys, looked up.

"You're home early," she said. "Who's coming?"

"My brothers," he said and ducked out again.

Asenath got quickly to her feet, asking Manasseh to watch Ephraim for a moment. Manasseh nodded dutifully and looked toward where his little brother sat holding the carved figure of a soldier. Asenath hurried out into the corridor. "Zaphenath!" she called. He paused as she hurried after him, her feet bare and her hair braided loosely over her shoulders. "Your brothers are here?" she demanded, reaching him, breathless.

Zaphenath shrugged. "I thought we should have a little feast."

She shook her head, reaching out, holding him by the arm. "Did you see him?"

He looked back at her, and she kept her eyes on his face. Then he looked down at his feet before saying, quietly "Not yet." He glanced up. "I hope"—he tried to smile, gesturing toward his face with one hand—"they don't frighten the boys, all beards and wool."

He walked away before any more could be said. She stood alone, watching him go.

Potiphar was scrutinizing the documents spread out in front of him, detailing the transactions of his household and the crop yield from the recently gathered harvest. He leaned down, giving closer review to several of the figures, while the newly appointed steward of his household stood somewhat nervously beside him.

Finally, Potiphar looked up. "You're sure these figures are correct?" Joseph nodded. Potiphar smiled, deepening the slight, fine lines around his eyes and mouth that had gradually been etched across his face in the time since he had first brought the young Canaanite into his household. "Because this is incredible." He clapped a hand on Joseph's shoulder. "You're making me a rich man."

Joseph—who had become Sasobek, man of Kemet, his body stronger and his face older and his person now fully a part of the household and his master's country, no longer bearing any particular resemblance to the disheveled young foreigner who had been brought as a slave, barely able to speak—inclined his head. "The gods have been gracious to your household."

"Yes," Potiphar said, "but you run the household. And you came up with the new planting system." Joseph shrugged and smiled. "You're earning this," Potiphar added, patting Joseph once more on his shoulder, which was broader now and covered by a loose linen overcoat, pressed with delicate folds, worn over his chest and shoulders and belted near the top of the smooth linen kilt that had replaced the simpler one he had worn as a domestic servant. "Now," Potiphar moved away, over toward the wooden chest in the corner of the room, "I have a question for you."

Joseph watched as his master knelt and opened the lid of the chest, digging around for a moment before pulling out two papyrus scrolls and closing the lid again.

"My father was the high priest at the temple of Ra," Potiphar explained, coming to stand beside Joseph as he unrolled one of the scrolls, "and he gave me both of these texts when I joined the priesthood." Joseph looked down at the unrolled papyrus. "This first one," Potiphar said, pointing at the inscriptions, "comes from this country. It's a text to restore life to the dead. I'm sure you studied something like it with the other scribes in the temple."

Joseph's eyes scanned over the characters—*Beginning of the Book of Breathings which Isis made for her brother Osiris, to make his soul live, to make his body live, to restore him anew . . .*"

Nodding, he glanced at Potiphar, who met his glance. "Now with this sort of text," Potiphar went on, looking back at the scroll itself, "the emphasis is always on the divinity of the soul in the *next* life—how that is the time when we can commune most fully with the gods and how death is the passageway that allows the communion to happen. The pattern is always death followed by a restoration of life, or breath"—he tapped his finger on the character for *breathings*—"which means an elevation to the realm of the divine—a unity with the gods—all using Osiris as the symbol."

Joseph nodded again.

"Now." Potiphar unrolled the second papyrus, revealing an illustration of two figures—a priest with the telltale leopard skin he wore to indicate his authority and primary role in the ritual, standing with his knife raised, and a reclined figure of a man stretched out on some sort of altar-bed.

"This text is very different," Potiphar said. "It starts out with a sacrifice, with death, again"—he pointed to the image of the man lying on his back—"but then the sacrifice is stopped, and his life is spared." He shook his head. "And it's *then* that the gods reveal their secrets to this man"—he pointed again—"who is still mortal. So the key here seems to be the sacrifice, which is like death but is not death." He paused. "Meaning, as far as I can tell, that this sacrifice becomes the portal to commune with the gods but in *this* life." Potiphar glanced at Joseph. "You're from Canaan, and so was the man who wrote this record." He pointed at the figure stretched out before the priest. "I assume this must all be founded on the beliefs of the desert people, so I'm hoping you might have some insight for me." He waited. "Is this how the desert people connect with the gods?"

But Joseph was staring down at the text, his eyes riveted to the words, feeling the strange, sudden pounding of his heart.

In the land of the Chaldeans, at the residence of my fathers, I, Abraham, saw that it was needful for me to obtain another place of residence; and, finding there was greater happiness and peace and rest for me, I sought for the blessings of the fathers . . .

"You can read it, I assume," Potiphar said.

And I, Abraham, talked with Jehovah, face to face, as one man talks with another; and he told me of the works which his hands had made; and he said unto me: My son, my son, I will show you all these . . .

Joseph glanced at his master. "How did you get this?"

"It's a priestly document," Potiphar said. "A sacred text."

"Yes," Joseph said, "but where did it come from?"

Potiphar seemed to weigh how exactly to respond. "It's from Iunu," he said at last. "The Temple of Ra." Joseph looked back at the document. Potiphar was watching him. "Do you do have records like this in Canaan?"

"My father had this record."

Potiphar's forehead creased in perplexity. "Not this precise record, surely?" He pointed back down at the scroll. "My father gave me this text, copied from a scroll in the temple vault."

As Potiphar spoke, in a flash Joseph saw again the sun, and moon, and stars, rising around him and heard his father's voice—a voice he never thought of, tried never to think of—reading aloud, in low, subdued thunder, *I show these things to you before you go into Kemet, that you may declare all these words . . .*

"It's a vision," Joseph said and closed his eyes, trying to center his thoughts, trying to steady himself. "The man's name was Abraham."

"Yes," Potiphar nodded encouragingly, "that's right. That's the name. One of your countrymen, yes?" He pointed at the text. "So your father did have this record?" Joseph nodded. Potiphar raised an eyebrow. "Is it well known outside of Kemet? I never imagined—"

"No one else has it," Joseph said.

It appeared that, rather than enlightenment, Potiphar's conversation with his steward was serving only to generate increased confusion. "But I believe that text is kept exclusively at the temple here." He shrugged, as if trying to come to terms with this strange new rift in the universe. "Though if this man traveled back from Kemet . . ." He gestured vaguely. "I just don't know what use it would be, outside the temples. I didn't imagine . . ."

"My father had it," Joseph said, staring down at the text, at the man bound on the altar, "because Abraham was his grandfather."

A still silence filled the room. Potiphar did not reply, and Joseph did not say anything more. Both men simply stood, looking down at the papyrus and its delicate script.

Finally, Potiphar said, "This man is your father's grandfather?" Joseph nodded. Potiphar looked back down at the scroll as well. "I see." He glanced at Joseph. "Shall we . . . discuss it some other time, perhaps?"

"If you'd like," Joseph said. His voice sounded distant.

"We have no more work to do this evening," Potiphar said. "Go and rest, if you'd like."

Joseph nodded. "Thank you."

Turning from his master and the scroll, Joseph brushed through the curtains, moving out into the candlelit corridor. He walked along dazedly in the dim light, following the familiar path until the corridor led out into the courtyard at the center of the villa, open to the sky. Slowing, Joseph looked up, standing exposed beneath the stars.

And it came to pass that the priest made an offering to the god of the king, and also to the god Ra—that was the diagram of Abraham, lying stretched out on the altar, with the sun-priest holding the knife over his body—*and as they lifted up their hands upon me, that they might offer me up and take away my life, behold, I lifted up my voice to my God, and my God hearkened and heard, and he filled me with the vision of the Almighty, and the angel of his presence stood beside me, and immediately unloosed my bands . . .*

The words came back to him unbidden, flowing, released from the text, his father's text, seeking him out across the desert and the night sky. Joseph closed his eyes as the words encircled him, wrapping him in recollection and the sudden hush that fell as he stood beneath the stars, hearing again the voice of the man whose life was so closely connected to his own, reaching out, summoning him—

Abraham—Abraham—my name is Jehovah, and I have heard you, and have come down to deliver you, and to take you away from your father's house, and from all your kinsfolk, into a strange land which you know not of . . .

Opening his eyes, Joseph looked down at the linen coat that he wore wrapped over his shoulders and cinched tight around his waist, a mark of his authority in the household of Potiphar.

Desiring also to be a greater follower of righteousness—Abraham's record, his explanation, his testament to his descendants—*and to possess a greater knowledge, and to be a father of many nations, a prince of peace . . . I became a rightful heir, a High Priest, holding the right belonging to the fathers . . .*

Melchizedek the prophet—it was his father's voice again, holding out the linen robe embroidered with the interlocking squares, the symbol of his birthright, the inheritance from his own fathers—*Melchizedek the priest . . .*

My name was Joseph, he thought, his eyes closed once more. Son of Jacob. Son of Isaac. Son of Abraham.

"Sasobek."

He opened his eyes. Djeseret, who was passing through the courtyard, stood staring at him, the moonlight falling over her face. "Are you all right?"

He nodded, rubbing the back of his arm with his hand.

She took another step closer, almost hesitant. "Are you sure?"

"I'm fine," Joseph said. "Where are you going?"

"I was just going to talk to Potiphar," she said. "Is he busy?"

Joseph shook his head, feeling suddenly cold in the warm evening air.

Djeseret looked at him a moment longer. "All right," she said, her voice soft. "Take care, then." He stood, listening to her footsteps along the corridor. Then he was alone again.

"Oh"—he heard Potiphar's voice, echoing out into the stillness—"Djeseret." Joseph took another deep breath and walked on through the courtyard. He was nearly at the front door when he paused, turning back at the sound of Djeseret's voice. "How can you say that to me?"

While he couldn't quite hear Potiphar's reply, he did hear a raised voice and sensed a harsh retort.

"No"—Djeseret's voice again—"you don't listen," and then another low, growling reply.

Joseph glanced around, relieved that none of the other servants were near enough to hear. He moved quickly, slipping out into the garden and pulling the carved, red-painted front door firmly closed behind. The red was to bar any demons, but the demons, it seemed, had already slunk their way inside.

The night sky sparkled on the reflecting pool. He looked back only once toward the house before moving on, past the moon and beneath the stars.

CHAPTER 26

Genesis 43:24–25

Walking along the dusty road, heading safely away from the official state buildings and the prison, Judah was the first of the brothers to catch sight of the breathtaking villa that sat beside the banks of the peacefully meandering River. The house and grounds of the estate were surrounded by a wall that was as cleanly whitewashed as the villa itself, and Judah could see palm trees dancing up over the artificial horizon of the wall, tossing gently against the bright blue sky. The sunlight felt warm across the back of his neck, and the reeds and grasses crowding along the riverbank swayed placidly. The overall effect was almost enough to soothe Judah's mind into thinking that perhaps, at last, all was actually going to be well.

He glanced back yet again at the guards accompanying them; the men seemed fairly relaxed and unbothered by their errand, and Judah hoped their attitude indicated that whatever awaited the brothers was not unpleasant.

"Have you ever seen anything so grand?" he heard Levi

murmur, with rippling comments of assent from several of the others.

Judah glanced at Benjamin, who walked close beside him, eyes likewise raised to take in the view. Benjamin gave a low whistle. "I've never seen anything like it."

"With any luck," Judah told him, "you never will again."

A guard standing at the gate waved them by, allowing the foreigners entrance onto the property. The villa itself was situated at the end of a tree-lined path, leading the eye directly to the house. Palm trees shadowed the walls, and fig trees surrounded a pool filled with floating lotus flowers. The guards seemed content to let the desert barbarians take in the wealth and luxury of the estate, but two or three servants on the grounds paused in their work, staring at a sight none of them had ever before seen—a whole tribe of Asiatics, in full desert dress and appearance, standing in the middle of their master's property. Even the presence of the armed guards did not appear to set them entirely at ease with regard to the visitors, and they whispered to each other, pointing.

As the brothers stood on the path, gazing around at this unexpected oasis, Judah turned toward the villa and saw a familiar figure emerge from behind an imposing, red-painted wooden door guarding the entrance to the home. It was none other than the young man who had met them at the prison, still arrayed in his handsome linens but no longer projecting so severe and formal a presence. Instead, he practically strolled toward them, as if enjoying the sun on his skin and the beauty of the day. Drawing close enough to speak, he raised a hand and called out in the unfamiliar language of Kemet, to which the guards responded in kind. The brothers glanced at one another, and the man came to a stop a few paces in front of them and smiled.

"I am Amon," he announced, as the guard who had translated stepped quickly forward. "You are at the home of Zaphenath-Paaneah, vizier of all Kemet." Glances rippled once more through the gathering of the brothers. "You are welcome guests at his home today. Follow me, please." Amon gestured with one hand, and murmuring to one another, the brothers hesitantly but obediently followed. They walked past the reflecting pool beneath the shade of the trees, following the linen-clad steward while the guards followed along behind, all heading toward a small, squat structure situated toward the outer walls of the compound. Judah could see three women, attired in the usual linen dresses with thin straps, standing outside this smaller brick building, smiling at their approach.

"This is where you will bathe," Amon announced, stopping in front of what Judah realized must be some kind of bathhouse. "You must clean and dress again before entering the home of Zaphenath-Paaneah."

Amon clapped his hands, and one of the women stepped forward, holding out a bundle of linens. Amon took the bundle and unfolded it, revealing a fine-spun linen robe meant to cover the chest and shoulders and a linen kilt to be worn underneath.

"This will be more comfortable for you in the heat," he said. "There is one for each of you—a gift of the fine clothing of Kemet."

Stepping back, Amon held out a hand, inviting the foreigners to enter the bathhouse, while the smiling women stepped aside. "These servants will assist you," Amon told them as they began shuffling forward, "and show you how to dress after you wash."

Benjamin glanced quickly at Judah. "Assist us?" he hissed.

Judah gave a helpless shrug.

"Well," Asenath smiled, "you two look very handsome." She crouched carefully in front of her sons, trying not to wrinkle her own dress while straightening the linen kilt she had managed to wrestle Ephraim into for the occasion. Manasseh stood beside his brother, decked out in a golden armband and a child-sized beaded collar that spread from his neck out toward his shoulders and swooped across his chest. The boys had both been bathed, and Asenath had carefully lined their eyes with dark kohl and rewoven the single slim braids lying flat against their otherwise bare heads. She turned to Manasseh. "You will make your father very proud."

"Who are the people coming?" Manasseh asked again.

Asenath, her own eyes also carefully lined, looked up at

her oldest son as she knelt in front of Ephraim, giving his kilt another twist. "They're very special visitors," she said, jangling the golden bracelets on her arms as she brushed at Ephraim's braid. "You've probably never seen anyone like them before."

"Are they Nubians?" Manasseh asked.

"Not Nubians," Asenath said. "And not from the lands near Kemet. She rose to her feet, smoothing her dress. "These men are Asiatics. They come from a place called Canaan."

"Canaan?" Manasseh repeated, wrinkling his nose, while Ephraim, his own armbands glistening on his tiny biceps, began chewing pensively on his finger. "Where is that?"

"The Red Land," Asenath said. "Now"—she set her hands on her hips, and Manasseh straightened his shoulders—"it is very important to your father that we be good hosts to these men. You know how to do that, don't you?" Manasseh nodded dutifully, while Ephraim just looked up at her with his wide dark eyes, still chewing on his finger. Asenath smiled. "Good. And part of being a good host means we aren't going to stare at them or say anything rude. They are not from Kemet, so they will look very different."

"Are they civilized?" Manasseh asked.

"In their own way," Asenath said with another smile, "I'm sure they are." She bent down again in front of her boys. "Your father will be very proud to introduce you." And she gave each of them a kiss on the cheek.

Judah raised his arms awkwardly while a serving woman tied a sash around his waist, and he glanced over at Benjamin, who stood straightening his own linen kilt. The other brothers were also nearly all dressed, washed and scrubbed clean from the dirt of the road, and the fresh linen felt soft and light against skin that was accustomed to the rough rub of spun wool. As the woman moved away, Judah looked down at what he was wearing—a linen robe that felt almost like an overcoat, covering his shoulders and neck and tied in around his waist—and experienced the same sense of unease that had followed him since their first journey into the Divided Land.

Benjamin wouldn't realize it—he wouldn't remember the garment his father had given to his chosen heir, before Jacob's other sons destroyed it—so Judah glanced toward where Reuben was standing. He met his brother's eye and pulled at one side of the linen tunic. Reuben glanced down at his own outfit, running his hand over the cream-colored folds, and looked back at Judah.

"It's his robe," Judah said, and Reuben looked back down at the linen with its fine weaving and delicate creasing.

"What's that?" Benjamin asked.

Judah turned back to him. "How do you like linen? I think it suits you."

Benjamin smiled a little nervously. "Why is he being so generous with us?"

"We're not sure he's being generous, yet," Judah said.

Amon appeared again in the open doorway, hands

clasped behind his back, and looked over the brothers, who had nearly filled the bathhouse with their broad bodies all crammed in together.

"Very good," he said, nodding approvingly, and the brothers glanced around at the freshly washed, linen-clad versions of each other. "Now," he beckoned with one hand, "come with me."

Thou breathest henceforth for time and eternity . . .

Amon comes to thee bearing the breath of life, he causes thee to breathe and come upon the earth . . . The Book of Breathings . . . is as thy protection; thou breathest by it every day . . . Horus protects [embraces] thy body and deifies thy spirit in the manner of the gods.

The soul of Ra is giving life to thy soul . . . thy soul breathes . . .

—*The Book of Breathings, lines 25, 39–42, 45–46*

CHAPTER 27

Sacred Scrolls

The sun had nearly completed its descent across the sky, sinking into the womb of the stars where it would await its rebirth the next morning. The horizon darkened into an exquisite deep blue speckled with stars, and the torches shimmered and spat in the outer courtyard of Potiphar's estate. Within the villa, candles burned in flickering rows along the walls and windows, and the sound of laughter drifted out into the garden, mingled with rhythmic clapping and the sound of delicately plucked strings, shedding melody out into the night.

It had been a hectic day preparing for the banquet, orchestrating and overseeing the food and the flowers and the dancing girls. The gardens had been under preparation for weeks, and the villa had to be cleaned and prepared to meet the master's exacting specifications. But when the guests began to arrive—all of whom were court officials like their host, all coming to congratulate Potiphar on the news that the king had decided to appoint him as the new vizier, second-in-command to the king, as soon as the current one retired—everything was in place. Now, as the guests feasted and laughed and applauded, Potiphar's long-suffering steward slipped out of the house, weary and sweaty, escaping into the cool of the garden.

Closing his eyes, Joseph breathed in the deep scent of the fragrant blossoms drifting across the reflecting pool, their green lily pads spread beneath the exuberantly open blue and white petals. The mighty, tangling fig trees, with their sprawling branches, cast shadows in the bright moonlight from where they kept their vigil along the outer walls, wise protectors of the estate and all who dwelt within. Potiphar's garden was a radiant and welcoming place, and it was here that Joseph most liked to come to sit, or think, or rest. And it was here that he stood, taking in the night air, looking up at the stars brought out so brightly now that the sun had passed on from the sky.

I am Ra in his rising, he thought. *I am Atum in his setting; I am Osiris in the night.*

He had been reading through the sacred scrolls with Potiphar, spreading out the texts and unrolling the delicate papyri in parallel, setting the words loose to mingle and converse. Potiphar's gods all flowed in and out of one another, it seemed—the sun called by the name of Ra in its rising and Osiris, lord of the underworld, at its setting, life and the afterlife all one eternal arc as life passed into death and the dead rose again in the quest to transform time into eternity.

And somehow, tangled up in these shifting gods and

mortal aspirations, was his own great-grandfather—a bearded foreigner, clothed in woolen garments, who spent his life in the desert beneath the stars and the vast expanse of heaven, a visionary who opened himself to the divine and was embraced by the light that created all things. Joseph had once read the words of Abraham as a vision of the cosmos, a glimpse into the creative powers of the universe. But now, when he sat in Potiphar's villa, he began to sense his master's gods weaving themselves into the fabric of his great-grandfather's visions, expressing the realities that lay beyond the language of the sun-priests of Kemet—guardians of the cosmic cycles, pacifiers of the forces that held the night sky in its orbit and brought the sun out of the womb of the stars each morning.

And yet, compared to the sublime symbolism of his master's gods, Abraham's god spoke with an intimacy that seemed unexpected from the force that held the sun and the moon and the stars in one unblinking gaze, who spanned the heavens and called all things into order at the moment of creation. Could it be that Abraham too was merely seeking to give a voice to these name-shifting forces, as Potiphar's fellow priests asserted, that he was simply seeking to speak out on behalf of the abstract Source of the powers of nature and the realities that lay beyond the limited comprehension of his creations?

Or had Abraham actually heard a voice and transcribed a divine communication that came not from the sun, or the moon, or the stars, but from One who had come to him, and comforted him, and talked with him face to face and sworn a covenant with him that his son and grandson and great-grandsons were destined to bear forever after?

Standing there beneath the stars, enfolded within the sweetness of the night air, Joseph's eyes traveled down the linen covering his body—the crisp, clean folds of the fabric rippling like waves on the River across the entire length of the garment, running from his shoulders down past his knees.

And he felt a tightness in his throat.

He did not often give himself cause to think of the home that had once existed beyond the bounds of Kemet within the world that had been stripped away from him, but now, ever since he had been so unexpectedly reunited with Abraham, a whisper would come, or a quiver, slipping out across the desert and through all the distance that spanned who he once had been from the man he now was—and he was sought out, and began to remember.

But the spell was broken as he heard a nearby rustling and turned, looking over toward the reflecting pool. His eyes adjusted now to the darkness, he could see someone sitting there, facing away from the water. He moved closer, wondering if one of the servants had perhaps had too much beer and stumbled into the fresh air to recover. But then he saw the smooth, unadorned arms, the delicate hands, and the loose, flowing dark hair that spilled down her back.

"Djeseret," he said.

She raised her face, glistening in the moonlight. His

footsteps brushed over the ground as he moved closer, and she sniffed, her large dark eyes turned toward him. He sat beside her on the raised rim of the reflecting pool with the lotus flowers drifting behind on their tiny sea of stars.

"Are you all right?" he asked, his voice quiet in the garden. Behind them, the villa glowed warmly, and the laughter and applause coming from within seemed at odds with the night's stillness and the shimmering on her face.

Her eyes shifted away from his, though she did not turn from him. "An argument," she said. "It's nothing."

Joseph looked down at his finely sandaled feet, feeling the evening breeze across his back. "I'm sorry."

She shook her head again. "I should be used to it." Then, trying to smile, she looked at him. "I remember when you could hardly speak to any of us, and look at you now." She brushed the palm of her hand across her cheek. "Running the estate."

Joseph glanced down at his hands, clasped loosely together. "That was such a lonely time," he said softly. "I'd seen so much cruelty." He glanced at her. "But you were kind."

She tried to smile and looked away, playing with the golden bracelet dangling loosely around her wrist. From the villa, the low, rhythmic beating of a drum started up, with a few appreciative shouts, and she glanced over her shoulder to where the candlelight from the house danced across the ground. "Has Potiphar been having you read the scrolls?"

Joseph nodded.

She sniffed again. "Have you solved the cosmic mysteries?"

"Not yet," he smiled, "but we're trying."

"So is there any chance for new life in this life?" She looked back at him, tried to hold her smile. "Or do we have to wait until the next one?"

"Well," he said, "the rites I've been studying are all for the living, so I imagine they must have some relevance for this life."

"Which ones?"

"Well, the Abraham texts, to start with." He paused, looking over the tops of the fig trees, out toward the night sky. "The thing about them is that they're so—intimate, somehow." He glanced at her. "My father spoke about God the same way, like God was . . . not a friend, exactly, but someone he knew. Who knew him."

"One God?" she asked.

Joseph nodded. "One God who oversees everything that is." He looked back up at the stars. "What Potiphar really wants to know is whether the covenant made with Abraham—the man who wrote the texts—can extend to anyone other than Abraham's descendants." He glanced back over. "I don't need to talk about it if—"

"No," she said. "It's fine." Another sniff. "What does he want to understand?"

Joseph looked at her. "He wants to understand this idea of covenant by sacrifice—with Abraham, before he has his cosmic vision, and also afterward, with his son Isaac, and the way each person who inherits the covenant also inherits the burden of sacrifice." He gestured with one hand. "It's a kind of ritual killing, making something sacred by passing it through the underworld." She looked down at her own hands. "It . . . seems to be some sort of key to the covenant."

"What's the covenant?" she asked.

Joseph thought for a moment, trying to recall the words. "I think the text says, *To be a greater follower of righteousness, and to possess a greater knowledge, and to be a father of many nations.* It's a binding promise between Abraham and his God." He paused. "That's what a covenant is. A promise, on conditions."

"All promises seem to have conditions." She glanced at him. "A father of many nations?"

Joseph looked at her and nodded.

"Well," she looked away again, "Potiphar won't find that with me."

"Actually," Joseph said, "Abraham and his first wife had only one son."

"His first wife?" Djeseret turned back. "Why 'first'? Did she die?" Joseph shook his head, and he saw her face change as she understood. "Because she couldn't have children." She looked down. "So he took someone else." Her voice had turned cold. "Is that part of the covenant? That his wife also had to be sacrificed?"

"That wasn't what it was," Joseph said, but Djeseret looked away.

"I'm not sure I think much of your God."

"He's—" Joseph began and then stopped.

"He's what?" Djeseret looked back at him. "He's your God, isn't he?"

"Think of it this way," Joseph said, moving a little closer, trying to close the sudden gap between them. "The Breathings text begins by talking about how the person, the initiate, is going to be called up to join Ra and his son Osiris in the horizon—the in-between place—and then, to prepare, the initiate is washed by the two goddesses. It's a birth symbol, a rebirth symbol, and meanwhile, here Abraham is talking about the cosmos and the creation, and the creation is a birth symbol, and birth is a symbol of the creation—"

Djeseret crossed her arms.

Joseph stopped mid-sentence. Quietly he said, "It's still the woman who brings life, Djeseret. Even in these ceremonies when there is no actual birth happening. Do you see?" Her expression indicated that she did not see. "The woman is the one who carries the breath of life inside of her," he went on, still trying, "and she's the one who transmits it—like the two women who come to wash the new soul in the Breathings text. They reappear at the final judgment, too, looking on as the soul is born permanently into eternal life."

"That's very nice," she said, "for them."

He gestured with his hand. "Well, whether it's Abraham or the texts here, I think both the ceremonial and the vision texts are imitating mortal life. Or mortal life is imitating the cosmic vision. There's some sort of connection—"

"Of course there's a connection," Djeseret cut in. "The

entire priesthood is based on the assumption that there's a connection. We align our lives with the movement of the sun and the stars. The River rises and falls with the sun and the stars."

"But if that's true," Joseph said, "then what you said—about whether there's new life in this life—then surely there has to be, don't you think?" She blinked. "If we go through the right motions, then new life happens in this life *and* the next." He pressed a finger into his open palm, as if indicating a word on a scroll. "That's what the texts seem to imply; that's why they're precious and sacred and kept so carefully—they hold the life secrets, in time and in eternity. That's the formula, over and over—*in time and in eternity.*" He could feel himself breathing a little more quickly. "And through our following the rituals and the patterns, the gods can release the power in the text and bring it to life—in anyone. Then that person becomes unified with the gods. She breathes again. She lives. It all means the same thing . . ."

Djeseret looked straight at him. "Those two women," she said, "who are involved in that ritual washing you're talking about—you know who they are, don't you?" She waited for a reply that did not come. "Isis and Nephtys." She narrowed her eyes slightly. "You're right about Isis. She is life—she brings Osiris back to the living, and she bears their son. But Nephtys is Seth's wife. She's death."

"She's a guardian," Joseph said, shaking his head. "And a nurse to the new soul as it passes through the transition."

"She's sterility."

"She's part of the balance." Joseph reached out to touch her arm, but she moved it away. "Djeseret, this is ridiculous. This doesn't have anything to do with you."

She looked at him. "It has everything to do with me." She shook her head. "What do you know about going through life"—she turned her face as her words caught in her throat—"with no idea of how you're supposed to fit into it?"

"Djeseret." Joseph looked at her and reached out again to touch her arm. "I'm a slave."

The laughter rose again from within the house, but neither said anything more as they sat there in the garden.

At last Joseph said quietly, "I'm sorry to see you so unhappy."

Her eyes were bright with moonlight, and she blinked, and they both looked away.

CHAPTER 28

Genesis 43:26–30

Amon smiled to himself as he watched the foreigners raise their widening eyes and step over the threshold into the interior of the villa. Trailing in through the front entryway, dressed in their new linen tunics and looking oddly between worlds with their unmistakably Asiatic appearance and the linen dress of Kemet, the men looked nervously subdued as they gazed around the open interior of the courtyard. Decorated with tumbling bursts of brightly colored flowers, scented with perfumed oils, and partially exposed to the softening pink evening sky above, the central space of the vizier's home had been transformed into quite a breathtaking vision. Small candles set into the walls flickered against the coming evening. A wide semicircle of carved wooden chairs, cushioned and elegantly detailed, were set out with stately circular platforms beside each one for the food and drink that would be coming.

As if sensing that the tribesmen had been sufficiently awed by their host's grand home, Amon gestured with his head to one of the servants. The man slipped out the front door and returned a moment later with another linen-clad foreigner, who let out a great cry. The others wheeled around at the sound of his voice and then cried out themselves in relieved happiness. Arms outspread and a great grin on his face, Simeon received the wave of brothers, surrounding and embracing him and asking a dozen questions all at once.

When he noticed Benjamin in the throng, Simeon reached out, clapping his youngest brother on the shoulder. "So you came to rescue me?"

Benjamin smiled. "If that's what I've done, then I'm glad I could do it."

"Who managed to convince Father to let this one come down here?" Simeon asked, turning to his other brothers, still chuckling.

Reuben, who stood slightly off to the side, said, "Judah did."

The chuckle faded, and Simeon smiled slightly and looked at Judah. "Well," he said, "thank you."

Judah inclined his head.

Amon, who stood apart observing the reunion, was the only one who saw his master enter the courtyard. The vizier was dressed in his finest linen, ornate and beautifully spun, with an elegant, shoulder-length wig. Golden bracelets adorned his arms, and around his neck he wore the golden chain given to him by the king. But for all his regal presence, he moved quietly and paused as he entered the room unnoticed.

For a moment, Amon wondered whether he ought to

intrude on this strange and fragile moment between the host and his guests; but then, catching his master's eye, he cleared his throat and announced, "His Excellency, Zaphenath-Paaneah, Tjaty of All Kemet."

Quickly the brothers turned. Seeing the man to whom they owed their liberty, they lowered themselves to the floor in a jumbling mass, and a fearful, respectful silence stamped out the laughter that had been echoing through the villa.

Keeping his eyes on their lowered forms and letting the silence ooze through the room, the vizier turned to the servant who had been translating for Amon and spoke in the quick, clipped native tongue.

"He asks about your journey," the servant announced. The words rang in the abrupt quiet.

"A good journey, my lord," Reuben replied, keeping his eyes down.

"And your father?" the servant asked, once the reply had been translated. "The old man? Is he still alive?"

The vizier was looking straight at Reuben.

"Yes, my lord." Reuben nodded quickly. "He is alive."

Hearing Reuben's reply, the vizier lowered his eyes, then looked up again and stepped closer. His gaze traveled slowly over the men's faces. A tense hush hovered in the room as he stood alone, facing the foreign brethren kneeling before him.

And then he saw Benjamin.

Judah watched Benjamin raise his eyes, tentative, as though feeling the strength of the vizier's gaze upon him.

The vizier's throat moved, swallowing. Then, keeping his eyes on Benjamin, he spoke again, softly, quickly, and the servant translated.

"Is this your youngest brother?"

Reuben looked over at Benjamin and then up at the vizier. "He is, my lord."

Benjamin had the same soft eyes he'd had as a boy and the same lush, curly hair inherited from a mother the young man had no memory of. And he knelt with such openness in his face, so strangely trusting of this official who had demanded his life to barter for his family's survival, so seemingly willing to be bartered.

"God be gracious to you," Zaphenath said, his voice hoarse. He flicked a glance at Amon, then turned and walked from the courtyard, disappearing back down the corridor from whence he had come.

As the vizier's footsteps receded and he disappeared from sight, the brothers glanced frantically at one another. Catching Benjamin's eyes, Judah mouthed, "What did you do?"

Benjamin shook his head, helpless.

"Please," Amon said, stepping quickly closer. The guard picked up the translation. "Make yourselves comfortable. You are guests in this house. We will bring you refreshment." He clapped his hands, summoning more servants bearing drinks.

CHAPTER 29

Genesis 39:7–9

Joseph winced as his foot splashed down into the shallows of the River, not quite making the leap between the edge of Potiphar's boat and the dry riverbank. He shook his sopping sandal, already weary from the hours spent among the waving ripples of golden wheat he had been out to inspect. Potiphar's lands lay upriver from the villa, and the day had been hot, but the short voyage back in the comfortable wooden boat had been pleasant enough until the wet sandal. Joseph watched to make sure the boat was under proper care by the waiting servants before moving on toward his master, who had accompanied him out for the inspections and stood waiting for him now. Making a squelching sound as he walked, Joseph sighed and looked up at the sky, shot through with rosy light, fading into a deep, slate-blue darkness.

"I suppose it's not enough for your god to send us a bountiful harvest," Potiphar said, following Joseph's gaze. "He has to paint the sky each night, too."

Joseph smiled. "Another harvest, in its own way."

"Even so." Potiphar waited for Joseph to fall into step

beside him, and the two men walked on past the gates and into the courtyard of Potiphar's property, awash in the sweet scents of flowers from the garden. "To think," Potiphar said, as their footsteps crunched over the gravelly sand of the paths, "the same god that spoke to Abraham comes now to bless my lands."

"If you believe it's the god of Abraham," Joseph said, "then he's always blessed your lands." He drew his outstretched hand across the darkening horizon. "And all of Kemet, and all that is."

Potiphar was quiet for a moment, then asked, "Is that what you believe?"

Joseph clasped his hands behind his back as he walked. "It's been a long time since I was in my father's household."

"You've adopted our gods, then?"

Joseph chuckled. "Perhaps they've adopted me."

The candlelight within the villa was flickering out through the cracks in the woven mats hung over the small windows cut into the walls and casting shadows out into the garden. "Abraham's god won't mind?" Potiphar asked as they walked by the reflecting pool.

"Oh," Joseph shrugged again, "he has my father and brothers to worry about. And I don't imagine any of them have much concern about me."

Potiphar slowed and then paused, standing in the garden with the stars beginning to peek through the veil of fading light. He turned his face to his steward.

"Sasobek," he said, and Joseph, standing beside him,

sensed a sudden gravity in his master's expression, "do you really believe that?"

Joseph looked at Potiphar, not expecting the question and therefore lacking any immediate reply.

"I've always understood our gods to be forces," Potiphar said, after a silence, "expressions of a deeper reality, symbols." He paused again, looking up at the sky. "But the god I find in your Abraham's writings does not strike me at all as a symbol." He paused. "He strikes me as humanly real and disturbingly present, and that"—he focused his gaze intently on Joseph—"is why I have not been able to leave those texts alone since my father first gave them to me. That is why I feel driven to understand them." He moved his head slightly to one side. "Do you feel nothing of this?"

Joseph, who could not tell whether he was being rebuked or merely interrogated, averted his eyes, looking down and away toward where the reflecting pool sparkled with its water canvas of nascent stars. But then he felt a hand on his shoulder and looked up.

"It was right to call you Sasobek," Potiphar said, and his voice was gentler. "Son-of-Sobek, the Crocodile, the water god."

"Why do you say that?" Joseph asked.

"Because water is the great in-between of the mysteries." Potiphar gestured toward the reflecting pool. "It holds the realm between earth and heaven, solid and sky. Even the stars are transformed into an ocean—the watery womb where the sun goes to rest each day. The in-between places are where the divine manifests itself—in the water, in the horizon." He fixed Joseph with a most earnest expression. "I very much doubt that Abraham's God—if he's the one watching over you—did not care that you were brought here." He shook his head. "Perhaps it is simply your destiny to swim through the in-between, like the crocodile." And he smiled. "Like Abraham."

Joseph felt a strange constriction rising deep within his throat. "Perhaps."

"Osiris was killed by his brother," Potiphar reminded him quietly, "and was brought back to life with even greater divinity. He gained it by passing through the violence and the shadow."

"I'm not Osiris," said Joseph.

"Or," Potiphar said, "perhaps you haven't met your Isis yet." He smiled. "Whatever—or whoever—it is that can bring you back to life." Joseph looked away again, and Potiphar reached out and put his hand on Joseph's shoulder. "All right," he said. "Forgive me. Come on. Let's have something to eat."

Joseph walked alongside his master into the flickering embrace of candlelight, leaving the stars behind.

Later that night, after retiring with Potiphar to his study to go over the last of the harvest calculations, Joseph said goodnight to his master and walked, alone, through the candlelit courtyard of the villa, quietly closing the front door as he stepped back out into the garden. He could hear the frogs croaking beyond the estate walls. Their faint, rhythmic ribbitting was a familiar and friendly accompaniment as he strolled through the night garden, a gentle assurance that the natural cycle of the world was still in order and another peaceful night had settled across the estate.

Passing back by the reflecting pool, he paused, watching the rippling stars, and he closed his eyes, taking a deep, fragrant breath of night.

Abraham—the words of the text came to him, whispered out of the stillness of the garden—*Abraham*—and he opened his eyes, looking up at the stars—*my name is Jehovah, and I have heard you, and have come down to deliver you, and to take you away from your father's house, and from all your kinsfolk, into a strange land which you know not of . . .*

It was the passage that came in response to Abraham's being lifted up on an altar, prepared for the sacrifice of his own life—*Behold, I lifted up my voice to the Lord my God, and the Lord hearkened and heard and he filled me with the vision of the Almighty, and the angel of his presence stood beside me, and immediately unloosed my bands . . .*

Joseph felt a sudden chill, even in the midst of so beautiful a night.

And then, amidst the stars and the frog song and the silent flowers, he heard a rustling footfall and turned toward where the path dipped among the fig trees, their branches spread out over whoever might be passing below. He squinted in the darkness and moved closer, leaving behind the drifting stars. The gentle fall of his footsteps mingled with the muttering frogs as he drew closer still, and he saw a murmur of shimmering white coming along the path toward him.

He slowed, and she slowed, and they looked at each other across the darkness.

"Djeseret." Her name, spoken out across the hush of the garden, brought the slightest of smiles to her face as she stood, safely sequestered beneath the branches that tangled the view of the stars, splattering the moonlight down in gentle patches.

"I didn't think there was anybody else out here," she said.

"I was just coming from the house," he explained, gesturing over his shoulder, and she nodded and looked down at the ground. He turned back to her, but she didn't raise her eyes, and he felt suddenly unsure what he ought to do as they stood in the quiet of the garden with the lowing frog song and the stars embracing the sky.

"Are you all right?" he asked.

She nodded.

"Well," he said at last, "I should go." He moved as if to pass her, but she moved with him, swallowing the distance back again, and when he turned around, his face was suddenly very close to hers.

"Please don't go," she said quietly. She reached out, tentative, and he felt her fingers slip through his; he felt her warmth against his skin.

There, in the night, he could hear Potiphar's voice, could

see the way his master had looked at him—*Do you feel nothing of this?*

And somehow, that voice became his father's, speaking out across the sky—

That is the symbol of Melchizedek—the prophet, the priest—

His father had put that robe with its symbols upon him, clothing him in an identity and heritage and folding him into the covenant line, a covenant his brothers had tried to tear from him the day that Joseph, son of Jacob, son of Abraham, was scattered into a thousand pieces—

A thousand pieces—

Until now, beneath the stars and the darkness and the hush of the garden, as he felt her breath against his body, the words came tearing back across the sky, rushing through all that had been and all that he was, and he remembered that the god had a name and that the god had known Abraham's name—

Abraham, my name is Jehovah—

—and that he was Joseph, son of Jacob, son of Isaac, son of Abraham, clothed in a promise that his name too was known to the God of his fathers and that he still, somehow, belonged to Him.

"Djeseret." His voice was unsteady, whispering, against the sudden pounding of his heart. "There is nothing your husband has kept back from me"—he took a slow breath—"but you."

He could feel her lower her head, brushing against him. "Am I his to give?"

He looked away. "Please don't do this." He moved his hand, loosening her fingers from around his. "I can't."

She looked up at him and let his hand go. He looked at her, at the open, plaintive expression on her face and the hopeful, trusting, frightened glint in her eyes. "Your god," she said softly, "is a god of abundance." She laid a hand on his chest. "Don't you think . . . he would give you . . . a child?"

How many times, he thought, had his mother pled with his father and his father's God—and how many times had her plea gone unanswered?

"I can't," he whispered.

He knew she had understood what he said, but her eyes betrayed that she did not understand. He turned his face away from hers.

He could feel her chin trembling.

And then she slipped away from him, like a pale shadow beneath the light of the moon.

He was left alone.

CHAPTER 30

Genesis 43:31–34

Zaphenath splashed cold water from the elegantly carved basin up over his face, the droplets dribbling off his chin, and pressed a cloth against his eyes with his wet hands. Letting out his breath in a slow exhalation, he lowered the cloth, rubbing the fabric over his fingers, and set it aside. Taking another breath, he lifted a small, polished bronze mirror that lay beside the basin, blinking at his reflection. Then he set the mirror back and plucked up the small reed brush, dipping it into the kohl pot and quickly relining the kohl around his eyes. Blinking again, he raised the mirror once more. He assured himself that he looked no worse than when he had left the gathering, which he could hear echoing through the house along with the lyrical voices of plucked strings, rising in their own mingled conversation, which meant that the musicians too must have arrived by now. Very well.

Setting the mirror aside, Zaphenath moved from the washroom back out into the corridor, head held high, regal bearing returned. The swell of voices grew louder, cresting as he entered the room. Amon saw him, and nodded, and clapped his hands.

The brothers turned to see the vizier's returning approach, and the hubbub of chatter grew quickly quiet as the brothers waited, respectfully, to see what their host intended. The great man drew closer, and looked over them all, and held out his hand.

From one of the rooms lying off the central corridor, a woman clothed in gentle linen emerged with two small boys by her side, each with a single dark side-braid of hair, dressed in fine linen kilts and armbands.

"The mistress and children of the house," the translator announced. The vizier's wife came and stood beside him, gazing out at the assembled guests—at their faces, their movements, struck by how fully like men of the desert they seemed with their broad shoulders and handsome beards and wind-weathered skin. She imagined that the servants would want to come and stare at these guests who were every inch men of Deshret, in spite of the linen garments they had been given to wear.

The brothers, struggling not to stare back, inclined their heads.

"You are welcome to our home," she said. Her welcome was quickly translated while the guests raised their eyes, gazing at their hostess—at her large, dark eyes, the splendor of her adornment, and the delicate beauty of her face. "I hope you will be comfortable here," she told them.

"We are very grateful for your hospitality," Reuben

replied, bowing slightly, and she smiled at the tall man with the gray hair and full beard. Then her gaze swept over the others, one by one—some taller, some broader, some not quite so tall or broad—before her eyes caught on one of the men standing closest to her, his hair not yet gray and his face not yet so weathered, and his eyes—

His eyes—

There, in that foreign, unfamiliar face, were her husband's own dark eyes gazing evenly back at her, with her eldest son's impish, intelligent smile.

You look like my husband, she thought, and the effect was so breathtaking that, for a moment, she could neither speak nor look away. You look like my son.

The two young boys stood between their parents. The older one looked back at the foreign tribesmen with a kind of hesitant fascination, but the younger child looked nervous and, at the first smile from one of the brothers, held up his hands for his mother. Smiling, she reached down and hefted him into her arms. He put his finger into his mouth, staring at the bearded men.

"The vizier and his family wish you to join them for a banquet," Amon announced, "so you can taste the hospitality of Kemet."

Judah looked at the vizier, then over toward Amon, then back at their host.

"Am I to understand," he asked, speaking carefully, "that our lord has no more suspicion of us?"

"He is satisfied," Amon confirmed, and Judah closed

his eyes, lowering his head in a wash of relief. "Please," he heard, "be seated," and the vizier extended his hand toward the seating for the banquet. Gazing again around the ornate room, the brothers made their way toward the seats while the vizier crossed toward Amon, speaking in a low voice and pointing. Amon nodded and moved toward the brothers.

"Here, please," he ordered, approaching Reuben and gesturing to the first seat that formed the semicircle where the banquet would be held. "Here," Amon continued, gesturing to Simeon to take his place beside Reuben, and he proceeded to seat the brothers at their places. As Judah sat down beside Levi, he was focused not on the room or the musicians or the décor but on Benjamin, as if still uncertain that there was truly no harm intended for him. But Benjamin was simply placed, last of all, at the end of the row, smiling.

Still, Judah felt another slight shiver go scuttling over his skin. He's put us in order, he thought. We're sitting in our birth order.

He looked toward Reuben, leaning forward to catch his brother's attention. Reuben leaned forward as well, peering at his other brothers, then sat back with an equally perplexed expression. But the music was playing sweetly, and the servants were beginning to appear, bustling out with pitchers to refill the drinks, and the tension in the room was relaxing so pleasantly that Judah could not but feel that it would seem rather dour of him to be so insistent in his fears. He looked once more toward Benjamin, who seemed merry enough, watching the pageantry and receiving the gracious smiles of the servants as they offered him roast goose and stuffed figs. At last, Judah sat back.

The vizier, whose family sat facing the foreigners, offered a seat first to his wife, then helped his sons nestle comfortably into their own chairs with arms and backs high enough to protect even the smaller one from toppling out, before sitting down himself, all the while observing the proceedings, Judah sensed, as closely as (or indeed, closer than) any of the brothers. Only once did Judah actually meet the man's eyes for a flickering moment. But then Judah looked away, turning to Levi to comment about the gigantic leg of beef currently being borne into the room by its escort of servants.

"Please," the servant announced as the food was brought out, "eat." Several of the brothers, chuckling now at their extraordinary good fortune, sat forward and began digging into the food the servants had set out on the low tables in front of them. Levi touched Judah's arm and gestured down toward Benjamin who, looking a little embarrassed, had received a very generous helping of the feast indeed—his portion inescapably larger than any of the others. Catching his brother's eye, Benjamin grinned. As if resigning himself to his position of favor, he lifted up a slice of beef and bit into the crisply fragrant meat. Judah looked down at his own serving of beef, a very fine serving, to be sure, but nowhere near so large as Benjamin's.

Levi was smirking. "Looks like the boy is the favorite even here."

But Judah felt another wave of the same creeping sense

of unease, unable to dismiss the suspicion that some discreet strangeness remained afoot. The other brothers seemed jovial enough, of course, laughing and eating and commenting on the delectable dishes offered up. From all appearances, the danger really was past and the accusations finally resolved, all with an unexpectedly wonderful outcome—dining at the home of the vizier himself, sampling the wealth of Kemet in a time of famine. Benjamin was happily watching the musicians and making by far the least progress on the piles of bounties offered to him, despite his obvious best efforts. Servants were even offering small, perfumed cones of wax, indicating that the brothers should place the wax on their heads—the cones would melt in the heat over the course of the evening, releasing sweet fragrances. Amused and curious, several accepted.

There's no more danger here, Judah tried to tell himself. How long could a suspicious conscience continue to color everything he saw, seeing danger in brother and stranger alike? How long would he keep bracing himself for the catastrophe that never came?

Benjamin is not Joseph.

It was finally time, perhaps, to let the desert bury its own secrets and no longer think there was retribution or restitution to be made. Or maybe this was his restitution—taking Benjamin and Simeon home. He had not been able to take Joseph back to his father, but he could take Benjamin back, and Simeon with him, and food enough to sustain them all through the famine.

Surely, now, it was enough.

And even if he could not quite convince himself—even if he could not yet believe that the price had somehow been paid, that it was forgiveness that had set this bounty before them and that the eye of the desert was upon them no longer—there was simply nothing he could do. He couldn't understand the series of events any more than he had when they all began.

So he plucked up a fig from his platter and bit into the plump, sweet flesh.

When Judah awoke the next morning, resting on a soft mat and draped in smooth linen sheets, he could not, for a moment, understand where he was. Pushing himself up, blinking in the new light, he looked around—yes, his brothers were all still there, surrounding him, their bodies rising and falling in a rippling sea of linens, and the gentle morning dawn was creeping in around the woven mats hung over the small windows of the room where they had spent the night. Benjamin was there, and Simeon was there, and they all were there, and safe—absolved of the accusations and loaded with grain for the return journey back to their father.

Judah let out his breath, lying back down as he closed his eyes. For the first time since they had taken their initial journey into this cursed Divided Land, he could feel the stirrings of relief.

Before long, the other brothers began to awaken, and soon the quiet of the dawn was replaced by the rustlings and laughter of preparations for their journey home. They dressed themselves once more in their heavy desert garments, shedding the briefly worn vestiges of their acceptance into the vizier's private company. At the steward's insistence, they bundled the handsomely made linen tunics to take with them, along with the new pair of sandals they had each been given.

"I rather liked being one of them for a day," Simeon said, pulling on his desert-worn sandals for the day's travel. "I felt very handsome."

"And scrubbed," Asher grinned, rubbing his hand over his head. "I still have perfume in my hair."

"The camels will hardly recognize you," Reuben chuckled.

Judah slid his feet into his own sandals. "The vizier certainly seemed to show some favor toward you," he told Benjamin. "He must not have thought you looked much like a spy after all."

Benjamin stuck out his tongue. "I've never eaten so much in my life." He patted his stomach. "I feel like a fatted calf."

"You look like one," Levi said, to the amused chuckles of the others. Benjamin chuckled with them.

Reuben straightened up with a wink. "Time to head back out of civilization, brothers."

They were reunited with their camels on the road outside the walls of the vizier's estate. The beasts were loaded down with tightly bound grain sacks, observing their masters with their usual dispassionate gaze. The vizier's young assistant was waiting to bid them a final farewell, with the translator's assistance.

"I hope you will find everything necessary for your journey," said Amon, inclining his head.

"We owe both you and His Excellency our greatest thanks," Reuben told him, pressing a hand to his chest. "We are deeply honored."

"The tjaty will be pleased," Amon assured him. "Perhaps we will see you again in Kemet."

Then he stood watching, as the men tethered the last of their belongings onto the animals' swaying backs. One by one, they guided the great beasts away from the villa, beginning the journey back out of Kemet and toward the Red Land, kicking up dust beneath the expansive blue sky.

When they were gone, Amon turned and slipped back into the walled estate.

CHAPTER 31

Genesis 39:11–15

She had awakened alone that morning, as she awakened most mornings. She lay in her bed, watching the light creep across the ceiling, listening to the scuffles and bumps of the household. It was a festival day—the festival of Min, god of the harvest and symbol of the fertility and vitality of the land and its People. Potiphar had risen early and left for the temple to take part in the festival worship with the other priests and court officials, many of whom were high government officials like himself. Later in the day, he and his wife would host a feast celebrating another year of bounteous harvests from their lands and, though no one would say it, another year of barrenness between them.

How long, the servants would murmur, until the master took a second wife or a slave woman to perform the duty in which his wife had failed?

And what other use for a woman, she thought darkly, could there be?

She sat up slowly, the linen sheets sliding from around her body. She gazed toward the small window cut high in the wall, with its hopeful beams of sunlight creeping in around the woven covering, and wondered—as she had wondered in the weeks leading up to this singular day—just how she would get through it. Bringing her knees in toward her chest, she wrapped her arms around her legs and rested her chin on her knees, looking around the room she shared with the man she had been so eager to marry and with whom she had imagined the happiness and affection everyone else had imagined for them. Now it was a room she shared with a man who was weary of her tears, a man she hated for his perceived negligence of her happiness—and a man she just as deeply wanted to love her as she had once believed she would love him.

But who was Potiphar, really? The child of a successful man, as she was—a son of privilege and promise, carrying a good name and the assurance of earthly comforts. They had barely known each other on their wedding day—or rather, what they had known was only as much as anyone else could see. She lowered her forehead against her knees. What had he seen? A girl who was beautiful enough, who was young and healthy, who would make a good wife and mother. But if she was neither of those things—neither a good wife nor a mother—what was left to her? It seemed hopeless to think of being her husband's friend or confidant, if she could not fulfill her primary purpose in his life. When she had felt her growing power as a younger woman and laughed in the confidence that came of knowing she was beautiful, she had not imagined that the day would come when she would waken and find that this particular source of power, so praised and doted upon, was in fact no power at all—it was always beholden to another, an admirer, a lover, blanketing her in an illusion of security that could fall away in an instant and leave her naked and nothing.

She slid her feet off the side of the bed, glancing down at the ground first to make sure there were no lurking desert scorpions in danger of being disturbed. Pulling her dark hair over one shoulder and running her fingers through the loose strands tangled by her night's rest, she rose to her feet. At least the house would be quiet for the morning with her husband gone and most of the men attending festival celebrations. It was just as well—she was happy to think of spending the morning alone. Perhaps she could walk in the garden, or sit by the pool, or even come back to her own chamber and rest. After a full night's fitful sleep, she still felt utterly weary. She had been snappish with the servants for the last few days and was certain no one would miss her if she kept to herself.

The worst part, of course, was sensing that they understood—a pitying glance, a soft reply to an angry accusation.

They felt sorry for her. She hated it.

She dressed alone, not bothering to wear a wig. She walked with bare feet out of her room and across the corridor, moving toward another chamber, quiet and far away from the public part of the house. She brushed past the curtain into a small private space with notches cut into the walls for little statues of the gods, golden and gleaming, tiny miniatures representing the forces of creation. A small crumble of incense lay piled in one of the wall nooks. She struck a spark, closing her eyes, and sank down onto her knees as the sweet scent filled the space, carrying her prayer heavenward. She opened her palms, resting the backs of her hands on her knees and reaching out her fingers to the unseen presence of the gods.

Today, perhaps, they would hear her.

Today, perhaps, she would find mercy.

Joseph's footsteps echoed through the abandoned central courtyard of Potiphar's villa. The house was quiet today in Potiphar's absence. There was plenty to do to oversee the preparations for the feast that would be held later that night in commemoration of another successful harvest and in echo of the fertility celebrations held to acknowledge the prosperous growing season and beseech the gods for their continued bounty.

But that morning his master's mind had not been on the details of the festival or even the calculation of the wealth his land had brought him under Joseph's careful stewardship. Instead, Joseph, who was usually up earlier than anyone else, had come upon Potiphar out in the garden, facing toward the newly risen sun with the sky soft and pink and the air cool in the day's first breath. His master was wearing only a linen kilt, his head uncovered and his eyes unpainted, standing as tranquilly as if he had just risen out of the reflecting pool himself and Joseph had come upon him during the first morning of creation.

When Potiphar saw his steward approaching, he smiled, and beckoned him closer.

"You'll go to the temple today?" Joseph asked.

Potiphar nodded. "Tell me," he said, as Joseph came to stand beside him, "does Abraham's God have any such days?"

Joseph looked up at the pinkening horizon. A burst of the chirping, bright-eyed song of the birds, who had also been awakened by the sun's ascent, scattered through the air. He said quietly, "I suppose every day is his day." He glanced back at his master. "Is there anything I can prepare for you?"

Potiphar said nothing for a moment, still looking up at the sky. "Do you suppose," he asked, "that your god would hear prayers in behalf of my wife?" Potiphar looked at his steward. "Every year at this time, she receives one more reminder that our gods haven't taken much notice of her pleas for children. Perhaps your god might be willing to listen."

Joseph lowered his eyes. "I'm sure he hears the pleas of anyone who speaks to him."

Potiphar nodded, then said softly, "She is suffering." He paused. "I'm sure she's spoken to you about it. She trusts you. I'm grateful she has found a friend in you."

Joseph said nothing.

"Well." Potiphar smiled again, but his smile was softer than it had been before. "Let's go back to the house, shall we?"

And so Joseph headed back to the house and oversaw his master's preparations for his departure to the festival. Then he went to the kitchen and took inventory of the produce and confirmed that all the necessities were accounted for.

Now, alone, Joseph took a deep breath, relieved in his own way for the quiet that the festival day would afford. It would be much easier to finish the final documentation and appropriation of the harvest without a full household to manage. Those who remained had their own duties to perform and wouldn't need any bothering from him.

And so he found himself walking alone through the villa's empty open courtyard, listening to the singing of the birds and smelling the sweet scents of the flowers from the gardens. Pausing, he began to imagine the blossoms that could be used to decorate the interior of the courtyard for the evening's banquet. They would bring in blue lotus blossoms, of course, as magnificent in scent as they were in appearance, with their petals bursting out like exploding stars. Should they add iris? Perhaps a scattering of iris, too . . .

He was still standing, molding the empty courtyard in his mind, when he turned, startled out of his Edenic visions and back into the bare mud-brick reality, with the harsh daylight falling across the undecorated interior space. He feared the surprise on his face would offend the woman standing there even more than he already had.

"My lady," he said.

She too seemed surprised, standing there, the two of them alone. "I was going outside," she said at last, pointing toward the door behind him. He could see the sallowness in her skin and the shadows beneath her eyes.

The silence thickened, filling the open courtyard with a strange stillness.

"Of course," he said and stepped aside.

She nodded and walked toward the door behind him while he looked away. When she reached where he stood, she paused and looked at him. He looked back.

She trusts you. I'm grateful she has found a friend in you.

Somehow, he knew what she was going to do in the moment before she did it. Yet in the instant that she moved not toward the door but toward him, and leaned in, and closed her eyes, he couldn't breathe, couldn't think, could only sense the way she held onto him so dearly, so desperately—and he was aware of nothing, nothing in the world but standing there, as if the universe were cleaving asunder in a violent spasm as past and present rushed together in a blinding burst of light—

He broke away, and she stumbled back. His tunic had been pulled down from his shoulder, and the fabric hung loosely around his elbow.

When at last he spoke, his voice was very quiet. "Don't."

Her eyes narrowed. Then her hand came wheeling toward him, lightning fast and stinging across his cheek. He jerked up one arm in instinctive defense. "Get out"—he felt her nails on his arm, tearing at the loose cloth—"out of my house—"

He jerked his other arm free, and the linen slid from his

skin, fluttering off his other shoulder and falling from his back, and she threw the tunic onto the ground in an angry, crumpled heap.

He was already backing away, hardly feeling the stinging on his skin for the shock, reaching up with one hand toward where the fabric had been ripped down over his shoulder, and he turned, moving faster, and he heard her crying, as if from somewhere far away—

And then he heard her scream.

CHAPTER 32

Genesis 44:1–12

The brothers and their ambling camels moved along the dusty highway, keeping to themselves as they walked among the other travelers crowding the road. Most of those they passed were native to Kemet, attired in the sandals and linen kilts of the People. There were far fewer among them who would be traveling on toward the forts and checkpoints, passing beyond the roads and the borders and the boundaries, and heading out into the Deshret, the uncharted Red Land.

A pair of soldiers passed, evidently keeping an eye on the pedestrian traffic. The constant presence of soldiers and armed guards, however peaceful, hinted at the rigorous enforcement that underlay the peace of the state. It was not so long since the time when the government of Kemet had all but collapsed, splintering central power outward into dozens of minor principalities and chiefs. It was not so different, Judah thought, from what still existed in the deserts of Canaan.

That time had passed now, after the great-great-grandfather of Senusret, the current king, had managed to assert himself over all others, and the people of Kemet had gradually folded back together. Now, the state was organized once more under one divine ruler who oversaw the protective unity that had elevated the kingdom to the height of its prosperity. But even beneath the heavily armed, militant presence of peace, there was a deeper unity that held the people of Kemet together—a philosophy of interaction, represented most often as a goddess with outstretched, protective wings, called *Ma'at.*

Judah had seen a representation of this bond, this *ma'at*—which bound a man to his neighbor in an interpersonal balance, ensuring that acts of goodness, kindness, and mercy would be returned to the one who had so acted and create continuing peace for the entire community—in one of the texts from Kemet that his father had inherited. The text was a depiction of a judgment scene, which his great-grandfather was said to have found particularly moving. A suppliant soul was shown standing before the gods, stripped bare of all he had been in his earthly life, while his heart was placed on a divine balance with a feather. The feather, it had been explained, was a representation of *ma'at,* as was the scale itself, depicted in the form of a woman with arms outstretched to either side.

At the judgment, the suppliant's heart was balanced against the feather, and his soul weighed against his practice of *ma'at.* If his heart was found to be in balance—and he had therefore lived according to just, peaceful, and merciful precepts—his soul would be rewarded with eternal life among the gods.

Otherwise, the heart was devoured by a waiting crocodile.

Shivering slightly, Judah reached up, rubbing a hand over the center of his chest. Trying to ignore any further thoughts of the lurking, beady-eyed creatures that patrolled the River of Kemet, he felt himself gradually coming back to an awareness of the road and his brothers and the day around him. He glanced toward where Benjamin was walking. Soon they would be outside the borders of the city, then beyond the borders of the kingdom and the final outposts guarding the road into Kemet from the desert. Then they would be free—free to return to their father, free from the strange and haunting events that had overtaken them on their journey, free from the fear of the desert's avenging memory overtaking Jacob's Son-of-My-Right-Hand, his beloved Benjamin.

Just as he had the thought, Judah heard some sort of tumult—raised voices and the sound of hurriedly scraping footsteps—and he glanced over his shoulder. A rising burst of dust had been kicked up several hundred paces behind. As he looked, he saw not the usual pair of soldiers but six armed men, running along together, freshly dispatched from some unseen force. The other brothers were beginning to look back too, and so were the other travelers on the road, quickly moving to stand aside and allow the urgent flurry of soldiers to pass on toward whatever urgent business required them.

As though watching in uncomprehending slow motion,

Judah suddenly saw a figure among the guards bumping along on some kind of elevated seat balanced cleverly on the backs of two trotting donkeys, easily keeping pace with the swift-footed soldiers. And in just the same, uncomprehending slow motion, he saw the person who was occupying that seat—the young man from the vizier's house, his cheeks flushed either with the heat or some strong emotion—extend an accusing finger toward them.

The servants of the household had seized Potiphar's steward, jerking his arms roughly behind his back.

He had seen her collapse—he had turned at the sound of her scream and watched as she fell to the ground with his tunic lying lifeless beside her. He had run back to her, and fallen to his knees, and tried to take her in his arms, and lift her, and help her—

And that was when the gardener appeared in the open doorway, and the master's half-clothed steward looked up from where he knelt beside the mistress, lying crumpled on the floor.

Two of Djeseret's serving women had come hurrying down the corridor at nearly the same moment, and one of them started screaming too, as Joseph realized, suddenly, that they were all staring at him. He could hear more footsteps, as if the entire household—wasn't the household supposed to be empty today, of all days?—had been summoned by her cries.

The gardener was a bulky man with hardened hands, and Joseph had not tried to run from him because he could not imagine that he had any reason to run. But as he heard Djeseret's voice and the terrible accusation that tumbled furiously, desperately, from her weeping mouth, his legs felt suddenly too heavy and too weak to move, and the gardener seized him with a growl.

I never touched you!—Joseph could still hear himself shouting at her, and she wouldn't look at him, she wouldn't even look at him—*you know I never touched you—!*

But the words came as if from some other body, some other world. He'd struggled against the gardener, demanding to be released, until the burly man struck him with a force that buckled his knees. Other servants were running in now, and he felt other hands seize his arms as he stumbled, and someone pushed him forward and his knees smacked against the ground in an explosion of light. She was still crying as he slumped down, gasping, and the serving women gathered protectively closer, shooting dark and disgusted glances that he couldn't quite see because his head was spinning and he could hardly breathe for the pain in his legs. His face felt numb and his mouth was wet and he could taste the sharp tang of blood as he had not tasted it since—

"You see?" Her voice, and he closed his eyes, his head suddenly too heavy to hold up any longer as he heard the words echo across the hall. "We bring in a filthy foreign slave, we trust him, and you see what he does—!" Her sobs choked off the words.

Joseph could sense the men gathering around him, muttering and grumbling to each another.

"Don't worry, my lady," he heard the gardener saying, "we'll protect you."

She looked toward him only once, and he raised his face, his lip swollen and smeared, and the tender skin along his cheekbone rising into a furious, bleeding bruise.

She looked away.

"I'm sure there's been some sort of mistake." Reuben was standing out in front of the other brothers where they had all gathered together in a loose, indignant bunch on the side of the road. The vizier's assistant stood facing Reuben, a translator beside him, and the armed guards just behind. The donkeys, still carrying the now-unoccupied chair across their backs, stood flicking their ears at flies, afforded a pleasant break by the occasion and evidently the only ones at all happy that the conversation was happening.

Amon crossed his arms. "Nevertheless"—he shook his head, as the language was quickly transmuted to the brothers—"my master's silver cup is missing, the one he uses for his priesthood duties. It is an item of extraordinary value."

Reuben could hear his brothers murmuring, and he glanced back at them before responding. "I assure you," he insisted, "there is not one among us who would have taken your master's cup. Especially not after the great generosity he has shown to us."

Judah could feel his heart beating beneath his robes.

Reuben shook his head again. "There must be a mistake."

"I'm afraid not." Amon clasped his hands behind his back. "No one else has been in the master's house."

"But there are servants." Reuben held out a hand. "Surely you are questioning the servants?"

"Of course we are questioning the servants." Amon puffed up his chest. "But I must insist upon searching your bags as a precaution." His voice was gentler now. "Please don't be offended. If you have nothing to hide, you have nothing to fear."

"When we first came to this place," Reuben said, and Judah looked concerned at the rise in his brother's voice, "we were accused of being spies, with no evidence except our foreign birth. And when we found the silver in our sacks, we returned it to you with further payment and gifts." He was taller and broader than the young man—one step closer and he would appear menacing. "Are we now to be accused of being thieves?" Judah stepped forward, putting a hand on Reuben's arm, but Reuben shook him off. "Whoever would dare such a thing," he said, looking back at the other brothers, "kill that man, and keep the rest of us as slaves."

Judah seized his brother's arm with a tightened grip and said, quickly, "You are free to search our bags"—he glanced at Reuben—"but I am certain you will find nothing."

"Nevertheless," said Amon, seemingly unswayed by either bluster or acquiescence, "I am sure you understand the necessity." He motioned to one of the soldiers, who stepped forward, drawing a knife from a pouch at his side.

Gesturing with his hand for Asher to step away from his camel, for it was Asher who was standing closest to the guards, the soldier ordered one of his fellows to remove the grain sack from the camel's back. The sack was pulled to the ground, and the soldier jerked his blade up through the cord binding the mouth closed. As the rope flopped, severed, to the earth, he reached down and rifled around through the kernels for any trace of the missing item. The other soldiers moved toward the other grain sacks while the brothers stood, arms crossed, their expressions a mixture of anxiety and affronted pride.

Judah glanced at Simeon, who caught the glance and frowned, and Judah turned away again. He could feel Reuben's gruff, angry presence beside him, radiating wounded dignity as he, the eldest son, was forced to watch these soldiers pawing through his family's food while he and his brothers were made to stand aside as though they were common highway robbers. Adding to the humiliation, passing travelers were warily eyeing the gathering with a variety of uncomplimentary expressions. One old man simply shook his head, as if he would expect nothing less from such foreigners.

"Just try to be calm," Judah murmured to Reuben. "We'll be on our way faster if we don't cause any trouble."

There was a sudden shout, and they both looked quickly over to where a soldier stood triumphantly beside an open sack of grain, holding up a glinting, silver goblet.

Then Judah saw the brother standing beside the guilty sack.

A terrible chill seized his entire body.

"And don't think you're going anywhere," Amosis snarled, "until the master decides what to do with you."

Joseph was kneeling with his bruised knees on the rough floor of the servants' sleeping quarters. He'd been marched unceremoniously out of the panicked villa and through the gardens by the gardener and his young assistant, both of whom waited in accusing silence with the disgraced steward until Amosis could be found. Joseph's authority was now superior to that of the stocky, bald-headed man who had selected him from the slave market and who still oversaw much of the work that went on in the grounds and fields of the estate. But that balance of power appeared to have shifted.

When the enraged Amosis arrived, he stormed first into the villa, where Djeseret had been taken to her room and the other servants were idling around like a confused flock of birds, and then came storming out to the servants' quarters once he learned where the despicable steward was being held.

Now, the strong-armed overseer was pacing back and forth in front of the battered captive. Amosis had dismissed the young gardener's assistant to go back to his duties but asked the gardener to wait outside, "in case the prisoner needs to be subdued."

But Joseph showed no signs of needing to be subdued.

"I should never have brought you into this household," Amosis grumbled, throwing a sidelong look at Joseph. "Should've known better than to bring in a filthy foreigner with no respect for the master, who," he said, raising his voice and coming closer, "will soon be vizier over all the land of Kemet." His voice grew softer as he stood before the kneeling steward. "Do you know what he can do to you?"

Joseph's voice was quiet. "I didn't touch her."

"I do not believe the mistress is a liar," Amosis growled, raising a hand. Joseph winced and turned his face away, instinctively protecting his bruised cheek, and Amosis lowered his hand again, mumbling a curse under his breath. Joseph's arms were bound behind his back, and as Amosis turned away, Joseph strained once again against the growing ache between his shoulders—to say nothing of the indignity of being guarded, bound and half-naked, by friends who were friends no longer.

Amosis turned back around, and Joseph met his eyes. "Do you know what the penalty is for adultery, Sasobek?" Joseph said nothing, staring back, unblinking. "Do you know what is done to betrayers?"

"I would not betray him." Joseph's breath was coming quickly now. "Or her."

Amosis walked closer—he was almost calm now as he looked down at Joseph. "Oh," he said, "I see. Did she come to you, then, steward? In the public part of the house?" The pitch of his voice rose, mocking, but Joseph kept his eyes fixed on Amosis's face. "I hope you understand," Amosis said, lowering his voice again, "that would be a very dangerous accusation for the mistress. Very serious slander from a slave." He watched Joseph, waiting to see this pronouncement sink in. "Life is sacred here. Trust is sacred. You have no reason to expect mercy." He leaned in closer, staring straight at his prisoner. "And neither would she." Joseph looked back at him. "Do you understand?"

Joseph understood.

"I didn't take it," Benjamin babbled, stepping away from the condemning silver cup, raising his hands, "I've never seen it before. I have no idea—"

The brothers stood as though transfixed by the unfolding nightmare. The vizier's steward gestured, and one of the soldiers came up behind Benjamin and grabbed his arms, twisting his wrists behind his back while the other soldiers closed in around him.

"No!" Judah cried, unable to keep his desperation silent as the guard handed Amon the incriminating cup, pulled like a demon from Benjamin's sack. Judah tried to move toward his brother, but Amon turned, facing him, and the look on his face froze Judah to the spot.

As silence settled over the gathering, Amon looked down at the silver item in his hand, as if contemplating the price that would be exacted in its behalf. "Well," he said quietly.

"Are you crazy?" Simeon shouted at Benjamin.

"I've never seen it!" Benjamin insisted, looking around wild-eyed for some explanation, some advocate, but the guards stood unyielding beside him, and his brothers looked away as Amon turned his gaze toward these men who had already been accused of one crime and now had been indisputably convicted of another.

"Well," he said again. Then he looked at Benjamin. "This," he said, his voice soft, "is how you repay the master's mercy."

"No," Benjamin shook his head adamantly. "No, I didn't—"

"This," said Amon, raising his voice, "is how you thank the man who spared your brothers' lives."

"No!" Benjamin cried out.

But Amon met Benjamin's imploring insistence of his innocence with an even, unflickering gaze. Benjamin tried to struggle against the guards holding him, and one of the men drew back his hand to strike the unruly prisoner.

"Don't hurt him!" Judah cried, and Amon, in the same moment, caught the soldier's arm and gave a single shake of his head. The soldier lowered his hand.

"You will come back with us to face the vizier," Amon ordered, looking at the stunned brothers. "All of you."

Holding the precious silver goblet in one hand, Amon turned and walked to where his chair was waiting with the placid, ear-flicking donkeys.

Moving slowly, as if in a strange, disbelieving dream, the brothers bent to tie up the grain sacks as best they could with their severed cords. The soldiers stood nearby, prodding the foreigners with their leveled stares, while Benjamin was marched over to where Amon waited. His beast was given to Levi to oversee.

"What will they do?" Issachar was whispering. "What's the punishment?" But Judah could not answer him because he could not take his eyes from where Benjamin was standing or join his other brothers in their frantic speculation as he watched his youngest brother's hands bound. One soldier seemed to be assigned particularly to the accused thief, while the others moved into position alongside the brothers—a dismal escort, Judah thought, for an already terrible journey. Other travelers passing by on the road now steered as far away from the accused party as the path would allow, evidently not wishing to be infected by whatever evil impulse had overtaken the bearded men with ashen faces.

At last, Judah turned toward Reuben, who looked as though someone had struck him with a blow from which he would not recover.

Kill whoever would do such a thing, and keep the rest as slaves.

As Judah stood there on the side of the road, seeing his brother accused and bound and taken toward what might prove his very death—and his brothers' death, and his father's death, and the death of all their people—he closed his eyes.

And remembered.

CHAPTER 33

Genesis 38:1–24

It had come to pass during the same time of year, when the spring was growling hungrily in the earth and the sunlight swept like a fresh breath across the land, that the man called Judah set out with his flocks to have their wool sheared in preparation for the lambing. The sun rose gently the morning of his departure, the inky richness fading like a soft song into a star-speckled twilight, and the gentle blue of the horizon nudged the darkness on its way.

While all the people were engulfed in celebrating the springtime abundance of the land and the fertility of the earth, Judah traveled quietly away from his home and youngest son, a bright-eyed lad named Shelah. Although Shelah was a man now, he would still remain behind, even if his name meant that he was one who was *sent away,* as he had sometimes jokingly pointed out to his father.

It was not the first time Judah had sensed how little Shelah understood of his name or of his place in his father's life—that the *sending away* had nothing at all to do with

Shelah but rather with the power the boy had over the demons that had haunted his father across the desert.

Shelah was Judah's third and last son, broader than his two older brothers and taller than his father. He was quick to laugh and seemed to have an easy prowess with everything his father taught him—so much so that Judah began to sense a certain jealousy from his older sons, Er and Onan, toward their charming and intelligent little brother. And though he could not explain it to them—not to his boys, certainly, for he could hardly bear to think of it himself—he was quick in his anger toward the boys' cruelty toward one another. He sent Er and Onan out to work among the flocks and the fields and guarded little Shelah safely at home. Shelah was older than either of the other two had been when his father finally began allowing him to travel with the flocks, which was to say, with his brothers.

How many years had it been now, Judah thought to himself as he set out on the road upon that springtime day, when Shelah was already a man—how many years? For it had been many years since Judah, or at least the young man he once had been, fled out into the desert, taking provisions enough to reach the nearest Canaanite city and leaving behind an unbearable weight of sorrow that threatened to suffocate everyone entangled within it. And he had done what he had intended to do—he had traveled beyond the edge of memory, beyond where the names of his fathers were known, beyond where the shadow of his brothers could follow. He was no longer Judah, son of Jacob. He was a man with no past to which he would attach himself and no parameters of family relations to set the bounds of who he was and what he was expected to be.

He had left his inheritance in the desert outside of Dothan, cast into a pit and left to die beneath the sun.

And so Judah sacrificed his birthright to buy his freedom and become a new man, wiping clean the trail of memory. He found kindness with the people he met. They accepted the young man from the desert and seemed to understand his urge to distance himself from whatever destiny he had been born to beneath the endless horizon that lay outside the safety of the townships. They gave him work, and he began to toil alongside the sons of the Canaanites. Soon, it was said that the man from the desert had a special gift, for all he touched blossomed into abundance beneath his hands.

That was the first time he realized that he had not yet escaped the inheritance he had received as his father's son—a strange gift of prosperity, an aptitude for increasing flocks and herds and fields.

Not all of his brothers had it. But now he knew that he did.

He had married the daughter of a Canaanite, and they had called their first son *Watchful,* and their second son *Prosperous.* But by the time Shelah arrived—several years after Judah's watchfulness and prosperity had established him as a man of some prominence within the community—he felt moved to give the child a different kind of name. The events that had caused him to flee into the embrace of a new people had faded further and further from his mind, and the arrival of another little life was almost enough to make him feel as though the desert really had forgotten—as if the God that had watched over his fathers would no longer threaten him with future vengeance, as if his sacrifice had finally been accepted.

So he named the child Shelah, an invocation to *send away,* to *let go,* as he had sent himself away and as he felt the God of his fathers had now let him go. The child was proof against the demons, a shield against the memories that sometimes stirred Judah in his deepest rest. It was a name of praise, a name of decision. What was done was done.

Yet, as Shelah grew, Judah could not but notice that Shelah looked different from his other two sons—both of whom were very much the image of their Canaanite mother and her family. Judah himself was not a large man, but Shelah was broad and strong and charmed his father utterly with his chatter and affection, even as a little boy. His face was not the face of his mother, or his brothers, or even really of his father. Shelah was the image of one of the sons of Jacob—sharing his grandfather's wide smile and strong shoulders and the family's rich, dark eyes.

And so while Shelah may have sent away the demons, he also called Judah's mind to that part of his inheritance that he carried within his very flesh, which could not and would not be evaded. And Judah began to realize that instead of escaping the heritage he had been born to, he had passed it to his own sons.

He told himself that he kept Shelah close because the boy was younger than Er and Onan, that he was bright and eager to learn, that he needed time to grow before taking on a man's responsibilities. When Er and Onan grumbled that their father favored the boy, Judah tried to make them understand that it was not a matter of favoritism but of practicality. But one day, when Judah came upon Er and Onan waiting for him with the flocks, he saw a look on their faces that he suddenly, frighteningly, recognized—because it was the same look he had seen Simeon and Levi give their own father and the look they had turned, later, on Joseph.

By that time, Er was old enough to be married, and Judah tried to take the matter in hand. He approached his birthright son and invited him to seek out whichever bride would be most pleasing to him, offering a handsome inheritance for brokering the necessary arrangements. Er eagerly accepted his father's offer and quickly set his eye upon a young girl who was one of the most beautiful to be found among the daughters of the Canaanites. Her name was Tamar, and she was round and comely and spoke pleasingly, and Er announced his intention of having her for his wife.

Judah was pleased and blessed the couple, and Tamar became part of Judah's household.

The first year of Tamar's marriage passed uneventfully. She remained round and comely and, for the most part, happy. But then the second year of her marriage passed, and still there was no sign of children, and Tamar became quiet. Judah's wife took the girl aside and spoke to her, offering small statues and amulets to encourage the gods who oversaw such matters to intervene. No such intervention came until the third year of their marriage, when Er was in the fields shearing his sheep, and the sharp, glinting blade slipped and sliced deep into his leg. First the wound bled, and then, as if it had taken to bleeding into his skin rather than out of it, the gash turned red and hot to the touch. The fever spread through his body and burned for three days while Tamar tended to her husband and her mother-in-law murmured charms and Judah stood outside and looked imploringly at the night sky.

On the fourth day, Judah's firstborn son died.

Er was buried while his widow looked on. Judah stood quietly with Onan and Shelah while his wife kept an arm around Tamar, and they wept together. At night, Judah would rage at the open sky, unable to understand why his eldest son should be so senselessly lost—cut off as a barren branch in the height of his life. But no answers came.

Judah had not really expected them.

His firstborn gone, Judah passed the birthright next to Onan. As was the custom, Onan received both his brother's birthright and his brother's widow, knowing that their children would belong to his older brother and receive the family's inheritance. However, there was still no sign of children on the day that Onan came inside and lay down, abruptly, at midday. He was not the first man in the village to show the symptoms of the illness that came upon him with such sudden fervor; by that night, he was unconscious and trembling.

Tamar sat at his bedside, just as she had with his brother, and just as she had with his brother, she was there when Onan took his last breath.

Shelah was still a boy, and Judah could forgive himself if he was relieved at the thought of not marrying his only surviving son to the woman who had already buried both of the boy's brothers. When Judah suggested that Tamar return to her father's house until Shelah was grown up to the age of a man, she agreed.

The birthright inheritance that should have been Er's and then Onan's passed now to Shelah. Judah taught the boy in reading and husbandry, taking him along to tend to the flocks and watching to see if the mysterious gift of prosperity would emerge under Shelah's careful hands. His son's quick eye and clever mind soon mastered whatever his father taught him, but it was not until one day when Shelah approached Judah, carrying a little lamb that he had found amongst the herd, that Judah was suddenly struck with a shiver of recognition at the way his son's large dark eyes were filled with compassion for the little creature. Shelah was gentler than his brothers had been, much as Judah liked to think he himself had been as a young man, but most inescapably, Shelah's look was reminiscent of the brother that Judah had fled into the desert to escape.

He felt his heart give a little tremble as he took the lamb out of his son's arms.

When Shelah was a man, handsome and grown, he

stood beside his father on the day his mother was lowered to rest beside her two sons.

"I am sorry that you should be so very much alone in the world now at the age that you are," Judah told him.

But Shelah shook his head and said simply, "I'm not alone, Father." He smiled. "I carry the birthright now."

Judah had not entirely understood what his son meant by that, but at the time he hadn't asked. Yes, Shelah would have a fine inheritance, but Judah did not see how that could mitigate the exquisite loneliness of isolation from his own family line—a loneliness Judah himself had known in all its terrible depths in the days before Shelah and his brothers had been born and which he feared he was perhaps now doomed to pass on to his only surviving son. He also feared what would happen when Shelah was married, to Tamar or to anyone else, because Shelah might forget him and become so concerned with being a man in his own right that he would have no need for the father who had raised and cared for him.

Shelah, he mourned, my son, my son. You are all I have.

Merely the wide-eyed stares of the natives who passed the awkward procession had become enough to make Judah wish they had never ventured back into the forsaken Divided Land. They would have been better off starving together in the wilderness of Canaan rather than standing helplessly by as their family was sundered one last time and their father's only remaining hope taken from under their care in such earth-rending shame. He could not speak to Benjamin because the guards were marching his youngest brother up ahead of the rest of them, but surely it was not possible, he kept thinking, surely Benjamin would not have been so idiotic, surely it must be a mistake, a nightmare, a reordering of the universe that would set itself right again, at any moment, in the next breath . . .

But the sun beat down in greater spasms of heat, and the road wound inexorably back toward the vizier's home—the vizier, practically the most powerful man in the most powerful kingdom of the known world and the supreme head of every court of law within Kemet, where their punishment and final humiliation would come. Judah could hear his brothers whispering furtively to one another amidst the unremitting crunching of the dust and sand beneath his feet. He sensed the stares and wide eyes of those they passed, but he found himself fixing his gaze on the back of Benjamin's bowed head.

Not one of us is innocent, Judah thought, except him. Not one of us deserves mercy, except him.

It was one thing to be accused of spying, or to spend the long hours of the night on the hard ground of a foreign prison, or to return shamefacedly to their father with their money in their sacks.

It was one thing for an old man to trust the sons he had

no reason to trust with the last child that he could love without fear of betrayal.

But not this. Judah stared at his brother's head, lowered like that of a submissive lamb. Not this.

He had made up his mind about what would have to be done long before they came to the villa. He had decided without speaking to Benjamin, without knowing for certain whether the boy was even guilty of the accusation, for the cup had been found in his sack and that was the death of whatever mercy might have been pled in his behalf. No eloquence, no tale of a forlorn father, no beseeching by his brothers would be enough to spare him.

Judah had made up his mind because there was only one possible thing to be done.

And he had decided upon it with a strange, heightened sense of surety that came from somewhere beyond his own will, beyond even the promise he had made to his father.

He would do it because he understood now what was required.

Er and Onan had both died at the beginning of the spring, just as the time of lambing and the celebrations of the earth's returning vitality dawned across the quiet land, and Judah could not but think of his sons as blighted crops, stopped in the cold ground before their proper time. Now the coming season and its accompanying rites of new birth and regeneration, sanctifying losses past with the promise of renewed life, circled back every year to mark their passing. But such rituals served only to mock Judah's sorrow, his sons committed to the ground like seeds never to rise and his wife now passed on with them. All the potency of all the little god-statues and the dances and the chants fell powerless beside the stark reality of his loss.

And of course, his sons were not the only ones who had been lost early in the spring at the time of lambing.

Judah felt no regret, therefore, to think of traveling before the beginning of the celebrations. He would go to Timnath and leave Shelah to care for the home and the remaining animals while he took the sheep for shearing before the lambs arrived. His friend Hirah would come with him—Hirah, who had been such a friend to Judah and was a native of the elegant city of Adullum that lay near the township where first he and then Judah had settled with their families. Sensing his old friend's growing loneliness, Hirah had offered to accompany him, and Judah had gratefully accepted the offer.

They set off on foot, walking with the trotting flock as the sheep moved like a great bobbing sea of wool across the open plain. The road to Timnath wound up over rocky ground, climbing in elevation. Sometimes the two friends passed the time in speaking to one another, and sometimes they merely walked, listening to the bleating of the sheep and watching the trail unroll like a great scroll beneath the horizon.

They came to camp that first night just outside a small township. They ate over a low fire, watching the sun dwindle down toward the edge of the world.

After eating, Hirah rose, stretching his arms. "I'll rest now," he said.

"Yes," Judah said, "yes, it is time to rest."

But when Hirah was gone, Judah still sat by the fire, staring into the flickering, spitting embers, feeling the shadowed heat dance across his skin.

When he raised his eyes again and looked back toward the town, he suddenly thought he saw some sort of shadow, perhaps, over by the side of the road, standing quite still, in the dying light.

It was unusual to see a lone traveler out at dusk, beyond the safety of the townships. Judah rose to his feet, clutching at the handle of his knife. As he moved closer, the shadow turned to face him—and Judah saw that it was not a bandit who stood watching his approach but a veiled face, with a body draped in light, flowing robes.

"Who are you?" Judah demanded, keeping his fingers wrapped around the handle of his blade.

"A priestess," said a woman's voice, her mouth hidden beneath the wind-danced veil. Judah came closer, loosening his grip on the handle as he moved. She stood calmly, watching him with her dark eyes, allowing him to approach. The night air was cool, and he could see the dim firelight from the town glowing gently against the sky. "You are traveling during the festivals."

"Yes." Judah was quiet for a long moment, and then he held out his hands, empty. "What do you want?"

Her eyes traveled from his face down toward his chest, and she reached out, fingering the leather cord hanging around Judah's neck. "Your signet ring," she said. Judah reached up and slid the leather cord from around his neck, revealing a small, burnished ring, concealed beneath his tunic, engraved with Judah's personal mark—his legal identity, his very word.

He coiled the leather strap down into her open hand, and she closed her fingers around the ring—the symbol of a man's place in the world, his birthright, bound up in a single sign—and smiled.

"Follow me," she said.

And he did.

CHAPTER 34

Genesis 38:25–30

It was nearly dark when Potiphar returned from the festival and found Amosis waiting for him at the gate.

"Amosis." Potiphar raised a hand. "You look very serious for someone who ought to be celebrating."

Amosis lowered his eyes, as though ashamed to look at Potiphar and speak the words he had to say. "Your steward—your wife has accused your steward of a terrible thing, Master."

"My steward?" Potiphar stared at Amosis, feeling the coming night pressing tightly around his body, as if the darkness itself would draw out the breath beneath his skin.

"The Asiatic boy," Amosis said. "Sasobek."

Potiphar was already moving, and Amosis was following, walking in brisk, long strides beside Potiphar, heading toward the villa. "We heard her screams," Amosis told him, "and found her, on the floor . . ." He shook his head. "The boy was there, and his tunic was off—"

"When did this happen?" Potiphar demanded.

"This morning."

Potiphar wheeled around. "Why was I not sent for?"

"Your wife asked that you not be disturbed."

Potiphar shook his head and walked on, with Amosis hurrying to keep up. As they reached the front doorway of the house, Potiphar slowed. Closing his eyes, he took a deep breath.

And then he went inside.

Joseph was not sure what time it was, only that the sun had sunk and plunged the world into darkness. At last he had been left alone, still bound and effectively incapacitated, while the other servants lingered anxiously in the villa, awaiting Potiphar's return. He had stopped trying to protest his innocence. He waited now in silence. His neck ached, and his shoulders gave a dull throb whenever he moved, and if he closed his eyes, he saw her face—heard her screaming—heard another voice screaming, buried down in the earth, and the harsh laughter of his brothers overrode her cries as he saw her, in a flash, once more stretched out upon the ground—

He blinked, hearing scuffling outside, and voices—someone speaking to another with a low, almost mournful voice—was it mournful, he thought, or furious? And then his pounding heart began to send tingling pulses up and down his arms, and he flushed cold.

The curtain was drawn aside, and the man with the low voice, silhouetted against the garden light, stepped inside.

They were alone.

"Sasobek." Potiphar's voice was very quiet. "What have you done?"

Judah told the priestess that he would return to her with a lamb and retrieve his ring after the lambing. But when he returned to Timnath, he could not find her. And while it had not troubled him in the least to hand over the ring to the mysterious woman when he felt assured it would be quickly returned, the reality of its loss weighed on him acutely. Where had the woman gone? What possible use was his ring to her? It was his seal, his mark, his identity that he had lost, and he felt it keenly and could not now imagine why he had been willing to barter it away so casually.

Because I did not think I would lose it, he told himself. Because I did not know I was giving it up.

When Shelah asked his father what had become of the signet ring, Judah told him it had been stolen.

"Stolen?" Shelah repeated, wrinkling his nose as if in distaste. "Why would anyone steal it?"

That was something his father could not answer.

Spring blossomed into summer, and the new lambs thrived, and Judah found that his flocks had increased yet again. But even this tumbling burst of new life could not turn his mind from the earth where his sons slept.

It was at about this time that Shelah set out to visit Tamar at her father's house and pay his respects to his brothers' widow. Judah was in the fields with the sheep when Shelah returned toward evening, and Judah watched as his son sat beneath the tall fig tree that stood a little distance from their home. Puzzled that Shelah had not come to greet him, Judah moved through his bleating flock, the scattering sheep trotting good-naturedly around his movements, stirring the dust.

When Judah reached his son, Shelah raised his eyes. Judah saw a strange paleness on the boy's face that set his heart beating.

"My son," Judah said, "you're not ill?"

Shelah shook his head. "No, Father," he said. "Not ill."

Judah waited, standing before Shelah as Shelah sat beneath the fig tree. "Did you see Tamar?"

Shelah nodded.

Judah looked at him. "What is it, Shelah?"

Shelah raised his eyes. "Tamar," he said, "is with child." He looked down at his hands. "What will happen to her?"

Judah sat slowly down beside his son. Somewhere in the fig tree, a bird began to twitter in the peacefulness of the evening. "There is only one thing," Judah said, "that is to be done."

There was one law of the land, one unquestionable expectation, one code of behavior that held all people together in a delicate and inviolate trust. If the truth had been violated, it had to be restored. If the balance were upset, restitution must be made. It was not simply a matter of punishment—it was a matter of imbalance, of chaos that would come if the forces that governed the world were left upended. If a person used her life to throw nature askew, that person's life was required to bring back the peace she had shattered. Mercy alone could not reset the balance, and no one spoke of mercy, and no one expected it.

Judah looked out toward the sky. "There has already been so much loss in our family." He shook his head. "We are a bare branch, Shelah."

And the order was given for Tamar to be burned.

Kneeling before his master, his arms bound and his face bruised, Joseph did not speak.

As he had waited for Potiphar to come, captive in the growing darkness, his mind had slowly begun to unleash scattering thoughts—and flashes of images—like the way the bloodied morning sky had dawned after the massacre at Shechem, and the dark shadows beneath his sister's unseeing eyes, his father's betrayed and furious face, and Reuben's shame, and the way Bilhah had cowered in fear for her life.

And then, in his mind, he had seen his mother. He saw her as he had last seen her, heavily pregnant with the baby who would cost her life, singing softly as she held Dinah in her arms, stroking the hair of the frightened, broken girl.

Joseph imagined his mother raising her eyes to his own and smiling, sadly, holding his sister and her own approaching death in her body, and willing—willing to sit with Dinah, willing to give her baby life, willing to carry the weight of it all. *This is the price we carry, Joseph,* he seemed to hear her say to him, *this is the price we always carry.*

As he sat there, alone, he began to wonder why he had even wondered what sort of punishment would await Djeseret if the truth were known. Whether answerable to the law of the desert or the governance of Kemet, the result was surely the same—the cowering, the fear, the sure and searing retribution of shame and disgust and blood. A life did not have to be taken for a life to be over.

She would know what she had done, now. She would realize that her husband might not believe her. An accused servant could be dismissed, sold, given over to a life much worse than the one he had—but his own life was not the one beyond all hope of recovery. And it was not her life alone—her shame was her husband's, her condemnation the end of all his happiness. A confusion of lives, all ruined in one afternoon.

Surely, Joseph thought, I cannot be more frightened than she is.

Then he glimpsed Dinah's face again, a face indeed from another life but a face that was still as much a part of him as his own soul. And he saw her curled up, as he had seen her in her tent, first after the prince of Shechem had raped her, and then after her brothers had violated the safety of Shechem and butchered the man who had taken their sister's honor before he became her husband—all while Dinah herself was wrenched back and forth between lives and peoples and without the chance to speak for herself.

She had lain there, without weeping—mute, listless, flattened, forgotten in the whirlwind of violent passions that stripped her dignity and her happiness.

And in his mind, as her eyes turned to him, he could see in her face what he had been too young to see then—

Please, she was whispering, *please, see me. Please see me.*

Now Potiphar stood before him.

Very quietly, he asked, "Is it true?"

But Joseph simply looked up at his master, seeing the bewildered betrayal and the wild, frantic look of a man whose world has just tilted inexplicably and thrown him into a wilderness from which he fears he will never return.

"I can have you killed," Potiphar said, his voice low, "or have you forgotten who I am?" Joseph did not shift his gaze from his master's face. Potiphar pointed back in the direction of the villa. "Speak."

But Joseph did not speak.

"You know what she accuses you of." Potiphar's voice was furious, pleading. "I command you to speak."

Joseph's skin was broken, purpled and stained, with one eye nearly too swollen to open. Yet he knelt without complaint. The shadows seemed to deepen the silence.

Slowly, Potiphar bent down and looked directly into Joseph's face—at the young man he had trusted, educated, come to look upon almost as his own blood.

"Sasobek," Potiphar said, his voice soft, "in the name of all the gods, you must speak."

Joseph looked at his master. "Your own opinion of me," he said, his voice even quieter, "can be my only defense. If I say . . . any more . . . I have to accuse her." He swallowed. "And for her life, and yours, I cannot do that." And again he lowered his head.

Judah left Shelah behind and traveled alone along the road to Tamar's father's house. Shelah had asked his father to let him come, to let him be there to lend what support he could in the difficulty that lay ahead, but Judah had refused. He would not ask his son to bear a burden that was not his to bear. Let each atone for his own sins.

Judah arrived at dusk and glanced only fleetingly at the stars beginning to emerge through the dying daylight as he moved on toward the small dwelling that sat beneath a giant spreading fig tree. Tamar's father met him at the door, holding a clay oil lamp with a sputtering wick, and led Judah toward the back of the one-room dwelling. The weak flame from the lamp leapt out ahead, throwing splotches of light along the wall and illuminating a small, curtained-off section that marked his daughter's sleeping quarters. He set a hand on Judah's shoulder and handed him the oil lamp. We are both old men now, Judah thought. We have seen too much lost already in this desert.

Judah took the lamp and pulled the curtain back.

Tamar was sitting on the ground, her hair covered and her body swathed in her robes as if in a burial shroud. She looked up. Even in her widowhood, even with the prospect of death staring unblinkingly upon her, her gaze was calm. "Please." She held out a hand. "Sit."

She did not beg for mercy he could not give, Judah thought, lowering himself to face her. She simply sat. He set the clay lamp on the ground. Shadows flickered across her face.

"Shelah tells me you are with child," he said.

Tamar looked at him with that unblinking, unruffled stare, not even bowing her head for shame. "Yes."

Judah took a slow breath. "Then you know what must be done."

Judah saw the briefest flash cross her gaze in the shimmering darkness. "So you take life," she said, "and turn it into death. You destroy your sons' only hope of increase."

"Shelah will be married to another," said Judah.

"But not Er," she said. "Not your firstborn. This child is rightfully his."

"Do not speak of my son," Judah snapped, but Tamar would not be silent.

"You have already been content to let your sons lie childless," she said. "You have refused to marry me to Shelah." And then, Judah thought, she did something extraordinary—she actually dared to reach out and touch his hand. "I know you have always loved him the most."

"I do not love any son more than another," Judah growled, pulling his hand abruptly from her touch.

Then Tamar reached up and drew a thin leather cord from around her neck—a thin leather cord with a single, dangling ring. Without a word, she held it out to him. The ring caught the weak reflection of the flame as it turned gently in midair.

Judah reached out, taking the cord and lowering it into his hand. He touched the ring with one finger as it lay in his open palm. He lifted the clay mark and scrutinized the carved signs. Then he looked at her. His quiet voice was dangerous.

"Where did you get this?"

She did not blink but said simply, "From you."

CHAPTER 35

Genesis 39:20

Potiphar face's was suddenly, heavily, weary. He raised a hand to his eyes, as if even the flickering light was too much to bear.

"How long have you been kept like this?" he asked.

Joseph swallowed. "Since this morning."

Potiphar looked at him. Then, rising to his feet, he moved behind his steward and bent down again, and Joseph felt the rough chafing of the rope sawing against his skin as Potiphar untied the coarse knots binding his wrists. As the bonds fell away, Joseph moved his arms gingerly, gratefully, wincing as the blood began to pulse. He turned, looking toward his master. "What will you do with me?"

Potiphar was quiet; he lowered his eyes. "If you will not speak," he said, "there is no choice. The accusation is too public." He looked at his steward. "It is the law."

Joseph lowered his eyes too. "Yes," he said, very quietly. "I know."

"Sasobek," Potiphar's voice was also quiet, and he put a hand on Joseph's shoulder, "you will go as a citizen, not a slave." Joseph looked at him. "I understand . . . what you have chosen to do. And I release you from your bond to me."

Joseph's throat was too tight to speak.

"And I promise," Potiphar said, and Joseph thought he could detect a tremor of unsettling emotion, "I will not forget you. When the times comes . . ." He paused, as if trying to gather the words. "When the time comes, I will make sure you are remembered."

Then Potiphar rose to his feet. He clapped his hands brusquely, twice, and the curtain jerked back. Amosis stepped inside. Potiphar looked back at his steward—his most trusted, most beloved steward—and turned his face away.

"Take him to the prison," Potiphar said softly.

Amosis bowed.

Joseph too lowered his head, exposed and naked, his tunic once more stripped away by the fury of his accusers.

Judah stared at Tamar, clutching the signet ring in his hand—thinking back to that night along the road and the darkness beneath the stars.

"What have you done?" he asked at last, his voice hoarse.

She took a slow breath. "I know Shelah is the dearest to your heart." She raised her eyes. "But"—her hand rested on her stomach, safely buried beneath her robes—"your responsibility is to all your sons, and to their children, and to their children after them." She paused. "You are only one link, as Shelah is one link, and Er and Onan too." She shook her head. "You might have been content to let your sons dwindle and remain barren forever, but I was not."

Judah could not speak, hearing her voice over and over again—*Your responsibility is to all your sons . . . all your sons . . . all your sons . . .*

And sons, he thought, as though the thought were not his own, *have a responsibility to their fathers.*

Her eyes were fixed upon him, no longer calm but beseeching, imploring. "This is your child," she whispered. "This is the future of your family."

Judah lowered his head, still clutching the signet ring in his hand. "The greater sin is mine," he said, hoarse and quiet. "The greater sin is mine."

He felt her touch on his hand. He looked up and saw her sitting there in the cramped sleeping space where she had waited, and waited, and waited.

"The sin is lifted," she said.

And Judah stared at Tamar, at this young woman who, mere minutes ago, had no hope of mercy because there had been no such thing—no such thing, until she brought it into the world and offered it to a mournful old man who had come to bring her death.

"My sin to my family," Judah said, his voice choking, "is not one you can lift, Tamar."

"Your sin to this family is atoned for," she told him. "I have done it, if you will spare my life."

"Yes"—Judah felt the warmth spreading behind his eyes—"yes, you will live, Tamar. You will live."

"And your family will live," she said quietly.

Judah bowed his head and wept.

And after the days were accomplished that she should be delivered, Tamar brought forth not one son but two, and the boys were named Pharez and Zarah, and it was as if Judah's two lost sons had been restored to him again.

And when he had seen the boys, Judah lifted up his voice, and wept, and took his family and journeyed out into the desert, toward his father's tent.

And that was how Tamar the Canaanite restored to Judah, son of Jacob, the memory of his birthright.

CHAPTER 36

Sacrifice

"What's going on?"

Zaphenath turned from where he stood in the garden of his estate, peacefully paused beside the reflecting pool, gazing toward some unknown piece of sky.

Asenath stood, hands on hips, waiting. "Well?"

"What do you mean?"

Her eyes narrowed. "Amon has gone after your brothers. All the servants are talking."

Zaphenath shrugged. "I sent him."

She shook her head. "What more do you want from them?"

"Benjamin." Zaphenath looked at her. "I won't send him back to be killed in the desert once my father is gone."

She looked at him, and when she spoke again, her voice was quieter. "How do you know they want to hurt him?"

"You don't understand life outside of Kemet." He crossed his arms. "Here, you honor life, but out there . . ." He shook his head. "Benjamin will have no one to protect him."

"It may be," she said, "that your brothers have not

changed, but you don't know that." She held out a hand. "Think of what you did for Djeseret."

Rarely, very rarely, had Zaphenath heard his wife speak that name.

"Why do you say that?" he asked, after a long pause.

Asenath moved closer. "Because," she said softly, "you knew, then, what mercy was."

Zaphenath looked away.

"I did that," he said at last, "because there was nothing else I could have done."

Asenath shook her head. "No one is merciful because there is no other choice."

"It was for my sister." Zaphenath's voice was quiet. "And for your brother."

"And Potiphar has no greater respect for any man," Asenath said, her voice softer still, "because you spared someone what had been done to you." She rested her other hand on his arm. "You were willing to set the world right again." She gazed up at him. "You are not the boy they put in the pit. You are a new man, now. You were changed by what you did."

Zaphenath looked at her, and she heard the tightness in his throat. "I can't let them hurt Benjamin."

She looked at him. "Benjamin had no part in what was done. They did"—she pressed a hand against his chest—"and you did. Keeping Benjamin here will not heal you. You know that."

"I can't send him away and never see him again."

She slid her hand down her husband's arm and took

his hand, intertwining their fingers. "Then don't," she said softly, and leaned up, very gently, and kissed him.

"Make way," Amon called out, "make way," startling the other pedestrians aside and leaving them to stare at the bearded man being led under guard and the—how many were there, nine, ten?—men trailing along behind, marched down the road by armed escort. Whatever brief words might have been exchanged between the captive brothers dwindled into silence as the sight of the vizier's ornate villa came into view. The gently swaying palm fronds above the white-washed walls created a strange visual disconnect from the devastation that awaited them within.

The warmth of the day, or perhaps just the events thereof, had been sending trickles of sweat down the back of Judah's neck. He looked over toward the River, where boats of near-naked passengers sailed briskly along with the current, their bodies open to the cooling breeze off the water. Anywhere he looked, it seemed, the condemning reminder was there.

You are not one of us.

The brothers shuffled in through the estate's opened, waiting gates, and their animals were taken by somber-faced, cold-eyed servants. Judah handed over the ropes to his own camel with a certain calm resignation. He knew he would not see the beast again. But let that be as it may, there was no freedom, he knew, in roaming the world at the price of a brother.

Go home, Benjamin, he thought, go home, and our father will live, and our family with him.

Benjamin would not be the required offering for the family's survival. Nor was there any reason that he, the youngest and most innocent, should bear the price of this strange and devilish retribution that had come lashing like a blinding sandstorm across a twenty-year chasm. Judah had come to understand it first from a young Canaanite woman in the flickering darkness, but he had come to understand it again now—there was no place where the memory of the desert did not extend.

And mercy without sacrifice could not be.

As he followed his brothers onto the grounds of the estate, he raised his eyes. It was almost as if he could hear Tamar's voice, speaking out of the darkness—

The sin is lifted.

"This way," the steward ordered. The front door into the villa was pulled open, and the soldier escorting Benjamin proceeded within. The other brothers followed behind, silently stepping back over the threshold they had so recently crossed in a passage of absolution, freed of all accusation and proven worthy to return to their father in triumph. Now, they were returning to witness their most innocent brother's condemnation—the required vengeance, it seemed, for a crime that his brothers had committed in the desert before the boy's real memory had even begun.

Judah glanced up toward the sky, seeing a bright flash of blue and hearing the call of a reeling, circling swallow, soaring effortlessly between heaven and earth. A slight smile came to his face.

"Come on," one of the guards grumbled, and although Judah could not quite understand the expression, the nudge was sufficient to communicate.

He stepped over the threshold.

Their accuser was waiting for them. In the same room where, just the evening before, they had been his guests, the brothers now slunk in like a row of the condemned. The vizier stood, arms crossed, watching from across the courtyard as they entered.

"There," the vizier's steward ordered, pointing, "wait against the wall." The brothers moved away, while Benjamin was brought forward, alone, with his hands behind his back. The soldier indicated that the prisoner should kneel. Benjamin knelt, lowering himself with a certain graceful dignity that struck Judah as oddly reminiscent of the mother Benjamin had never known and the brother who was more a composite of other people's memories than of Benjamin's own. Perhaps it was the boy's birthright, somehow, also to be sacrificed—as his mother had been to bring him into the world and as his brother's blood had sealed up a terrible unity amongst his bickering brothers.

But a birthright, Judah knew, could be given to another.

CHAPTER 37

Genesis 39:21–23

Darkness, and a strange damp cool in the midst of the heat, captive to the sounds of the shadows and the movements of men who carried swords and crossed in and out, marking the passage of days by their comings and goings. The new prisoner, it was whispered, had been an important member of an important household. Some scandal had brought him here, some betrayal. He had been brought in late one night on order of the captain of the guard and, though foreign, was apparently a proper citizen of Kemet rather than a common slave. There were no official charges, simply an order that he was to be kept at the royal prison. The guards, who were used to dealing with sensitive and confidential crimes, did not ask for details.

Mostly, the prisoner sat alone, staring sightlessly into the shadows. He did not make any trouble, although most of the prisoners who came here were men of reasonable enough breeding (or at least exposure to it) not to make much trouble. They were usually those who had the misfortune to be accused of crimes in high places, of intrigues or embezzlements, and there were rarely more than a handful of them in the central cell where they remained until their fates were decided. Some would be released back into the world, cleared of their crimes (or with friends powerful enough to secure the repayment of their debts), while others were taken away to other places, unknown places.

Only the very highest forms of betrayal—plotting against the king or the state—were likely to face the possibility of execution. Life was honored here in Kemet, but those who would risk catastrophically unbalancing the delicate fabric of *ma'at,* or the government that held it in place, could not be left free or, in some cases, alive.

It was not at all clear, therefore, what crimes this foreigner had committed. One or two of the other prisoners thought at first that he looked familiar but could not quite place where they might have seen him. The unshaven stubble around his jaw was growing by the day into a new dark beard, and his shaven head had sprung up rich, curling shoots across his scalp. It was as though his very flesh had already begun to forget him—shifting away from the face of Sasobek, steward of Potiphar (the man, he eventually heard, who was now the vizier of all Kemet) to the face of an unknown desert man, an anonymous Asiatic of no family or name. In his captivity, he was powerless to hide it.

And so the days passed, and no one came either to absolve or confirm whatever accusations had brought him there. He was a foreigner clothed in the simplest dress of Kemet, a free man who had become a servant who had become a prisoner, belonging to no household, and no country, and no people.

He had fallen between all distinctions, belonging to no one at all.

At first, he believed that Potiphar would come for him, just as he had once believed his father would come. Djeseret would speak to her husband, or he would speak to her—and she would weep and repent, unable to stand what she had done to the man she had once cared for, perhaps more than any other. Perhaps a certain amount of time had to pass, the proper days or weeks of observance, and then someone would be sent. He would be told there had been a mistake, a misunderstanding, that time had passed and there was no shame in returning to his former position of influence and belonging.

But even as he clung to the lingering memories of Potiphar's house, his changing appearance carried him steadily toward his new reality, as if in revelation of the person he now was, and paying no heed to his dwindling hope, or his wishing, or his dreams.

Yes, the dreams, the dreams that came in the darkness were confused jumbles of flashes and snatches of words that he couldn't understand—the broken vision of his life, the distorted monsters of a future he could not see. He would wake in the same darkness that had lulled him to sleep, feeling no change, no transition from sleeping to waking or night to morning. Where once his dreams had been the transport of a bright future or whispered insights from the troubles of his days, it was as if even his dreams no longer knew how to make sense of so senseless a life.

Once he dreamt of his father and saw his father's worn, weary face and wondrous white beard, but he awoke in Kemet, and he was still alone, and still no one came for him. No one had ever come for him. Who would come? He was nothing, no one—not a son, not a brother, not even a slave.

As the days drew on, and his hair grew, and his flesh lost its bronzed strength, he began to drowse to pass the time. And as he began to drowse, no longer coiled so tightly in his own anger or submerged into a grief beyond despair, different dreams began to come, dreams that allowed him to slip gently between sleeping and waking, like a crocodile floating in the River. He smiled as he, who had been called Sasobek, thought of it. The dreams came in washes of sound and sensation but few images—he would find himself surrounded entirely by landscapes or splashes of color, bright and indistinct. The dreams were warm, like sun on the sand, and they let him drift, unbothered.

It was in those dreams that the words began to come.

At first, they came only in snatches and in a voice he did not recognize—hardly a voice at all, more like a passing thought or a whisper drifting in from a word spoken to someone else. The first time, he was standing in the desert, far beyond the borders of the Black Land, looking out toward the horizon, and he heard a word that he recognized as the identity that he had been given before he came to Kemet—

Joseph—

He awakened, still hearing the echo of his name.

And the name came back to him again, always in that in-between moment of sleepiness, where he was not quite conscious but somehow not fully asleep, and somewhere else—somewhere amidst the colors, in the splash of desert landscape where he could stay without fearing the nightmarish collision of images and sounds that came from the deeper dreams.

And then, early one morning, he heard the words he had read with his father and then with Potiphar.

Joseph, Joseph—

He was standing in the desert, looking out over an empty, windswept plain, and he heard the narrative that he surely should have known by now, down to his deepest core.

—my name is Jehovah, and I have heard you, and have come down to deliver you.

He stirred, surfacing again into consciousness. He was not sure whose voice it was, for it was not a voice that he knew, but it was one that brought him a strange, calm comfort, like the sound of a forgotten friend. He was also quite sure, as he thought about it, that it was the same voice that had spoken out his name before. He realized that he felt oddly comforted to know that someone else in the universe, whether in his own mind or not, would still call him Joseph.

From that day on, he no longer introduced himself to the new prisoners that drifted in and out of his cell as Sasobek, Son-of-the-Crocodile. He told them that his name was Joseph. And instead of just asking their names, he began asking about their homes, their people, and the worlds they had left behind. There was another steward, and a servant from the king's court, and a scribe accused of thieving from his master. They were with him only a few days, though, before the missing items were recovered, and the scribe was released, and the steward was quietly sold off to another household, and the servant was taken away to work in the fields.

But Joseph remained behind.

There were days when criminal activity appeared to have dwindled in the upper echelons of society, and the prison grew quiet. Joseph, who had still received no direct sentence one way or another, was left to himself. He did not provoke much attention from the guards beyond the occasional suspicious glance from the new ones, who seemed curious as to why he had been kept there without any seeming resolution. But with the appointment of a new vizier, the more senior guards explained, it was easy for prisoners like this one to slip through the bureaucratic cracks. Since the foreigner caused them no trouble, they caused none for him either.

Joseph began to drowse again during the day, and the dreams returned, though now the bright colors of the horizon had faded, blurring, the way a fresh gray morning hovers over water. He stood within the mists, turning, looking up and around, but he did not know where to go. So he began to walk—effortlessly, moving through the mist over soft, solid ground but at times losing sight of even his own hands stretched out in front of him.

It was when he awoke from the first misting dream that he heard the voice distinctly. The voice did not pass through his ears, and there was no particular sound or timbre that would identify it as male or female, but it seemed friendly. He was blinking himself awake from his wanderings, wondering what had happened to the bright colors of the desert, when he heard it.

You're not there anymore, said the Voice.

Joseph paused, not aware that he had intended to respond to his own half-thought question. But the response had come with such swiftness that Joseph nearly looked around the shadows to see what invisible old meddler had interjected himself into his private contemplation. He paused and then, as if not really meaning to, asked—

Not where?

Not there, said the Voice. *Do you understand?*

Joseph didn't especially understand.

You remembered your name, said the Voice. *That's a good beginning.*

Thank you, thought Joseph, feeling a little strange.

You're welcome, said the Voice.

And so began their acquaintance. Joseph could not seem to summon the Voice according to his own will, and sometimes it became very quiet, especially if he was stewing about Djeseret, or when he suddenly saw a flash of his terrible brothers or his father, and he started working himself into silent, frothing anger over the injustice of his situation.

Sometimes, though, it did speak to him right then, though usually without words, especially when the weary weight of his own frustration began to gape and give way, chasm-like, to a sinking, bottomless despair, hollowed out through fear. At those times, he felt the Voice come and sit beside him. It usually didn't say anything, but he was glad to have the company.

And so, day by day, he began to make friends with the Voice. It most often spoke to him as he woke from his dreams and was always willing to talk as he lay awake in the deepest hours of the night. When he had been Sasobek and was first shut into the prison, he would have brushed the Voice away, finding it an aggravating annoyance and certain it was nothing more than the frenzied workings of an aggrieved mind. But he had been in the darkness long enough that he was not quick to dismiss any company that came to him, and he knew the darkness well enough to know that the Voice was a pleasant respite from the shadows.

One day, almost jokingly, he asked, *Are you trapped here too?*

Of course not, said the Voice. *I'm here because you are.*

And how long will I be here? Joseph wanted to know, but the Voice said nothing more.

Another day, Joseph asked, *Why did you call me Joseph?*

Because that's your name, the Voice said, as if Joseph ought to know.

It was about that time, when Joseph began to feel as though the Voice were waking him up from a long and strange night of dreams and he had begun to come to himself again, that the keeper of the prison began to notice how this mysterious prisoner was developing a way of bringing out an ease and comfort of confidence among his fellows. Several times the keeper had overheard prisoners who growled staunch denials of their guilt open up to this quiet foreigner, confessing household intrigues and pressures that had driven them to become involved in whatever entanglement had landed them in prison. Other times, prisoners had continued ardently to insist upon their innocence until the man—Joseph, he called himself, a proper foreign name to go with his bearded countenance—had a private word with the keeper and assured him that he was quite sure the accused was indeed innocent, or unfairly burdened by pressures, or truly quite bad.

And thus far, Joseph had not been proven wrong about the character of his fellow prisoners. It was as if all who came into contact with the man seemed to blossom open under his presence, from the most taciturn scribe to the most obstinate and nervous courtier. The keeper knew that this man had been none other than the steward to Potiphar, when Potiphar was still the captain of the royal guard; he knew that no clear accusation had been brought against him and that his case, from all appearances, was either sufficiently open ended or so secret as to warrant no written record. So at last he sent word to the office of the vizier, inquiring about the prisoner and whether he were, in a word, dangerous. Not long afterward (which was most unusual for a reply from the vizier), he received word that while the vizier had reviewed the case and was unable to take any legal action on account of the prisoner's lack of defense, if the keeper were so inclined, the vizier himself would highly recommend the man's abilities and even allow for his release, provided he remained, for legal purposes, under the keeper's care.

The keeper grunted at the reply. He knew the new vizier had a reputation for being careful to avoid any hint of abusing his power. It seemed that the poor former steward would require a pardon from the king himself to have his case resolved.

And so, one quiet afternoon, the keeper approached Joseph. An inspection of the royal prison was coming up, to be conducted by none other than the vizier himself, and the keeper wanted Joseph's help in getting everything organized and prepared. The keeper would move Joseph out of the cell, and he could have a small sleeping space set up close to where the guards stayed.

Joseph eagerly agreed to all of this. At last, he would see Potiphar again, and surely—surely—Potiphar would remember him.

That first night, as Joseph lay outside the cell for the first time since the fateful day of Potiphar's banquet, he wondered for a brief, startled moment if this meant that the Voice was going to leave him now.

I'm still here, came the reply. *Go to sleep.*

So Joseph slept, and he dreamed and found himself once more in the desert, standing beneath the open night sky. As he stood gazing up at a moon the color of linen, a cascade of words came whispering out of the stars, words from texts he had read before but now blending together, spinning into a new text he had never before read, only he wasn't reading it so much as being enfolded within it, surrounded and filled and tumbled by the words.

This is the beginning of the Book of Breathings—it was Potiphar's voice, reading from one of his sacred scrolls—*which Isis made for her brother Osiris, to make his soul live, to make his body live, to restore him anew.*

How many times had he read through those words—practicing his new language or seeking alongside his priestly master for the secrets hidden within the text—of the woman who raised the man back to life, of the initiate who found a way to approach the gods, of the steps undertaken to return to the presence of the divine.

And then came the words he had read along with the story of Isis and Osiris, the sojourn into the stars that he had read as a child in the desert. *Finding there was greater happiness and peace and rest for me*—and it was his father's voice—*I sought for the blessings of the fathers . . .*

Justified!—that was the voice, once more, of Potiphar the priest—*Thou art pure, thy heart is pure, cleansed is thy front with washing, thy back with cleansing water . . .*

Abraham—now the god called out, with his words transmitted through the voice of his father, Jacob—*Abraham, behold, my name is Jehovah, and I have heard you, and have come down to deliver you, and to take you away from your father's house, and from all your kinsfolk, into a strange land which you know not of . . .*

Thou enterest by the great purification, the Breathings text instructed, and now it was Djeseret's voice, and her eyes and her touch that reached out—*with which the two Ma'ats have washed thee*—two women, Isis and Nephtys, life and its passing (*I am Nephtys,* she had said, *I am Nephtys*), for it was through life and death that the soul was bathed and renewed and prepared to ascend beyond, to begin again, to remember itself, re-member itself, draw body and spirit back together, and fuse into an eternally restored identity—

Behold, Abraham was promised, *I will lead you by my hand, and I will take you, to put upon you my name, even the Priesthood of your father, and my power will be over you*—

Thou breathest henceforth for time and eternity—washed and re-membered and brought to remembrance, and now the voice was his own, reading from his master's scroll—*Amon comes to thee bearing the breath of life*—a soul restored to itself, the breath of life received through a sacred kiss—*he causes thee to breathe and come upon the earth*—the Breathings text was triumphant now, the moment of sacred creation and re-creation had come—

My son, my son—the god had called Abraham his son—*behold I will show you all these. And he put his hands on my eyes, and I saw those things which his hands had made*—the sun and moon and stars, the earth and women and men and all things that are and were and would yet be, all were one and all were his, and the voice was his own, as the dream had been his own of the sun and moon and stars and the way he had been carried up into the heavens—

I dwell in the midst of them all; I now, therefore, have come down to you to declare to you the works which my hands have made, wherein my wisdom excels them all, for I rule in the heavens above, and in the earth beneath—

Horus embraces thy body—this was the promise of Potiphar's text, the purpose for the restoration of the breath, a body raised in life to reunite with its spirit, fusing once more into its full identity—*and deifies thy spirit in the manner of the gods*—raised out of the earth and up into the horizon, fusing with Ra and the Light-of-All-That-Is as the sun passes back up out of the womb of the stars and the soul rises out of its washings to ascend alongside—

Abraham—that calm, familiar voice, that was now not quite his and not quite his father's—*you are one of them, you were chosen before you were born—and you will be a blessing to your seed after you, that in their hands they will bear this ministry and Priesthood to all nations—*

And Joseph, son of Jacob, son of Isaac, son of Abraham, opened his eyes.

The soul of Ra is giving life to thy soul, he heard, *thy soul breathes,* and he sat up, rising out of the swirling words and the shadows. He breathed slowly, and deeply, and deliberately, staring into the dazzling darkness, and turned and looked toward where the keeper of the prison stood, his arms crossed, his bowed head nodding, listening to the low whisper of a guard who had just come on duty.

Then the keeper of the prison looked toward him.

And Joseph learned that Potiphar was not coming.

All the court that day was abuzz with the news—the vizier's wife had, at last, borne her husband a son, and the child was strong and healthy and well, and the great man and all his household were in mourning.

Ben-oni, Joseph thought, *Son-of-Pain*—that was the name his own mother had given his brother as her life bled away, but his father had shaken his head. *No,* he said, *no. Ben-jamin. Son-of-My-Right-Hand.*

His mother too had carried life and death within her body to bring a child into the world—Isis and Nephtys, Sun and Stars, Time and All Eternity.

I am Nephtys, Djeseret had said, and he lowered his head at the news and closed his eyes at the feeling that welled between sorrow and reverence.

And now you are Isis, he thought. *Life-bringer. Light-bringer. I am come to myself again.*

For it was in the prison that he remembered. And it was she who had brought him there.

CHAPTER 38

Genesis 44:14–34; 45:1–14

Zaphenath-Paaneah, vizier of all Kemet, stood with his arms crossed, decorated in his fine linens and jewels and watching with cold, elegantly painted eyes as the men filed into the courtyard of his home. Amon was ordering all of the Canaanites to stand against the wall except for the accused prisoner, who was brought forward to kneel between his brothers and the offended vizier.

The young man kept his head down. His hands were bound behind his back.

Zaphenath watched the others looking on with hollow eyes and broken faces, disoriented, weary, and frightened. Apart from the shuffling of feet and the admonitions of the guards, the courtyard was quiet—none of the brothers spoke as they moved to their appointed places. They simply stood, fidgeting, or staring at Benjamin's bent back.

Surveying the foreigners and satisfied that they were properly in place, Amon turned and approached his master. He bowed, holding out the stolen silver cup. Zaphenath took the cup from his steward's hand and held up the offending item, perhaps weighing its worth against that of the offender. Then he nodded, and Amon bowed again, and stepped back.

Holding the silver cup, Zaphenath moved closer, walking with slow, measured steps. He looked first down the line of brothers, from one to the next to the next. Only one or two dared raise their eyes in return. But none of them spoke, and none of them moved.

Finally, Zaphenath looked down to where Benjamin knelt on the floor, head bowed, his body crouched, perfectly still.

"This is how you repay my hospitality." Zaphenath's voice came low and cold, and the brothers shook their heads in vigorous unison at the translation, but Zaphenath raised his hand against the beginning swell of protests, and the wave broke and settled once more. "I am told you offered me the life of the guilty one." He looked down at Benjamin, at his brother's dark curling hair and the eyes that so perfectly matched his own, and thought for a brief moment, How is it they cannot see?

But of course, he was no longer the boy who had been their brother, no longer even the young man who was sold in the slave markets of Kemet. When he was summoned out of the prison to interpret the desperate king's troubling nightmares of devouring, skeletal cattle and insidious stalks of corn, and the Voice had whispered the visions of coming famine in a way that transcended words and flooded his mind with clear understanding, he had been given the name Zaphenath-Paaneah and raised to stand beside (or nearly beside) the Son-of-Ra, God-on-Earth, King Senusret II. Zaphenath had embraced the name as his new identity and his elevation as his resurrection, and it was as Zaphenath that he had been known ever since—even to Potiphar, the departing vizier who, just as the king's dreams began, had expressed his wish to devote himself to the priesthood and to his young, motherless son. His whispers in the king's ear had not been inconsequential in his former steward's elevation.

And when Zaphenath had met the boy Amon, he assured his former master that he would look forward to the time when Amon would assist him with his many important duties. And Potiphar—who had seen to it that Joseph was watched over in the prison and continued to receive reports from the guards as to his former steward's well-being, and when the keeper of the prison at last created the opportunity by suggesting it (for Potiphar himself could not appear to abuse his authority), quickly had his former steward elevated as the overseer of the prison, where he could prove his abilities while continuing to have food and shelter and protection—yes, Potiphar was well pleased.

Zaphenath believed that he had come to understand the words that swirled around him in the darkness, the mysteries of the texts that he and his father and Potiphar had all studied so diligently—new life came through the passages, the process of an elevation of the spirit from one understanding to another by experiences endured. *Ma'at* was restored in the sacrifice. Abraham had to first be on the altar before he could see the stars. Joseph had died first in the desert, once more in the prison, and then had risen as Zaphenath-Paaneah, vizier and counselor to the king, inheritor of the priesthood secrets of Ra and Abraham and transformed, as the sun is transformed in the womb of the stars, to rise again.

When he was married to Asenath—daughter of Potiphera, high priest of the Temple of Ra, and sister of Potiphar, the departing vizier, who was charged with arranging a marriage for his newly appointed successor—and as she prepared to bear him a child, Zaphenath had been nearly out of his mind with fear that he would lose her, as his mother and others he had known had been lost.

But Asenath was breathless only with radiance, and the baby boy was strong and shrill, and Joseph, who by then was Zaphenath, wept as he held the child in his arms and called him *Manasseh*, for in the moment he held him he could not remember the pain of his father's house or the taste of betrayal or the years of his imprisonment. There was only his son and Asenath, the woman who brought their child into the world and who smiled at him now, who carried life within her and only life, who had caused him at last to forget.

He could not speak, and she understood.

When a little brother was born, also before the onset of the years of famine, Zaphenath named the boy *Ephraim* as an expression of God's abundance, an acknowledgment of what had been and a reminder for the times that would shortly come. He had received his own name from his father as an acknowledgment of God's increase, and he hoped that this son would carry that blessing of abundance with him as well, an inheritance from his father and his father's fathers. And still Asenath was strong and well, and for the first time since the day his father's coat had been torn from his shoulders, Zaphenath no longer feared that his happiness would be taken from him.

So it was no surprise that his brothers did not know him as he stood hidden behind his new name and ornate dress and extraordinary mantle of power, facing the men whose beards were gray and bodies weakened by the passage of the years that had separated them. And Benjamin knelt before them all, helpless and exposed, offered up like a lamb.

"Did you think I would not know?" Zaphenath asked, his voice soft. Not one of the brothers dared raise his eyes to meet the accusation. "I know a man's guilt." His assertion hung unchallenged in the silence. "I know." He looked down toward Benjamin. "His life is mine now." He paused. "But I am a merciful man. This one will remain behind only as my slave." He held out a hand, the most powerful hand in all the land beside the king's, with the golden ring of power glinting on his finger. "The price of your dishonor is paid. The rest of you are free to go."

But suddenly and without speaking, the foreign men lowered themselves to the ground, kneeling behind their brother, faces toward the earth. Zaphenath stared at them, at the way their outstretched hands seemed to reach toward their captive brother, calling out to his accuser.

"Get up," he said and felt his voice waver—*Behold, I*

dreamed a dream, and the sun and moon and eleven stars bowed down to me—and he swallowed. "You are free to go."

Benjamin was raising his head, slightly, as if sensing a change in the current of the air.

"Please." One of the men raised his head, gazing directly up at the man who held the life and death of his family in his outstretched hand.

Zaphenath looked at the one who had dared to speak, seeing, in a moment, the man's faded beard and lined expression, his weary eyes and his face so open, so hopeless, so determined.

The other brothers also raised their heads, turning uncertainly toward the sound of Judah's voice.

Still kneeling, still with his hands upon the ground, Judah kept his eyes focused on the vizier's face, strongly suspecting he was violating some sort of protocol yet feeling compelled that he could not do otherwise.

"My lord." Judah's voice was quiet in the expanse of the courtyard, surrounded by the walls of wealth and authority, unable even to speak directly with the man who seemed intent on destroying them. The open sky itself seemed to be staring pitilessly down at his bowed back. "What shall we say to you?" His words dropped like rippling stones into the quiet, reverberating out into the still. "How can we clear our names before you?" He took a slow breath. "If your servants are guilty, my lord, it is not before you but before God—" and he could feel the echoed intake of breath from the brothers surrounding him as he said it, but he pushed on—"and we will all stay behind as your servants."

Benjamin had raised his head further, glancing halfway over his shoulder, as if so distracted by what he was hearing that he had nearly forgotten where he was—as if he too was simply unable to resist turning toward his brother.

Zaphenath kept his eyes on the one who dared to speak. "Only the man found in possession of my cup will stay behind," he said, speaking to the man whose name, he knew, was Judah. "As for you"—he fought to keep the hoarse edge from his voice—"get you up in peace to your father."

He clapped his hands and turned, walking from them, feeling his throat tighten.

"Oh—"

Zaphenath stopped and closed his eyes, because the voice was his brother's, and all the years and the bitterness of his betrayal could not erase his recognition of the voice that called out to him.

"—my lord," Judah said, making himself fully prostrate on the ground as the vizier turned back toward him. "Let your servant, I pray, speak a word, and do not be angry."

Zaphenath hardly heard the unnecessary translation. He simply stood, unmoving. When no reply came, Judah hesitantly raised his eyes.

"You asked us," Judah said, speaking faster now, as if sensing that he was being granted a brief dispensation to plead, "when you first believed we were spies, if we had a father or a brother." Judah nodded, as if to reaffirm the truth of the story. "We told you that our father is an old man and that our brother"—he gestured to Benjamin, who still knelt, bound—"is the youngest, the child of his old age." Judah raised his eyes to Zaphenath's face. "And you asked us to bring him to you, so you could see him and know that we were truthful." He shook his head. "And we told you, my lord, that this brother could not leave our father, because the boy is his very life. But you ordered us to bring him if we ever wished to see our other brother"—he gestured then toward Simeon—"or you, my gracious lord, ever again."

Zaphenath's chest rose and fell, and his brothers were staring at him, and Judah plunged on.

"And so," Judah said, "we told our father what you said, my lord." It was as if Judah were holding out his hands, imploring, pleading, with his very voice. "And our father sent us back with the child of his old age, his most beloved son." Judah's voice was trembling now, and Zaphenath bit down on his lower lip to forestall the burning that threatened behind his own eyes. "Now"—Judah's voice came stronger—"seeing that our father's life is bound up in the boy's life, when we return and the boy is not with us, our father will die." He bowed his head. "It was on my word of protection that he came with us, my lord." He raised his eyes one last time. "Let this boy go up with his brethren, and our family will live. I will stay here in his place."

Judah's voice fell into silence. Not even the translator spoke. For a breathless and brief and terrible moment, Judah feared that perhaps his plea would not even be heard and he had spoken in vain.

But when he raised his eyes, he saw the vizier gazing back at him, and the man's eyes were shimmering, even as his own.

"Go," the vizier ordered suddenly, clapping his hands, and the guards in the room looked at each other. "Go," Zaphenath repeated, and Amon cleared his throat, reaffirming the order. After another hesitation, the guards withdrew, and Amon glanced only briefly at his master before following them out.

Zaphenath stood alone.

Benjamin raised his head and looked at the vizier. The powerful man's own head was bowed, and he covered his eyes, the golden ring glinting on his finger. Then he wiped his hand across his face, and the tears glistened on his skin like the River beneath the newly risen sun. He looked at Benjamin, who knelt, gazing up at him in terrified wonder, and then turned toward Judah, who looked up at him with the even gaze of a man who knows he has no hope and must hope anyway.

"I am Joseph," the vizier said, and he pressed a hand over his heart. "Is my father alive?"

Judah blinked, staring uncomprehendingly at what must surely be an apparition, the strangest and cruelest vengeance the desert had yet taken upon him. He could not understand how their accuser could suddenly speak to them as if he were Joseph himself—as if he were the very brother they had murdered in the desert—it was some piece of sorcery, some horrible vision—

But the vision stood before them and wept.

And then he came closer, moving toward Benjamin, the accused thief staring at him with trembling eyes, and the vizier bent down and untied the bonds that held Benjamin's wrists.

The frayed rope fell to the ground.

Benjamin gingerly moved his arms from behind his back, and the vizier rose up to his feet and slid the elegant wig from his head, and—

And it was Joseph.

It was Joseph—Joseph, who let the wig fall to the floor, his dark, curling hair matching Benjamin's exactly. His face was Joseph's, and the painted eyes were Joseph's—Joseph, who had haunted them since that day beneath the terrible sun at Dothan—

"Please," he said, his voice breaking as he held out his hand, "come."

Judah rose up from the ground.

For a moment, neither of them could bear to speak or dared to breathe, and then Joseph clasped Judah by the arm, and Judah felt the solidness of his touch and knew in one terrible, joyful, sweeping moment that this was no apparition.

It was rushing upon Joseph now, the words of his fathers *I show these things to you before you go into Kemet* and the words of the sacred texts *to make his soul live, to make his body live, to restore him anew—*

"Our family will live," Joseph said, and Judah nodded, chin trembling. "Hurry back to our father, and tell him I'm alive, and bring him down to me." He looked out over the faces of his brothers. "All of you will come, and stay here, and be near to me," he blinked, spilling more tears over his face, "and you will be protected here. Please." He looked back at Judah. "Will you go to him?"

"We will," said a voice.

Joseph turned, and his touch fell away from Judah's arm as he stared at the man who had been his brother—a child who had been only a small boy and to whom he had been nothing but a whisper, a dream, a far-off memory tenaciously clung to during all the years they had been apart.

And though they had wept much in the years that had separated them, Rachel's sons wept together now once more.

Asenath—who could not understand what was being said as she stood outside the courtyard, listening because she and all the household had heard her husband weeping so openly—understood.

And she smiled.

CHAPTER 39

Genesis 45:28; 46:5–6

He came upon Asenath standing outside in the garden, very early in the morning, watching the first light beginning its ascent into the fresh sky. She turned when she heard him and smiled. The soft, sweet scent of open lotus flowers drifted in the air. The wise fig trees spread their branches out toward both ends of the horizon.

He came to her beneath the trees and beside the pool where the petals drifted peaceably in the new light of unspoiled day, and he leaned down, very gently, and kissed her. Neither of them spoke, while the morning all around them went on singing softly in the rustle of the breeze across the reflecting pool and the call of the birds stirring near the River.

"You are my star of Isis," he whispered. "You have brought this harvest in a time of famine."

She looked up at him, resting her hand against his chest. He pressed her hand against his heartbeat.

"I will call you Joseph," she said.

"It doesn't matter," he said, but she shook her head.

"It does matter," she insisted. "A name matters very much."

He leaned down, touching his forehead to hers. "Asenath," he smiled. "Daughter of the war goddess."

"I wasn't named for war." Asenath gave him a little nudge. "I was named for water. Creation." She leaned in against him. "Neth is the great mother-goddess. I am Daughter-of-Neth, mother of Ra, and brave enough to nurse the crocodiles." She closed her eyes. "You know why my father named me."

Joseph nodded, running a strand of her hair between his fingers in the morning light. "Brave enough to nurse a crocodile," he repeated, quietly, and she closed her eyes and stood there with him, man of two names and two peoples.

"What are you doing in the garden?" he asked at last.

She smiled. "I wanted to see the sun rise today."

So he stood with his arms around her, watching the new sky shed its shadows and awaken in shudders of glowing light. They stayed that way, together, until the sun sailed back out of the stars, and the gentle moon faded softly into the horizon.

The clatter of the caravan crept along the desert highway, drawing up over a cresting slope and stumbling upon the first glimpse of the border towns guarding the entrance into the land of Kemet. Their white-haired leader stopped, looking out at the foreign land that would be his home now and his family's home. Then he turned and looked back toward Canaan, the land promised to his grandfather Abraham, the land of their inheritance.

But his promised land had disappeared long ago into the horizon.

"How long?" Jacob murmured, and Judah leaned closer, as if he had not heard. "How long?" Jacob shook his head. "This is not our home."

Judah looked out over the unfolding plain. "The famine leaves us no choice, Father."

Jacob nodded. "And Joseph—" His voice still grew a little hoarse when he spoke of his son—his son, his son whom he could hardly bear to speak of without seeing him, without knowing for certain—

Judah lowered his eyes. "Yes," he said. "Joseph is alive."

Jacob looked back over his shoulder at his family—who, in one generation, had flourished from a solitary refugee into an entire tribe, with twelve sons and their wives and children, and his daughter, Dinah, who, of all of his children—the woman, daughter of four women—would have no husband and bear no children. Jacob had a glimpse of her face, veiled from the sun, before looking back toward the stretched-out horizon, arching over the land that would become his family's home until God saw fit to lead them out again and fulfill his promise to Abraham.

Somehow, this too was their birthright—to have place and to have no place, to inherit and to wander. He had been born the Displacer, but it had been his destiny to be displaced.

But Joseph was alive.

It was enough.

His inheritance would be the survival of his family. His son would be his promised land.

Without another word, Jacob walked on and did not look back again toward Canaan.

A NOTE TO THE READER

The perceptive reader, upon reading a story set in ancient Egypt, will no doubt wonder why there are no Egyptians.

And that is a very good question.

The short answer is that ancient Egypt was not called Egypt at all, and the term *Egypt* isn't Egyptian but Greek, and the Greeks didn't show up in Egypt until many centuries after the time of Senusret.

Set in a time before Egypt was Egypt, the story takes place during ancient Egypt's Middle Kingdom—as opposed to the Old Kingdom (which saw the construction of the pyramids) or the New Kingdom (responsible for the Valley of the Kings and the temples at Luxor), or the Late Period (marking the arrival of the first Persian kings), the Ptolemaic Period (the Greeks, including Cleopatra), or the Roman Period, amongst others. To be more specific still, the novel's central action is set principally during the reign of the Twelfth Dynasty king Senusret II, who reigned from approximately 1897 to 1878 B.C. and who did instigate a major irrigation and land reclamation project in the area known as the Faiyum or Faiyum Oasis, located near the assumed location for the Middle Kingdom capital of Itj-Twy and south of the Old Kingdom capital of Memphis, near modern-day Cairo.

Throughout the novel, effort has been made to avoid admittedly better-known terms, such as *Egypt*, *Pharaoh*, and *Nile,* that were not actually in use during the Middle Kingdom, referring instead to *Kemet*, the *King*, the *River,* and, as the citizens of Kemet thought of themselves, the *People*.

As far as possible, the descriptions, events, and concerns of the various characters, both Egyptian and Hebrew, are meant to be appropriate for their particular time and place. That being the case, a certain amount of additional context, history, and culture may benefit from some brief explanation.

Chronology: Joseph in the Middle Kingdom

The chronological setting of the novel is, of necessity, somewhat arbitrary, but it is not entirely so. While there is no general consensus as to when Joseph actually arrived in Egypt (indeed, there is plenty of debate about whether he existed at all), a few tidbits at least make the reign of Senusret II an interesting time.

Working with the Genesis account of the genealogy of the Patriarchs—meaning Abraham, his son Isaac, and Isaac's son Jacob—we will assume, remarkable longevity aside, that Abraham, the founder of his people and a fellow sojourner in

Egypt during a time of famine, was easily one hundred years older than his great-grandson Joseph. If we put Abraham's arrival in Egypt sometime around 2000 B.C. (at the very beginning of the Middle Kingdom), Joseph could have arrived relatively close to 1900 B.C., which would mean that the same dynasty would have been in power and Abraham's earlier visit and teachings could certainly still be remembered by the time of his great-grandson's arrival.

For the sake of simplicity, to avoid skipping through too many kings and because the story must be set at some point in time, the chronology is therefore calculated upon Joseph's arrival in Egypt in the year 1900 B.C., at age seventeen, during the long reign of Amenhemhat II, and becoming the vizier under Amenhemhat's successor, Senusret II. A nice touch to this chronology is that Senusret would still have been alive when Jacob and his family arrived in Egypt.

The Middle Kingdom is an intriguing time in Egyptian history. Interspersed between the Old, Middle, and New Kingdoms were so-called Intermediate Periods, when central governmental power was weakened or disintegrated. In fact, the political history of ancient Egypt is essentially an undulating wave of central authority—where strong centralized power under the king wanes, splintering away from the native monarchy and out into the hands of other (sometimes multiple) rulers, only to have the centralized government reinstated by a new native dynasty, which in turn subsequently crumbles and again dissipates power.

Egypt's Middle Kingdom emerged amidst all of this

undulating and is often referred to as a sort of golden age, both for its stable prosperity and its cultural outpouring (The Story of Sinuhe, a highly copied and frequently studied piece of literature, was composed during this time). Egypt did not really become a nation of warriors and empire builders until the New Kingdom and the overthrow of the foreign Hyksos rulers, who took power during the Second Intermediate Period. Their overthrow, it has been suggested, turned the Egyptian mind toward the necessity of conquest and warfare in maintaining their independence. In contrast, the preceding Middle Kingdom appears to have generally been a time of relative peace and prosperity.

Speaking of the rise and fall of dynasties, the astute reader may also be wondering where all the pyramids are. Alas, the great age of pyramid building had already passed away with the decline of the Old Kingdom, which ended around 2200 B.C. With the end of the Old Kingdom, there was movement away from the old capital at Memphis (near modern-day Cairo) to the new capital at Itj-Twy (about two hours south of Cairo), near the marshy Faiyum region. Had he lived during the Middle Kingdom, Joseph, whose life centered near the king and the government, would not have been especially close to any of the Old Kingdom pyramid sites. If he did see them, they might have been a notable lesson in resource allocation to the foreign vizier: the end of the Old Kingdom was likely precipitated by the collapse of the government, rather than by external conflict or the dissipation of natural resources, and the government may well have bankrupted itself with building projects.

This collapse of central authority shifted the balance of power away from the king and out toward a handful of powerful regional rulers called nomarchs who appear to have governed largely without a strong central government. Known as the First Intermediate Period and lasting around two hundred years, this time appears to have lingered in cultural memory as a chaotic and unstable period, beset with danger and darkness.

It's hard to say whether things were actually as desperate as later records indicate—a change in regime often necessitates unflattering comparisons with the period just preceding it—but not long after 2000 B.C., the First Intermediate Period ended as a new generation of native kings came to power, and the prosperous Middle Kingdom began. Amenhemhat I (along with his son, Senusret I) moved the ruling capital to Itj-Twy (not, interestingly, to his native Thebes, which became the capital during the New Kingdom) and unified the country once more under the Twelfth Dynasty. The Twelfth Dynasty (that is, the twelfth family of rulers, including one ruling queen) is synonymous with the time frame of the Middle Kingdom and lasted about as long as the preceding chaotic period (approximately 1990–1780 B.C.).

King Senusret II therefore came to power about one hundred years after the rise of the Twelfth Dynasty, when the cultural memory of the First Intermediate Period and its accompanying woes were, if not exactly fresh, inevitably still present. Thus, a certain comparative pride in the stability, prosperity, and accomplishments of the Middle Kingdom—though likely not without concern about reverting to the country's previous instability—would likely have been the dominant sentiment of the day.

Beyond the Middle Kingdom

One other chronological candidate, not represented in the novel, deserves mention, because placing Joseph in the Middle Kingdom is admittedly less common an approach to biblical chronology. While Joseph himself may not attract too much attention in regard to his chronological setting, the much later exodus of Jacob's descendants out of Egypt, which is inevitably tied to Joseph's own arrival in Egypt, has often been set, whether in academic or cinematic conjecture, in the aggressive New Kingdom, often under the Ramesside kings of the Nineteenth Dynasty.

Even taking the Genesis account at its own word, calculating the time between Joseph's arrival and the later Israelite exodus is a little tricky. For example, Abraham prophesied that his descendants would sojourn for four hundred years, and it's unclear whether the four hundred years should be calculated from the time of Abraham or the time of Joseph, and so on. Nevertheless, it does seem that the later Israelite exodus fits nicely into one of the New Kingdom dynasties, after the expulsion of the (possibly Semitic) Hyksos kings, whose rise to power ended the Middle Kingdom and whose overthrow ushered in the New Kingdom thereafter.

Assuming a New Kingdom exodus, the question for Joseph is which preceding period makes the most sense: the Middle Kingdom or the Second Intermediate Period, which fell between the Middle and the New Kingdoms? In the novel, he comes to Egypt during the Middle Kingdom; however, it has also been suggested that placing Joseph's arrival during the Second Intermediate Period, during the reign of the foreign Hyksos kings, might better account for his rapid political ascendency.

Along with shaping the New Kingdom's cultural and political consciousness regarding the necessity of aggression and empire building (an attitude that certainly seems to fit with the oppressive conditions that open the record in the book of Exodus), the overthrow of the Hyksos rulers ushered in the new Eighteenth and Nineteenth Dynasties of native Egyptian rulers. A change in political power and a new family of rulers would certainly explain the enigmatic opening line of the book of Exodus: "Now there arose up a new king over Egypt, which knew not Joseph" (Exodus 1:8). Putting Joseph in the Middle Kingdom would probably put the Exodus in the Eighteenth Dynasty; dropping Joseph in among the Hyksos rulers would likely push the Exodus into the Nineteenth Dynasty.

As you may be sensing, at the end of the day no one really knows—though this is no reason to deny anyone the delicious pleasure of hearty speculation. Ramses II (whose name means Born-of-Ra), of the Nineteenth Dynasty Ramesside kings (that is, kings named Ramses), is not infrequently suggested as the ruler who might have instigated the Exodus. Tuthmoses, meanwhile, which shows up as the name of several Eighteenth Dynasty kings, means Born-of-Thoth. And if you think you recognize the *mss* root in both of these New Kingdom dynasty names—a root that means "born of" and, by itself, might simply mean "born of an unknown or unnamed god"—as the name of a Hebrew baby adopted by an unnamed but probably New Kingdom Egyptian dynasty, you do.

Geography: The Black Land and the Red Land

Throughout Egyptian writing and religion, there is a strong preoccupation with the way the forces of harmony and justice (*ma'at*) are in constant conflict with the destructive powers of chaos and instability. This metaphysical construct of harmony constantly battling destruction was also reflected starkly and literally in the demarcation of the land itself. The area where the Nile flooded was called *Kemet*, or the Black Land, named after the residual, nutrient-rich mud spread over the landscape by the annual flooding. The four-month flooding season actually forced the People to travel by boat outside their homes, thanks to the rise in the water level.

Egyptian civilization clung closely to the part of the land nourished (exclusively) by the Nile floods. The region along the River allowed for agricultural cultivation and provided a constant bounty of water, fish, and plant life. In contrast, the area beyond the sustaining reach of the Nile—the *Deshret*, or Red Land—was considered hostile, sterile, and without a source of natural nourishment or the steadying hand of civilizing governance. A hapless traveler was simply and solely at the mercy of the unbridled forces of nature and the whims of the desert tribes.

Egypt's geography also created a certain regional dichotomy, which may well have contributed to the country's undulating political stability. The country divided quite naturally into an Upper and Lower Kingdom—which distinction corresponded, confusingly, to southern (Upper) Egypt and northern (Lower) Egypt. Instead of indicating relative latitude, the distinction was instead oriented to the directional flow of the Nile, which runs north from southern Egypt (the Upper Kingdom) toward the Nile Delta in northern Egypt (the Lower Kingdom). Not surprisingly, the two regions of this sizable country, parts of which were invariably separated from their king by quite some distance, routinely struggled to maintain their identity as one unified kingdom. The king's double crown of red and white was itself a hopeful symbol of the two regions' unity.

Time and All Eternity: Life and Afterlife in the Middle Kingdom

Along with political shifts and a sustaining, dualistic worldview, the Middle Kingdom saw important changes in the practice of religion. In the Egyptian (or Kemetian, if you like) worldview, kings were divine and directly connected with the gods. The king oversaw the law and order of the state and helped to maintain the delicate balance of *ma'at* so that interactions remained peaceful and relationships beneficial. He (or, in the occasional case of a ruling queen, she) also had the added benefit of divinity: the king was considered the son of the sun god Ra ("Son-of-Ra" was one of his titles) and was particularly associated with and protected by the hawk-headed god Horus, son of Isis and Osiris (themselves also children of Ra). Moreover, the king was believed to become fully divine after mortal life and was therefore buried with the necessary spells, rituals, and supplies to ensure a comfortable and successful transition into eternal life. The royal tombs were representative of the wealth and influence the king enjoyed during his lifetime and would continue to enjoy as a god.

During the Old Kingdom, only the king or nobles of great status seem to have had hopes of this glorious afterlife. At the very least, they were the only sort of people routinely buried with the necessary treasures and funeral texts—called the Pyramid Texts because of their exclusive appearance in aristocratic tombs—which contained a collection of the necessary rites, spells, and rituals for passage into the afterlife. However, after the collapse of the Old Kingdom and the proliferation of power into the hands of men besides the king, spiritual power seems to have experienced a similar democratic surge. The possibilities of immortality apparently began to extend to men and women besides the king and his relatives, and by the time of the Middle Kingdom, the chance at eternal life appears to have encompassed all men and women who could undertake the proper preparations and obtain the necessary spells and rituals.

This spread in religious ritual is evidenced by the spread of funeral texts and inscriptions once found almost exclusively within the royal pyramids. Copies of these religious rituals begin to appear in the tombs and among the personal possessions of nonaristocratic citizens and, to differentiate these records from the earlier Pyramid Texts, the Middle Kingdom funeral texts have consequently become known as Coffin Texts. By the New Kingdom, these collections of rituals and instructions proliferated into the myriad versions of what is now known as the Book of the Dead. Often kept as private documents that were then buried with their owners (though particular sections and spells also show up on tomb walls), the Book of the Dead and the preceding Coffin and Pyramid Texts all contain various assortments of instructions, spells, and rituals to aid the dead through the trials and impediments encountered between death and the entry into immortality and eternal life.

In the spirit of full anachronistic disclosure, the specific Breathings text quoted throughout the novel does not date to the Middle Kingdom. This particular document, which would have been used as a private ritual text by the original owner and buried with him at the time of death, comes from a later, likely New Kingdom, date. However, while the religious ritual of the Egyptians evolved to some degree over time, the essential ritual steps, whenever they were written down, appear to have remained relatively constant and uniformly old. Several spells from the Book of the Dead appear to date back to the Pyramid Texts of the Old Kingdom, meaning that the rituals were transmitted over hundreds or even thousands of years. Quoting this particular text is more like quoting from a twentieth-century publication of a collection of Shakespeare—the actual document is newer than its content and would be equally recognizable (or unrecognizable) to a reader in 1714 as in 2014.

However, even with the necessary rituals and preparations, immortality depended in large part on conforming one's life to the principles of *ma'at.* Such conformity meant that a person lived properly, justly, and in harmony with one's neighbors and the forces that govern the world. Amongst the spells in the Book of the Dead, which exist in various abbreviated or elongated forms, depending on the specific copy, there is a specific rite for successfully undergoing divine judgment, and the famous judgment scene gives us an explicit look into what such judgment entailed.

A soul's heart was placed on a balance against an ostrich feather (a symbol of *ma'at*) in the presence of watchful gods, including the goddesses Isis and Nephtys, who helped prepare the soul for judgment. Sometimes, Osiris himself—the god of the underworld and a potent symbol of resurrection—was present as an onlooker. In fact, suppliants were explicitly identified by the name Osiris throughout the recitation of the funeral texts (as in "Osiris-[name]"), taking on the god's identity in imitation of Osiris's own successful passage through the underworld. If the heart of the suppliant balanced against the *ma'at* feather, the person would be revealed as one who had lived according to the precepts of *ma'at* and would be received into eternal life. If not, the unworthy heart would be devoured by a crouched, crocodile-headed beast named Ammit, and eternal life would be forfeit.

All things, in the Egyptian view, thus had spiritual undercurrents. While there was clearly an acknowledgment of both good and evil, such awareness does not appear to have carried over into creating alliances with one force over the other. The presence of all divinity saturated the everyday world, and the Egyptians conducted their daily lives in constant acknowledgment of ever-present spiritual forces (even Seth, the murderous brother of Osiris, had his own cultic following). The Egyptians therefore worshipped a great variety of gods and goddesses, who appear to have represented the various forces and aspects of the spiritual realities underlying everyday life. Many homes appear to have had small rooms where members of the household could engage in private worship, burning incense and keeping small statues of the gods they particularly wished to supplicate, such as those who oversaw fertility, childbirth, or domestic prosperity. Annual public festivals of worship and celebration similarly kept the Egyptians aware of both the community and the divinity that bound up their world.

Further underscoring the intermingling of religious and everyday life, the priesthood was not a full-time occupation until the New Kingdom. Men held professions outside their sacred work and would serve in the temples for only a certain amount of time (say, three months out of the year), rather than devoting themselves full-time to religious duties. They were required to shave their bodies and maintain a state of purity while serving in the temples, but they would return to their outside lives upon the completion of their service. Priestesses, too, were known to exist, though they appear to have served in different capacities and sometimes appear as sacred singers and dancers. The office of the high priests of the various religious orders (such as the high priest of Ra) were often political as well as religious positions. It would not have been unusual for men in significant political positions—like Potiphar and Joseph—to hold priesthood offices as well.

Culture: The People of Kemet and Deshret

Kemet

A multitude of other peoples lived beyond the boundaries of Egypt, including the Asiatic desert tribes and their Nubian neighbors. The Egyptian kings sent out expeditions both for diplomacy and for trade, and there were even mining operations stretching out into the Sinai for copper and turquoise. The average Egyptian, however, would likely have had little or no interaction with any of these foreign peoples. Foreigners would have come into Egypt primarily to trade (tourism was not yet in Egypt what it is now) or been brought in as slaves. Although there was apparently a great influx of captured Canaanite slaves during the Middle Kingdom (and the Canaanites primarily appear to have served as domestic servants), it would be a stretch to imagine the Middle Kingdom as particularly cosmopolitan.

However, the Middle Kingdom Egyptians would likely have been suspicious rather than hostile toward foreigners simply from lack of exposure. After all, it was not until the New Kingdom that Egypt began to take a deliberately militaristic attitude toward neighboring peoples. And throughout her remarkably long history—exceeding three thousand years of unbroken civilization—Egypt never became a mighty military empire in the model of the Assyrians, Babylonians, or Romans. Instead, the country and culture were, and essentially always remained, fundamentally peaceful, agricultural, and self-sustaining. In fact, this mighty agrarian empire far outlasted any of the other ancient powers in that region of the world by several thousand years. Not until the incursion of Alexander the Great (in the fourth century B.C.) did Egypt fall permanently under foreign rule, and it was only following the defeat of Antony and Cleopatra (the queen who was the last of the Ptolemaic, or Greek, rulers) in 30 B.C. that Egypt was finally subsumed into the Roman Empire.

Along with being a remarkably stable civilization, ancient Egypt was also notably humane. The concept of *ma'at*—that difficult to define sense of social justice and harmony, if not righteousness—was the foundational philosophy of all interaction and law. Those with power were expected to advocate on behalf of the weak and the powerless, and rulers were expected to be law abiding and just. Even slaves, rather than being considered merely as chattels of their masters, were endowed with certain rights—including the ability to own and bequeath property, the option for male slaves to marry free-born women, and even the possibility of eventual freedom and citizenship.

Although they did not appear to hold many positions outside domestic life and they married early, usually as teenagers, Egyptian women possessed equal rights with Egyptian men. Women could own property, pursue legal action, instigate divorces, serve in the temples, and inherit the throne (although female rulers were far more rare than their male counterparts). Literacy was not widespread among men or women, but there is evidence that well-born women may have had the opportunity to be educated alongside their brothers. Marriages were rarely arranged, and couples were expected to be monogamous. Children were considered a great blessing, and infertility might result in taking another wife or slave-women to bear children in the wife's place. Fidelity and marital happiness were considered natural and desirable, and adultery would have been considered a serious breach of *ma'at* and the social law of the land.

Add to their relatively humane worldview the details regarding dress and hygiene for both men and women—shaved bodies, frequent bathing, wigs and elaborate hairstyles, makeup, perfume, linen, and abundant jewelry—and you begin to get the sense that Kemet would have been an abrupt contrast with the world Joseph left behind.

Deshret

Indeed, in many ways, Judah's world could not stand at greater contrast to his brother's. Deshret, or the Red Land, was home to isolated and often warring tribes and scattered townships. Rather than being home to relatively peaceful and unified citizens of a highly bureaucratic and organized state, the Red Land presented a much starker picture of survival—tribal, often nomadic, and, within the scope of the Genesis narrative, saturated with both secular and sacred violence. Yet despite violence, violation, death, famine, and betrayal, Jacob and his family survived with tenacity, courage, and extraordinary spirit.

The absence of bureaucracy, of course, did not mean the native Canaanites were a people without order. There were towns and cities full of Canaanite inhabitants who led a much more settled life than the nomadic desert tribes and who have left to history their own collection of cultural relics. Indeed, many of the descendants of these people were still living in Canaan—Abraham's promised land—when Jacob's descendants (hereafter Israelites, as opposed to Canaanites) returned from their nearly five-century sojourn in Egypt. Much of the early history found in the book of Judges records the Israelites' conflicts with these other native Canaanites, whom they were forbidden to marry or join and with whom they waged an incessant series of territorial and cultural battles.

Like the other Asiatic tribes and ancient powers, including the later Babylonians and Assyrians, the Canaanites worshipped multiple gods and goddesses. Several of these deities—such as the god Ba'al, who apparently liked human sacrifices, and his consort, the fertility goddess Astoreth—continue to show up quite late into Israelite history, even making an appearance in the clash between the much-later queen Jezebel and the Israelite prophet Elijah. As long as the two peoples lived alongside each other, the Canaanites' enticing religious rites evidently remained a constant and alluring temptation for the chaste, monotheistic Israelites.

Religious, tribal, and family identities were all closely intertwined in the Israelite tradition; indeed, the violation of any one part of this composite identity could compromise the identity in its entirety. Like their Canaanite neighbors, the Israelites tended to be heavily patriarchal, with sons inheriting from their fathers and men standing at the head of the family. However, sons could also lose their spiritual and secular inheritance through violation of the tenets of the covenant. Marriages were to be undertaken exclusively with other inheritors of the Abrahamic covenant, though the early record indicates that such inheritance could come through birth or conversion (Dinah's new husband, Shechem, was murdered after undergoing the ritual requirement of circumcision). To marry outside the covenant was one sure way to forfeit tribal and spiritual privileges, as well as one's core identity, and to threaten all of one's descendants with the forfeiture of their birthright as Abraham's heirs.

The frequent incursion of non-Israelite women into Israelite history—including the wives of Joseph and Judah and several ancestors of the illustrious king David—remains, therefore, one of the most intriguing aspects of the record.

The Brothers

As the astute reader has also no doubt noticed, the rituals mentioned in the Breathings text (including the transference of breath, washing, ritual interaction with two distinct women, and Osiris's eventual reunion with his father, Ra) align with notable harmony alongside the experiences of Joseph and Judah. Their experiences also align quite remarkably and in ways all recorded in Genesis. Indeed, the two brothers' lives are inextricably intertwined. After all, it is Judah whose suggestion spares Joseph's life and (albeit in the novel, inadvertently) sends him on to Egypt, and it is Judah whose plea on behalf of the falsely accused Benjamin eventually reunites his long-lost brother with their family more than twenty years later. At the same time, the very different worlds that Joseph and Judah inhabit influence (at least within the novel) each brother's engagement with the fundamental conflicts inherent in the larger world—good and evil, harmony and chaos, justice and corruption.

Egyptians and Israelites

The Israelite worldview was one in which mortal man was engaged in a constant struggle between personified forces of good and evil, symbolized in the story of the Garden of Eden. The world and all of its inhabitants were irretrievably broken, fallen from the presence of God without hope of return, save for the power of a single, personal, redeeming God who had power over the inevitable conditions of physical and spiritual death. And it was this God that the patriarch Abraham sought out and who, he taught, had opened his mind to visions and entered into a redemptive covenant with him and all of his descendants after him.

As part of this relationship, Abraham and his descendants practiced sacrifice—both literally, with the symbolic offering of animals, and figuratively, in obediently conforming lives and habits with divine will—as they sought atonement. This at-one-ment was literally a reunion with the divine, brought about by conforming one's life to God's teachings and thereby activating divine mercy and salvation. The definition of a life properly lived centered on cultivating this personal relationship, through obedience, between an individual and God. And despite the constant search for a promised land, there was not, in the lifetime of any of the Patriarchs, any true and lasting refuge in the world, aside from God—Abraham's heirs were simply "strangers and sojourners" (Genesis 23:4) to the end.

The all-important purpose of life, from an Egyptian perspective, was not explicitly focused on seeking a personal relationship with a personal deity (and using the deity's commands as a basis for human interaction) but rather in cultivating and conducting proper, harmonious, and just relationships with one another based on the more amorphous concept of *ma'at.* The practice of *ma'at*—frequently personified as a winged, protective goddess—along with religious practice (which focused on worshipping and acknowledging a multitude of divine forces) and the strong rule of a divine king (considered the ultimate link with the gods) helped keep Kemet in a state of proper balance and order. Kemet herself was seen as a bastion of civilization, order, and justice, albeit under constant threat from the upending forces of disunity and chaos found beyond her borders. Like the Israelites, a life in conformance with a higher divine will, personified in the practice of *ma'at,* was the ultimate requirement for peace in this life and passing into the exalted afterlife. But in contrast to the wandering Israelites, to the Egyptian mind the Red Land that lay beyond the peaceful, orderly borders of Kemet—*Deshret,* from which we get the English word *desert*—was nothing to be desired. It was a place of disorder, death, and chaos. The Egyptians even buried their dead on the west side of the Nile—facing toward the uncharted Deshret.

Reunion

Along with spending their adult lives in very different worlds, Joseph and Judah are also the only two of Jacob's sons of whom we have any record showing significant time spent away from their father and family. In the story, therefore, they grapple with the fundamental questions of identity and survival in a different way from their more insular brothers. They are equally pursued by recurring questions regarding their true identities: Joseph as a displaced and inadvertent citizen of Kemet, an heir who becomes a slave who becomes a prisoner who becomes the vizier who eventually saves the brothers who betrayed him, and Judah as a refugee (and, he fears, a murderer), a man of some stature among the Canaanites, and, eventually, the brother who plays the other pivotal role in unifying and saving his family. Each undergoes a process of transformation and recollection in his sojourn, being alternatively humbled and enlivened by his experiences. Each ultimately comes to remember (or re-member) himself as Jacob's son and Abraham's heir.

The larger issue of remembrance—re-membrance, re-membering, a literal piecing back together—is a significant one, and so it should be, coming from a biblical text so wonderfully full of resurrection and reunion imagery. Potiphar's sacred writings, which come from the Egyptian Book of Breathings, are no less saturated with restoration imagery. Indeed, the central theme of the Breathings text is essentially one of resurrection by reunion: a reunion of body and spirit, of mortality and divinity, of man and the gods.

In the Israelite story of the Garden of Eden, the man Adam is tricked by the serpent, Satan, and doomed to suffer physical death and permanent isolation from God as a result of his changed nature. His hope turns to the eventual promise of a redeemer, who will have power over death and possess the ability to restore his divine nature. In Egyptian mythology, the god Osiris, with whom the initiate identifies himself, is killed and dismembered by his jealous brother; he is then literally "re-membered"—pieced back together and regenerated—by his wife, Isis. Even the word *breathings*—*snsn*—apparently has strong implications of union, or reunion, as well as life-breath. It is life restored through the restoration of body, soul, and divine association. The giving and receiving of breath is thus a sort of divine embrace, a sacred, life-reviving kiss.

Joseph's story is perhaps the perfect blend of Israelite and Egyptian restoration imagery, particularly in regard to the episode in which his coat (the symbol of the covenant and the birthright) is dismembered and he himself is thrown into the earth as a dead man and separated from his home and birthright. Happily, when he is eventually reunited with his father and family, he has the power to restore life to his family—ironically, but in keeping with both the Egyptian and the Israelite redemption narratives, as a direct result of an earlier treachery.

Such a deft touch in the Genesis narrative can hardly be coincidental.

Caveat Emptor

The characterizations and structure within the novel have sought to be reasonably supported by the original narrative, though they may not necessarily follow its most familiar interpretations. At times, language and cadence are directly borrowed.

The characters of Amon, Asar, and Joseph and the others of Potiphar's household staff are entirely fictional. There is also no explicit evidence that Joseph's wife, Asenath, has any particular relation to the elusive character Potiphar, who is only ever identified as the captain of the guard, not the vizier. However, we do know that Asenath's father is "Potipherah, priest of On." On is Heliopolis, or the Temple of Ra, and Potipherah and Potiphar are the same name. Incidentally, this is also the same name that appears in Abraham's account of his near-sacrifice at "Potiphar's Hill" (Abraham 1:20), though the full implications of this detail remain to be explored another day.

The name *Potiphar* indeed means "Given-of-Ra" and derives from the divine name of the sun god, the dominant royal deity of the Old Kingdom. Although Osiris appears to have become the dominant deity figure by the Middle Kingdom (and is the god with whom initiates identify themselves in the funeral texts), Ra, the father of Osiris, remained a powerful and important figure. The Temple of Ra at Heliopolis (Greek, "City of the Sun")—called by its native name "Iunu" in the novel and "On" in the Genesis account—served as a religious site of enormous importance. Indeed, it may well have been founded to commemorate the first moment and first geographic spot of the original creation—where a sacred mound rose up out of the primordial waters and was struck by a ray of light.

Finally, the events presented in the novel have been juxtaposed for the sake of elucidating the parallels, foils, and repetitions nestled within the original narrative, all of which can be studied, poked, prodded, and researched but never improved upon.

Works Cited

The Book of Breathings text quoted throughout the novel is taken from Hugh Nibley's translation of the ancient Egyptian text of the same name, published in his book *The Message of the Joseph Smith Papyri: An Egyptian Endowment* (Deseret Book and Maxwell Institute, 2005). Any alteration of Dr. Nibley's translation is the author's own.

The writings of Abraham are taken from the Pearl of Great Price, as translated by Joseph Smith and published by The Church of Jesus Christ of Latter-day Saints, 1981. Again, any alteration is the work of the author.

Works Consulted

Additional sources consulted in researching and writing the novel include *The Ancient Egyptian Book of the Dead,* translated by Raymond O. Faulkner, London: British Museum Press, revised edition, 2010; *The Oxford Companion to the Bible,* edited by Bruce M. Metzger and Michael D. Coogan, Oxford University Press, 1993; *The Oxford History of Ancient Egypt*, edited by Ian Shaw, Oxford University Press, 2000; Jan Assman, *The Mind of Ancient Egypt: History and Meaning in the Time of the Pharaohs*, translated by Andrew Jenkins, Metropolitan Books, 2002; Mark Collier and Bill Manley, *How to Read Egyptian Hieroglyphs,* revised edition, University of California Press, 1998; Rosalie David, *Handbook to Life in Ancient Egypt,* revised edition, Oxford University Press, 1998; Leon R. Kass, *The Beginning of Wisdom: Reading Genesis*, University of Chicago Press, 2003;

Derek Kidner, *Genesis: An Introduction and Commentary*, Tyndale Press, 1967; Hugh Nibley, *Abraham in Egypt,* 2nd edition, Deseret Book and Foundation for Ancient Research and Mormon Studies (FARMS), 2000; Hugh Nibley, *The Message of the Joseph Smith Papyri: An Egyptian Endowment,* 2nd edition, Deseret Book and FARMS, 2005; R. B. Parkinson, *Voices from Ancient Egypt: An Anthology of Middle Kingdom Writings,* British Museum Press, 1991; Donald P. Ryan, *Ancient Egypt on 5 Deben a Day*, Thames & Hudson, 2010; Joyce Tyldesley, *Myths and Legends of Ancient Egypt,* Penguin Books, 2010; Gordon Wenham, *World Biblical Commentary: Genesis 16–50,* Thomas Nelson, 1994; Avivah Gottlieb Zornberg, *Genesis: The Beginning of Desire*, Jewish Publication Society, 1995.

ACKNOWLEDGMENTS

My thanks and love, first and foremost, to my family—to my mother, who read to me; to my father, who brought me books; to my sister and brothers as partners in crime and dearest friends; to my little rascals; and to grandparents who opened the world to all of us. My thanks and love, too, to those friends who have become family and who have been my light in dark places, and to those mentors who have stepped into my life and given light to my path. And many thanks, of course, to those whose time and talents have transformed a manuscript into a book. Merci à tous.

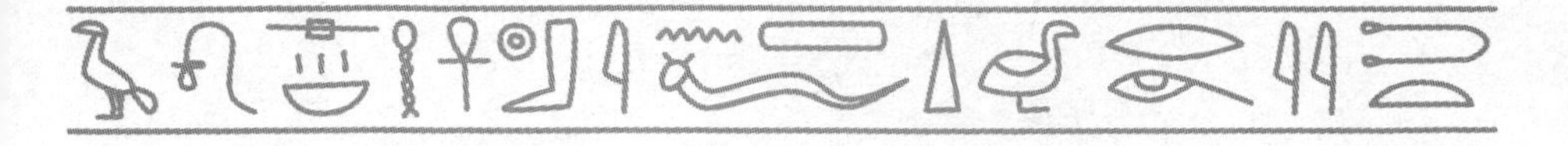

ABOUT THE AUTHOR

Courtesy Rachel K. Wilcox

After spending her high school years in the south of France, Rachel K. Wilcox studied philosophy, literature, and film at Brigham Young University, where she graduated as the class valedictorian. After college, she moved to West Africa to make a documentary film and instead used her camera to co-found a humanitarian project. She has been a researcher and case writer at Harvard Business School and writes and researches in the interdisciplinary fields of law and the humanities. She is in her final year of law school at Stanford University.